EVERYDAY PEOPLE

EVERYDAY PEOPLE

The Color of Life—A Short Story Anthology

Edited by

Jennifer Baker

ATRIA PAPERBACK

NEW YORK LONDON TORONTO SYDNEY NEW DELHI

ATRIA
PAPERBACK

An Imprint of Simon & Schuster, Inc.
1230 Avenue of the Americas
New York, NY 10020

First Atria Paperback edition August 2018

ATRIA PAPERBACK and colophon are trademarks of Simon & Schuster, Inc.

For information about special discounts for bulk purchases, please contact Simon & Schuster Special Sales at 1-866-506-1949 or business@simonandschuster.com.

The Simon & Schuster Speakers Bureau can bring authors to your live event. For more information or to book an event, contact the Simon & Schuster Speakers Bureau at 1-866-248-3049 or visit our website at www.simonspeakers.com.

Interior design by Kyoko Watanabe

Manufactured in the United States of America

10 9 8 7 6 5 4 3 2 1

Library of Congress Cataloging-in-Publication Data

Names: Baker, Jennifer, 1981– editor.
Title: Everyday people : the color of life—a short story anthology / [edited by] Jennifer Baker.
Description: First Atria Paperback edition. | New York : Atria Paperback, 2018.
Identifiers: LCCN 2017060013 (print) | LCCN 2018000990 (ebook) | ISBN 9781501134951 (ebook) | ISBN 9781501134944 (paperback)
Subjects: LCSH: Short stories, American. | American fiction—21st century. | BISAC: FICTION / Anthologies (multiple authors). | FICTION / Literary. | FICTION / Urban Life.
Classification: LCC PS648.S5 (ebook) | LCC PS648.S5 E93 2018 (print) | DDC 813/.0108—dc23
LC record available at https://lccn.loc.gov/2017060013

ISBN 978-1-5011-3494-4
ISBN 978-1-5011-3495-1 (ebook)

Dedicated to Brook Stephenson
We love you.
We miss you.
We cherish the time we had with you.

CONTENTS

Introduction   ix
JENNIFER BAKER

Link   1
COURTTIA NEWLAND

A Sheltered Woman   27
YIYUN LI

High Pursuit   49
MITCHELL S. JACKSON

Do Us Part   69
NELLY ROSARIO

Mine   89
ALEXANDER CHEE

Wisdom   111
NANA EKUA BREW-HAMMOND

Boy/Gamin   139
BRANDON TAYLOR

The Kontrabida   157
MIA ALVAR

The African-American Special   187
JASON REYNOLDS

Long Enough to Drown   195
GLENDALIZ CAMACHO

If a Bird Can Be a Ghost   209
ALLISON MILLS

Last Rites   229
DENNIS NORRIS II

Moosehide   245
CARLEIGH BAKER

Surrender   255
HASANTHIKA SIRISENA

Reading List of Contemporary Works by
Women, Nonbinary, and Transgender Writers
of Color/Indigenous Writers   275

About the Authors   311
Permissions   319

INTRODUCTION

For a while I had this long-standing joke that when Black babies are born they are smacked to encourage their first cry of life, swathed, and placed on the bosom of the person who brought them into this world, and then they're handed a copy of *The Black Poets*, edited by Dudley Randall. *The Black Poets* was the quintessential book I'd see on the shelves of my fellow Black writer friends. If you were into literature, especially poetry, as an African American, then you had to have this book. It verified your commitment to the cause and for the *culture*. If you don't have it, why not? How will you learn about those who came before us? Where we're going and where we've been? No shade, but I have my copy. Whether I got the book soon after coming into the world or not, I cannot say.

There are other seminal anthologies used for study and inspiration, such as *The Scribner Anthology of Contemporary Short Fiction* or E. Lynn Harris and Marita Golden's *Gumbo*, a celebration of African American voices. I'd like to think that *Everyday People: The Color of Life—A Short Story Anthology* will be that type of book over time. On shelves not only for reference but for pleasure, a book housing short fiction from an array of wonderful contemporary writers both established and emerging that speaks to experience, loss, fulfillment, and also being at that fork in the road where decisions must be made yet are not always pursued due to failings of moral fortitude. Each story will always speak to our humanity and the universality of who we are as People of Color/Indigenous People.

As I told the contributors when I approached them, *Everyday People* isn't "my baby" in terms of inception. This book was birthed through the ingenuity and enthusiasm of the late Brook Stephenson, a wonderful person and literary citizen who loved books as much if not even more than I do. He wanted to see a new collection celebrate PoC voices. The aim here is to continue what other writers have cobbled together of not only Black voices but Asian/Pacific Islander, Indigenous, and Latinx ones as well. At a time when "diversity" is used as a buzzword, Brook sought to invest in the stories that people may not be seeing. The name of this anthology is not meant to solely focus on the racial composition of the writers or characters but to showcase the larger story and relationships depicted as well as the landscape—be it in New York City, Maine, Alabama, Great Britain, South Korea, Ghana, or Sri Lanka. As the Sly & the Family Stone song of the same name goes "I am no better and neither are you / We are the same whatever we do . . ."

I inherited this anthology after Brook passed away suddenly and Atria was gung ho about seeing it come to fruition. From there I solicited and corresponded with contributors during a very tense time (the 2016 US presidential election). I was heartened by how eagerly those I reached out to wanted to add their names and fiction in any way they could, or even offer a hand after the fact. In 2017, I found that reading their submissions reinvigorated me with the power of the written word when things seemed bleak. In addition, the versatility of our experiences as expressed in each story fortified me in new ways. These stories, mostly new and some republished, pack a punch in all their iterations, leaving me sated knowing that the world will have a chance to also engage with these characters and writers. From the political to the personal, from familial strife to geographical displacement, from heartbreak to ego checking, stories that gain inspiration from Langston Hughes's Simple series (Jason Reynolds) to expounding on the depths of grief (Glendaliz Camacho), each contributor draws from a well of work that can be studied and should be savored.

I hope that in this time when people seek to be more inclusive and representative in their writing *and* reading that *Everyday People* will be that compilation reached for and sought after for the bevy of short fiction that doesn't relegate the authors or characters to their "status" as much as recognizes their skill.

I want to extend a tremendous amount of thanks to every contributor (Courttia, Brandon, Alex, Nana, Allison, Mitch, Carleigh, Dennis, Yiyun, Mia, Nelly, Hasanthika, Jason, and Glendaliz) for sharing not only these stories with me but for the continuous work you do in your craft and your unyielding support of other writers in this industry so that we may see more PoC/Indigenous voices rise up. And thanks/blessings to Brook Stephenson, who is greatly missed. I'm confident we did you and your vision for *Everyday People* proud.

—JENNIFER BAKER
November 2017

LINK

Courttia Newland

AARON FELT IT for the first time, a pulsing at the back of his skull, firm pressure between his eyes. A throbbing ache behind his ear, low ringing. He'd made a call the night before, half believing nothing would come of it, only to wake up with sensation invading his head. An answer. There were others. He called again during breakfast, his mum fussing around as usual, and felt three stronger replies from three directions. The back of his skull, between his eyes, behind his right ear. He relaxed into the warm, steady pulsation, chewing until there was nothing left but lonely oat kernels, Mum going on about him doing the housework while she was at the hospital, Aaron ignoring every word.

He should have known what to expect before he got there, might have if he'd thought about it harder, but he'd been more concerned with his own nerves alongside the jarring pain of the too-bright, too-loud veneer of normality, a glistening, shifting bubble on all sides. The cheap glow of budget clothing stores. The counterfeit stall selling defrosted E-number cakes they claimed were organic and homemade.

The row of fruit and veg stalls, the lightweight shack of the CD hut, its walls thin black material, rippling as the masses walked by. People, too many, too fast or slow, darting through gaps in the crowd or halting right in front of him until he swore and sped past the lurching granny sideways on, guilty for subscribing to group consensus. He hated the old center during the day.

It was almost a relief to swerve into the pissy-oasis of the car park entrance, a small enclave leading to oil-dark steps. He climbed past two olders, hunch necked, puffing a ripe blunt, smoke and urine filling his head, making Aaron cough, them stare. He trotted upward until he met swing doors, pushing into the expanse of the first floor. Breathed deep, tasting exhaust fumes, smog. Sighed. He wandered across concrete, taking the steep incline of driveways instead, up and up until he reached the sixth floor.

They stood by thin railings looking at the streets. The downturned meringue peaks of the bus station awning, the glass underground entrance and panoramic Westfield steps, the six times removed hum of the crowd. There were three, of course. Two girls, one boy. It took a moment before he clocked that he knew them. Not well, not to talk with, just from around. Live anywhere your whole life and you're bound to see the same faces, *Groundhog Day* for real, only less dramatic, more tedious. Crossing the street to the corner store, standing in line for Maccy D's, sitting rows from each other on the bus. Only one he'd ever wished he could talk to, or thought about longer than the time it took to walk by. But he knew all three as surely as the silent boasts of tags on street signs, or missing digital letters on the countdown. They all belonged to the bits, were all home.

The tall kid wore a school blazer, was lanky and broad with a face like a pinched raisin, the lopsided mini-Afro of a younger. The 'fro looked like a disabled black dorsal fin, making his screw face infantile: a man's aggression beneath a toddler's hairstyle. Aaron stifled a laugh. The girl was short and BRIT Award thin, a few years older than himself, blond hair tied back, falling to her waist, brown leather jacket with bare zips, sensible shirt, trousers, and flat shoes, the dark rings of a part-time weed smoker around her eyes. He'd seen her going in and out of the dentist's opposite his GP's surgery for long enough to assume she worked there. She was hard-faced and gaunt, smoking a withering fag, looking more like thirty than the early twenties she really was.

The other girl was a manifestation of dreams. Tall as Aaron, tight storm cloud jeans betraying a curve of hips, snug roll-necked gray top tucked in at the beltless waist, as gorgeous above as below. Aaron saved the best for last, after he'd taken in the rest—deep brown skin, unblinking eyes, lips maintaining a perpetual pout. The slim denim jacket, blue LDN fitted and rare matching Nikes that told the world she was not only down but prided herself on originality. Normally the type he sneered at inside his head knowing he felt unworthy, except she was here and that made her different from the others, a woman of substance rather than image.

All three lived within a square mile and passed each other randomly at least once a week, possibly more.

He approached, only really seeing her, heart leaping at the odds of her being one of them. The others lost clarity and focus, becoming peripheral. He was smiling, and she noticed, recognition curving her lips upward, Aaron drawn by the strength of a connection he'd not known existed until now. He almost reached out a hand toward her, managed to stop himself (too soon, way too soon) pushed his glasses up on his nose and widened his grin.

"Oh, *hell* nah, not him, too, are you lot bloody serious?"

Old Girl, expression wrinkled, shook her head with even more violence than her words, hair whipping her back and shoulders. Tall Kid spat laughter. Dream Girl's smile didn't exactly grow, but didn't disappear. *Damn it. Skinny bitch.*

He ignored her, stopping before them, eyeing the younger two without saying anything. Actually he didn't know what to say but an older cousin had told him silence often made him look confident if he pulled it off right.

"Are you shittin' me? You lot seriously trying to say that's him?"

They stared him out, daring him to say the real reason he came up to the sixth floor acting like he knew anything. Dream Girl seemed uncertain. Tall Kid's swaying body, hard eyes, and clenched fists made him look as though he wanted an excuse to spark him, and would probably enjoy it.

"They're not saying it's me. I am, because it is. I called you. Last night I said I could feel you, all of you, and I meant it. Now I want to know why."

He let that sink in, concentrating on the white trail scribbled across blue sky behind their heads, fading into wisps, then nothing but molecules, hearing low gasps, mutters, feeling the atmosphere change. Dream Girl and Tall Kid relaxed. Old Girl felt it, too, sucking hard enough on the fag to hollow her cheeks and make her eyes bulge, enhancing her death stare, which roamed in all directions until she threw the blazing stub at his feet, where it exploded into a bouncing trail of sparks. Aaron refused to move or acknowledge what she'd done. He stared into her eyes, waited.

"Have fun on yuh play date, then."

And she was off, brushing his shoulder lightning fast, muttering curses all the way to the fire doors, which clapped sudden thunder after her. He scratched his head, turned to the others.

"What's her problem?"

"She thought you'd be older."

"How'd she know I'm not?"

Both smirked. He felt himself grow hot and tried to shake it off. Be cool. He had to be cool.

"She thought we'd all be."

That was better. Tall Kid stepped forward, eclipsing Dream Girl with his broad body. Aaron could see her aura glowing on all sides. He imagined he could even feel her heat. Then the fist was high, up in his face.

"Limo," Tall Kid said, less hard, practically smiling. Except he couldn't quite do it, could only manage a sneer.

"Huh?"

"My name. Limo."

"Oh, cool. I'm Aaron."

They connected knuckles, Aaron wincing at the force of contact as always, teeth clenched trying to hide it. He never understood why they couldn't just shake hands, or at least slap fingers.

"Christie."

Damn, bruv. She was even hotter close up. Teardrop hazel eyes, long, dark lashes, brown skin underlit with red infusion, cute dimples on both cheeks. She smelt of something sweet, consistent. He smiled as much as he dared without foiling his cool, and didn't know how to greet her, so he settled for doing nothing, disappointing himself. It speared him deep inside to think she might have felt the same way. He fought against his insecurities again.

"She's not even that much older than us."

All nodding, conceding defeat. Old Girl's view had won, right or wrong. She'd left them feeling like the kids she claimed they were.

"So what now?" Christie said.

Aaron didn't even have to think about it. He'd been doing enough last night, nursing that very topic like a sore muscle. His first troublesome thought was their obvious opening question.

"Show us." He pointed at the railings. "Down there."

They walked that way. Bodies bent, they looked at the streets below. The nearest were the hoards waiting by the lights for traffic to slow to a stop so they could cross. Christie went first, seeing as she'd asked. He tried not to snatch a peek at the blue jeans stretched taut against her bum and thighs, to keep his eyes on the roads, but it was tough.

"Which one?" Limo propped on his elbows, searching the crowds.

"Him," she said. "Bald guy, blue suit."

"Don't point." Aaron heard himself, bit his lip. Granddad.

"Sorry," she said, lowering her hand, shooting him a look he felt, not saw. Not malice, regret. It made him like her just that little bit more. She understood he wasn't being an arse, only cautious.

"Just so they don't see us," he told her, still feeling bad.

"Sure."

"He's crossing," Limo warned, and then her attention was back. Her threaded eyebrows lowered.

"No he's not," she muttered.

The green man was flashing; beside him yellow digital numbers fell from 10. Blue Suit stopped in the middle of the crossing, head pivoting. A small kid bumped him, looked up in shock, and went around, dragged by the hand and momentum of a woman who was probably his mother. The surge of pedestrians flowed around Blue Suit like a river around a stone, slowing to a trickle until he was alone. The green man disappeared. The count reached zero. Blue Suit remained in the center of the crossing. Limo sniggered, covering his lips. The red man returned and a BMW revved, leaping forward. Blue Suit looked perplexed but stayed where he was. Horns beeped. Drivers got out of cars. It was all getting too much when Blue Suit did a strange robotic turn and went back to the mall side of the road where he'd started. A driver made to follow—red in the face, trackie bottoms, and XXL T-shirt. Christie grunted surprise, leant forward. The driver walked back to his car just as purposefully as he'd left, got inside, and roared away. Blue Suit blinked into the faces of his fellow commuters as if they could tell him what had gone wrong. Christie backed away from the railings.

"Classic," Limo said, slapping brick with an open palm.

"Well done," Aaron said, meaning it. She gave a teeny smile, something less focused in her eyes. This time he tried to avoid them.

"My turn," the Kid said, a little too eager for Aaron's liking. He watched him, not the road.

Hunched like a cat, the Kid's chin rested on the cradle made by his folded arms slowly licking his lips. When he saw what he wanted he rose, stiffening. "This'll be bare joke," he grunted through half-closed lips, nearly too low to hear. Aaron saw pure concentration, more focus than Christie.

"Don't do that," he heard her say. "*Don't.*" Then she turned away from the street below. Aaron, alerted, slipped into the space next to Limo.

A gathering of boys about the Kid's age. Blazers and thick school jumpers, pointing. Work commuters passing, heads turned as if to view an accident, still walking toward the crossing, shaking their heads. A woman, megaphone in one hand, Bible in the other, placard at her feet—JESUS SAVES—calling God's vengeance, pointing at the homeless man with his arms and legs wrapped around a lamppost, hips moving, slow grinding, rubbing against hard, grubby metal. Peals of laughter reached them. Aaron gritted his teeth, said nothing. When the British Transport Police approached the homeless guy, Limo let him go, bringing him back to face heavy hands on his shoulder, protesting as he was led toward a waiting patrol car.

Limo slapped brick even harder, creating solitary, one-handed applause. Aaron looked back at Christie. She was frowning at her box-fresh trainers, arms wrapped around her own body.

"That's not funny," he told him.

"Is to me." Limo towered over Aaron, concrete hard again. "Each to his own, innit?"

Aaron tried a look that said he was beneath some schoolkid's Grime-based posturing, turning back to the railings.

"Fair enough," he said beneath his breath, tuning out Limo's rigid face and grubby blazer.

The air filled with perfume. Christie had come closer, but he focused on the streets and another homeless dude. This one was sitting by a wall just beyond the totem pole of train station signage, a series of varied transport symbols stacked on top of each other. Behind the dude, who stared into space oblivious to the hoards tramping by him, stood a quartet of bright ATMs.

"Him," Aaron said, tilting his head. He heard their complaints, felt them jostle him on both sides, trying to see past the disgusting *Day of the Triffids* sculptures the council put up during the Olympics—to hide the old center from the world, many had said. Probably to hide the people too. Now the shimmering yellow and green petals worked in reverse, blocking Westfield and all routes out of Stratford. He silenced the thought. Concentrating, he found his target.

She was a young businesswoman who might have been going home after a long day in the office. Brunette, legs tanned, suit well fitted. Tall and broad-shouldered, possibly Eastern European, but that was just a guess. He made her type in more cash than she needed without a receipt. When the wad spat from the machine he made her take it quick, walk three steps, and drop it into homeless dude's lap, gasps of shock exploding like cloudburst from spectators, then had her sprint toward the bus station as a 25 rounded the corner, pulling up at stop B. Knowing what was good for him, homeless dude shot to his feet as if the ground were electrified. He gathered his dog, loose change, and blanket, shuffling off before any spectators fully reacted to his luck, disappearing into the backdrop of commuters. Unable to find him, Aaron let the woman go, turning his back on her wheeling on the spot, heels tap-dancing against the pavement.

"*Sick!*" Christie came closer still, deliciously embracing him, even kissing his cheek. Aaron blushed, shivering at the warmth. "Proper sick! I love it!"

"No problem," he said, trying to stare out Limo, who wouldn't allow it. The Kid was vex, no doubt. His bottom lip stuck out, his eyes tracked tarmac. His arms hung, huge fists useless by his side.

"So what, you lot on a link ting now?"

She let him go. Immediately, Aaron missed her. They stood apart, looking as guilty as people who had actually done something wrong.

"No."

"It ain' even about that. Aaron done a good thing. Why you goin' on weird?"

"Yeah, carry on." Limo honestly looked hurt, as though Aaron's actions were an affront to his moral center, an act that had to be purged in some way, perhaps by the undertaking of more evil. "I see how this'll run. You lot are on some couples vibe, an' three ain' magic. Catch you later, yeah?"

And he was gone too, arms swinging, leg limping, fire-exit doors flapping until they closed. The silence afterward was awkward, dense, Aaron unsure what he should do next. He didn't want to say it but the urge was sweet, compelling enough to take the risk.

"He's not wrong, though, is he?"

He turned to face her, seeing that bright, beautiful smile. Christie sized him up as though he'd pleased her.

"No, he's not," she said, and took Aaron by the arm, leading him toward the swing doors.

They went back to his, seeing as Aaron's mum was mopping floors and sterilizing hospital surfaces until late that night. He tried not to think about it, the hard work she was forced into just so he could have a painless education. Her only reward a future that saw him comfortable, a good job, wife, house, two good, beautiful kids. Aaron dismissed those vague, misty images with more purpose. Too far, too distant. When he asked Christie where she lived, she pursed her lips, head twisting to follow the exhale of a passing bus, breathed, "Not far." Aaron smiled. He got it. Enough said by her hand in his, the slip of her arm between his inner bicep and ribs. What more did he want?

They didn't even run to catch the 25, just let it idle to allow people on, an old Asian lady struggling on the upward step like a toddler. When they finally got aboard and tapped Oysters, the driver snapped alert, looking from Christie to Aaron as though they were mythical, like he already knew their secret. Aaron bowed his head, hid his grin. He walked her to the raised seats in the back, radiator hot, thrumming. Christie rested her head on his shoulder. It was all he could do not to look each and every passenger in the eye, to ensure that they took note. This was him. With her.

His room was dark and tidy, which always made Aaron wonder why his mother caused such a fuss about house-work. He made sure the place looked like his personal space, even cooking on occasion. He was responsible. He owed Mum that much. Christie slow spun, taking in posters, his pinboard, the jammed bookcase and full shelves, his tiny writing desk beneath the window, his DVDs. He sat on the bed, swallowing nerves. When she'd made the whole 360, bending to inspect book covers and cut out newspaper clip-pings closer, her neat eyebrows were arched in surprise.

"You march?" she said, pointing at the largest poster. A

red star superimposed with black letters: LBR—and underneath that, an explanation: London Black Revolutionaries.

"Yeah, course. Not every one," he said, blushing, chin touching collarbone. "But sometimes. You?"

"Yeah, course."

He tried not to show his pleasure. "I didn't think you'd be political."

She shrugged, walking over. When she sat, springs gasped and the mattress indented, taking Aaron with it. He moved toward the wall.

"Sorry," he said. "It's a bit old."

"Don't be."

She took his hand. She was staring in a way that made him feel weird, intense and unblinking, but she was so beautiful he felt himself doing the same.

"Which way you voting?"

"Huh?"

She peered at the poster and he shivered.

"Remain."

"Course."

"Course."

She kept peering downward, running her hand across his. He wanted to close his eyes—her touch made him sleepy—but was worried that might say more about him than he wanted her to know. He tried to sit up straight. She was the first girl he'd had up to his room in four years.

"This is nuts." Half laughing, coughing to hide it. "We only just met."

She slid soft fingers along his bare arm, focused on what she was doing. Her lips shone, parted. She leant forward until she'd pushed beneath his T-shirt, reached his shoulder.

"Uh-huh," she said. Perfume clouded him. Their lips met.

Nothing but sensation. No sound, no feeling, not even thought. Everything happening on the inside, like closing his eyes in a dark room only to see the delicate, butterfly swirl of phosphenes. Something composed of nothing. Like falling, a feather, not rock. Like nothing to push against and nothing to hold, a lightness he'd always felt inhabited his body were it not for bones and liquid and muscle and soft tissue. Were it not for himself. He might have smiled, tried to, but as the feeling glowed and expanded there wasn't the familiar stretch, the noise of separation, a touch of hard teeth against soft lips. Everything had flattened, merged, spread like clay. There was no way to tell what belonged to him, or anything else. There wasn't anything else. Only touch.

■ ■ ■

He was on the bed, head fuzzy, ceiling spinning. A quick check; he was fully clothed. Another; Christie was gone. He sat up, palms flat against the mattress, checking every dark space and crevice as if the ability to shrink had been added to her powers. He squinted his desk from a formless blob back to its original shape. Found his glasses splayed on the bed, put them on. An open book facedown by the empty chair. He checked the spine: *Other Britain, Other British*. No sign of Christie.

There was nothing left but to put out a call. He did so tentatively, a little scared of what he might learn. When the pressure returned between his eyes, a soft migraine, he closed his eyes, lying back. Allowed a smile to touch his lips. He curled on the bed, sensation pulsing at his forehead, and that's how his mother found him when she opened the bedroom door just before two a.m. Sleeping fully clothed, a pillow clutched to infinity beneath his nose, still smiling.

He put out a call at breakfast before his morning classes and heard nothing. That didn't faze him. He wolfed down bran flakes and left the house before his mum woke for her customary coffee and low-energy grumbles. He sailed through his lectures with an enthusiasm that made staff and students alike look twice, wondering if he was the same person they'd seen for almost a full term. In the afternoon, when he powered from the building with secondary-school energy, his classes done for the day, a trail of smiles, head nods, and raised fists bubbled and frothed in his wake.

She leant against the lamppost directly outside his college. Short denim skirt, tights and Timbs, slim tank top, and bright furred gilet. Hair pulled back and gleaming, frost chip eyes and high cheekbones. Nearly every guy who passed her turned to get a better look, and those who didn't stiffened, walking self-consciously, swag depleted. Christie seemed lost in another world until she saw Aaron and stood to attention, overjoyed at something as mundane as the mere sight of him. Damn. She even had a lollipop, ruby gleaming, which she gave a final lick, crunched into shards and pulled from her lips, dropping the white stick behind her, grinning.

"*Hi*," she sang, embracing him. A collective gasp rode the air. Her perfume, a tang of something sensual, something her. Crunching, the scent of flavored sugar on her breath. The dark of his closed eyes felt good, like the night before. He wallowed.

"How you doing?" he said, letting go to look at her. *Damn*.

"Good." She was jittery, blushing. "Thought we could do something. At the polling station? You voted?"

"I haven't."

She sent a quick image across real time vision. He watched, sightless, nodding. Pretty good idea.

"We can hang out after if you like." Head ducked toward dark pavement, giving him the zigzag line of her center parting. "Maybe go to Nando's? My treat?"

Aaron was in love.

The polling station wasn't far, an old church he'd ignored most of his life, signs outside stating its new, temporary persona. A tall woman with thin lips, cornrows, and a council ID hanging from a poppy-red ribbon smoked and shivered against the damp wall, eyes distant. Christie waited not far from the woman while Aaron made his mark and slid his vote into the ballot box, joining her after. They leant against open church doors, playing sullen-eyed teenagers, nothing more on their minds than the time on their hands. They didn't have to do much. Just a simple look in the direction of anyone who passed, a gentle probe inside their heads, a nosey around. If the person was voting their way they left them be. If they were going against their interests, or unsure, a suggestion was planted. Often, when that happened, the person would jerk, frown as if they'd forgotten something, and continue on, a little more determination in their step than before.

The Tall Woman went inside after fifteen minutes. When she came back an hour and a half later to see Christie and Aaron still there and a number of people halt, jerk, and look puzzled, she turned toward the teenagers, uncertain suspicion in her eyes.

Aaron didn't see her until Christie nudged him twice. He watched the Tall Woman for a long while, pushed out a command. She jerked, too, harder than the others, all scrutiny blinded. Opening her cigarette box, she fumbled one to her lips and began to smoke hard, nonstop. Finished it and started another. And another. When they left the polling station around ten p.m., she was smoking cigarette butts she found on the grass, one after the next. Her colleagues beside her trying to pull at her arms while the woman elbowed them away, kept searching.

They bought a whole lemon and herb chicken and double large fries to share, taking it to the shopping center where they found a place to sit huddled by closed Holland & Barrett doors. Around them, the swish and clatter of roller skates and skateboards, white noise beneath Grime pumped by youngers outside Costa watching their mates with grim, negligent pride. Others with their backs pressed against JD Sports glass, or sat on benches lacing up, speeching fresh-faced teenage girls or staring into space, meditating on their next move, carnal or athletic. Afropunks, mostly, hair mixtures of blues, reds, oranges, and a rainbow of chemically enhanced colors, shaved close or flowering in full bloom, beaded, loxxed, weaved. Straight-haired blondes and brunettes styled much the same, long hair tied thin to avoid accidents. A trio of girls in Khimars, skates rattling trains, rolling west, all laughter and shouts and streaming dark material until they went unseen, trailing ghosts of echoes. Ripped and rolled-up jeans, exposing bare knees and glistening ankles, polished Doc Martens and fresh Timbs. A reflected haze of bodies on floor tiles, colored wheels pulsing like distant landing lights. Some spun on the spot, ballerina slow, trapped in worlds belonging to them alone. Others leapt for harsh ceiling lights, wheels erupting noisy landings, wobbling but upright, expressions betraying they expected no different.

In their midst, pedestrians crossed from one side of Stratford to the other. Late-night students, red-eyed workers, young lovers, families pushing bully buggies, their walking children finding a grip wherever they could. Silver-screen aficionados, shambling drug addicts and their alcoholic cousins, pensioners bored to blindness with dull four walls. Skaters wheeling through everybody, unseeing, perhaps uncaring. A handful of high-vis security guards stood to one side, serene as though dreaming white light and ambience. Homeless men and women set up for the night, laying sleeping bags flat, clutching steaming teas. The cinema-sized flatscreen above the West Mall showed boy bands and London Met ads on continuous rotation.

Christie motioned at the Nando's bag. He tipped it toward her and she burrowed for fries, stuffing a handful into her mouth. Raised voices barked loud. Stiffened people, looking. There, just beside the lime-green lettering of Osbon Pharmacy, they saw him.

"Christie . . ."

They got to their feet.

"It's him, right?"

Craning to see, one hand on his arm. "Yep."

"We better go over, in case."

She seemed reluctant, yet moved with him to the central area where Limo, even taller in huge black skates, loomed over a broad man much older than himself. The man had lank black hair plastered to his head, a dusty red hoodie, and a rolled up *Metro* in his fist. Both shouted at each other,

Limo pointing in his face, the man gesticulating with his paper. Aaron couldn't make out what was going on, caught between the thin girlfriend trying to pull the broad man away and Limo's friends tugging in the opposite direction, the Kid shrugging them off, shouting, "I didn't touch you, though," louder each time.

In one swift moment the broad man's face changed. Eyes narrowed, his face seeped red until he was spitting, "Who the *fuck* d'you think you are, eh? *Eh?* Wait until mornin', you'll see, you lot'll be sent back where you come from pronto, d'you hear me? This is *my* country. *My* country."

Maybe he didn't really mean it. Maybe it was only a counteraction to what the Kid was saying, brought on by the vote and the intensity of the argument, but Limo stopped shouting as though he'd been slapped. His expression lost all animation, blanking until he regarded the man with no more interest than a frayed bootlace.

Christie tensed, Aaron felt it. The broad man turned on a scuffed heel, brushing past his confused girlfriend, walking toward the marigold Amazon lockers on the northern end of the mall. He stopped and smashed his head against the metal, again and again, the sound of it like someone beating a tin drum. People screamed. Security guards ran over, trying to grab his arms, one pushed away by the man, falling and skidding across the polished floor on his arse. He got up and tried again with more of his mates and they were all pushed back even harder. The metal lockers banged, rocking steady time, growing dented, smeared red. Limo's friends backed away, their expressions pale and sick.

And the Kid stood there, focused on the man butting the lockers, a sneering half smile twitching at his lips.

Aaron stepped forward, not even thinking until he felt a hand on his forearm. Christie shook her head, eyes holding his. He frowned *Why not?* and she shook her head even harder. A surge of anger swelled in his chest. Why not? When he turned back, Limo had seen him, his smile broader, eyes dilated, the whites seemingly larger. He winked at Aaron and let the man fall, unconscious. The watching people gasped, rushing to his side. The man's girlfriend had long fainted, but no one noticed her. Limo spun on the spot, skating away with long, graceful strides, the lights in his boots blinking. Aaron watched the glittering red, blue, and white. His body grew light, and the spiral ascent opened in his head. The shopping center faded, returned, faded, and returned. Prickles of rage burned his eyes.

Christie saw his anger; he knew that. She grasped him by the shoulders and led him away from the people and the fallen man. He let her walk him outside, into the cold night, toward the bus stop, where she pushed him aboard the first 86 to pull up, guiding him to the upper deck. She sat him in the space behind the stairs by the window and leant against him so he could feel her warmth. Aaron saw dull lights, slow-walking people. He felt so tired. He wasn't even sure what was wrong; all his energy had left him. Somewhere farther along the main road she hauled him down the stairs and onto the pavement, crossing roads until they came to another stop. They climbed aboard the next bus. She sat him down, putting her arms around him to quiet his shivering. He had a vague sense of where he was. He gave up learning more, or perhaps lost interest. His body felt loose and floppy, no bones.

He blanked out completely after that. When awareness

came back they were entering a house—hers, he guessed. A featureless hallway with one framed picture; an aerial shot of a beach, an orange and red outlined word in a corner: Bantayan. He had a vague memory of two people: a snub-nosed man in a blue-checked lumberjack shirt, red-eyed, tiny brown marks dead center on his lips, sucking on the tiniest roll-up Aaron had ever seen; and a plump woman, lively in a fading way, wearing a little blue apron and regarding him as if his presence was of little importance. There were names, a round of nods before lengthy silence, yet Aaron didn't understand the words. He was tugged upstairs before he had time to ask if they were her parents. He might have even said it, but he didn't remember Christie answering, or being sure whether he'd actually voiced the question. The next thing he knew a door was closing. He sat on a sagging single bed mattress pretty much like his own.

The room was dark, very warm. That strange redolence in the air like nothing he'd known, pleasant and enveloping. Like the undercurrent Christie brought whenever she was near him, yet stronger, richer, headier. He tried to see the walls and objects in the room to get a better picture of who she was, but struggled to find anything to hold on to, just vague black forms and a light from the hallway that disappeared when Christie shut the door. He thought she'd flick the switch, waited forever for the click, the quick ache at the back of his eyes, a sudden reimagining of the formerly blank space. He felt a dip, then solid warmth beside him.

"We gonna sit in the dark, then?" His tongue felt thick. He could barely free the words. She snuggled next to him, hair tickling his ear. It bothered him that he couldn't move. Speaking felt uncomfortable.

"I always wanted to go to the Philippines."

She giggled, kissing him beneath his ear. He closed his eyes.

"You're Filipino, right?" Mumbling, barely able to free the words.

She did it again, a trail leading to his lips, turning his chin and kissing him fully. Everything inside him relaxed.

He was there again, floating in darkness he remembered, and this time it was better because of anticipation. When the freefalling came he let himself stretch and surge, be carried wherever the flow took him. This time he went deeper, a sensation like rich, soft liquid removing every physical sense of who he was until he was enveloped by it and he moved without will. He heard a low creak, similar to crickets only it sounded synthetic. Then something else came, hotter, a little searing. Later he would think it was like steaming water being poured into a cooling bath, followed by the rapid awareness it wasn't that at all, more like hot water being poured inside himself from the top of his head to his toes. Except there was no head, no toes, and the water was scalding, painful, and he tried to open his voiceless, mouthless lips to scream only to find it was impossible; he had to wait until the pain faded into the dark of the room.

The bed. The dark. Nothing further. He tried to crawl, to find something solid he recognized by touch. When his fingers brushed objects, there were only corners and right angles, rectangles and squares, flat surfaces nothing like household items, or an object someone owned. Even the bed, when he went back, had no legs, just a smooth, cool material akin to plaster reaching from the mattress to the floor. He frowned. Crawled to the bedroom door. Fright built inside him as he imagined there might not be a handle, he might be trapped, until he eventually found it, opened, could stand.

The passage wreathed in shadows. A blurred arc of light below was enough to see down the stairs. He stepped quietly, trying not to make any noise in case Christie's parents were sleeping. Perhaps she was watching TV or crashed out on the sofa. If the last were true, he'd leave and call in the morning. The television, a sudden loudness, something about the vote that caught his attention; he tried to descend fast without making a sound. At the living room door he stopped, peeking around the frame, self-conscious. He didn't know these people, barely knew Christie. White light flooded the room. Something odd was going on with the sofa, but he ignored that because Farage filled the screen, baring teeth amidst flashing lights and bouts of applause, saying it was Independence Day for England, and he listened, feeling that falling sensation again, only quicker and inside his own body, solid, rooted, causing him to slump against the doorframe.

As his eyes adjusted, the sofa became a shape he knew better. Three strange, writhing masses in a row. Not matter, not as he knew it, these were spheres of persistent energy, patterns shifting and swelling on each surface like plasma on the photosphere of a star, waves rippling, tendrils emerging, testing the air every so often before receding into the central mass. Even worse, discarded flesh lay in a draped pile beneath the rounded balls of energy like snakeskin. When he dared to take a step closer he saw fanned hair and glimpses of clothes flopping from sofa cushions onto the carpet, realizing the husks were the shed carcasses of *them*—Christie and each of her parents, the skins creased and partly inside out, veined and pale.

The spheres eased into deeper colors, darkening. Somehow they rotated. The closest ball to Aaron reached out a slow, probing tendril. It curled like smoke, stretching toward him.

He ran. Out of the door and into the street, down the empty, orange-lit road. He sprinted across roads, feet slapping pavements wet with morning dew, night buses bathing him in stark light. He didn't stop and didn't pay any mind. There was no point. They knew where he lived. They also knew where he was *right now*. He and the creatures were forever linked. He'd thought he was smart, the leader, the one who'd called them all, when really, from the start, it was her.

He collapsed against a lamppost, slid to its concrete root, and when he could stand again he walked. His lungs burned, his legs weak. The streets were shimmering lake water. The high road stretched into the distance.

There was nothing else to do but go home, let himself in, and wait. Aaron shivered at the thought of his mother asleep in her room, snoring loud enough to be heard downstairs. He walked, alert to every sound, craning frightened looks over his shoulder whenever he heard a noise. No one was ever there.

In the kitchen he poured cold water and sat at the table, the silence a solid force. The walls ticked and the sporadic creak of floorboards made Aaron wonder if they could teleport. No matter. Not now. There was nowhere he couldn't be found. After an hour he heard shuffling at the back door. A hazy shape formed in frosted glass, blurred as their true form. A series of soft taps against wood. One, two three.

He got to his feet. His hands shook as he unlocked the back door.

She looked the same. Just as beautiful, not frightening, or perhaps there was something in her eyes. Not shy, downcast, only steady appraisal. That was it. She studied him without pause, without feeling.

"Sorry you had to see us."

He lowered his head, not wanting to remember his panic, heart thudding like pounding escape in his chest.

"We were going to tell you. You woke sooner than we planned. I knew you were strong from the start."

Aaron looked at the ground. On another road, not far away, a car changed gears, engine fading.

"So what now?"

"You come with us. We'd prefer by choice."

He released a sigh, his swirling breath.

"Okay. Okay."

She said nothing, did nothing, not even nod. Just stepped back to let him pass.

They took the bus. It was dawn, a trickle of commuters seeping through glass station doors and past the shuddering arms of barriers. On the tube, Christie sat next to him, back stiff, face blank. They did not touch or talk. He kept his chin tucked into his chest. She was like a carving or, better yet, a mannequin, more anatomically correct, more real. He looked from the corner of his eye to see if she'd react to anything, but she sat motionless, life bled. It was eerie. He wondered if the other commuters noticed. They seemed buried in their papers, and he didn't want to risk a better look in case she suspected he was up to something, trying to communicate what they were doing, that he wasn't going along.

At Westminster she stood and he followed. Up escalators, out through barriers, into the streets and the morning crowd. The sun cracked the sky pale orange and red. The clouds were dark-bellied, gloomy. They walked along Whitehall at a rapid pace, Aaron treading fast to keep up, but she kept on and didn't look at him once. Halfway down the long, wide road, they stopped outside black gates. Two policemen stood on either side eyeing them. A sign above their heads said what he'd feared: Downing Street.

"Here?" He stood directly in front of her, a vague challenge, trying to see beyond those deepwater eyes. "Seriously?"

She turned toward him, her unfeeling expression fathomless. It scared him. He backed away.

"Okay. Okay."

Someone brushed his shoulder. He started, turned. Limo and Old Girl. Their faces blank, unseeing. Other young people were at their side, equally blind and entranced. They pushed forward, Aaron following. They walked up to the barrier, all of them, and the policemen guarding the street stepped aside, opened the gate, let them enter.

At Number 10, they did the same thing.

A SHELTERED WOMAN

Yiyun Li

THE NEW MOTHER, groggy from a nap, sat at the table as though she did not grasp why she had been summoned. Perhaps she never would, Auntie Mei thought. On the placemat sat a bowl of soybean-and-pig's-foot soup that Auntie Mei had cooked, as she had for many new mothers before this one. "Many," however, was not exact. In her interviews with potential employers, Auntie Mei always gave the precise number of families she had worked for: a hundred and twenty-six when she interviewed with her current employer, a hundred and thirty-one babies altogether. The families' contact information, the dates she had worked for them, their babies' names and birthdays—these she had recorded in a palm-size notebook, which had twice fallen apart and been taped back together. Years ago, Auntie Mei had bought it at a garage sale in Moline, Illinois. She had liked the picture of flowers on the cover, purple and yellow, unmelted snow surrounding the chaste petals. She had liked the price of the notebook, too: five cents. When she handed a dime to the child with the cash box on his lap, she asked if there was another notebook she could buy, so that he would not have to give her any change; the boy looked perplexed and said no. It was greed that had made her ask, but when the memory came back—it often did when she took the notebook out of her suitcase for another interview—Auntie Mei would laugh at herself: Why on earth had she wanted two notebooks, when there's not enough life to fill one?

The mother sat still, not touching the spoon, until teardrops fell into the steaming soup.

"Now, now," Auntie Mei said. She was pushing herself and the baby in a new rocking chair—back and forth, back and forth, the squeaking less noticeable than yesterday. I wonder who's enjoying the rocking more, she said to herself: the chair, whose job is to rock until it breaks apart, or you, whose life is being rocked away? And which one of you will meet your demise first? Auntie Mei had long ago accepted that she had, despite her best intentions, become one of those people who talk to themselves when the world is not listening. At least she took care not to let the words slip out.

"I don't like this soup," said the mother, who surely had a Chinese name but had asked Auntie Mei to call her Chanel. Auntie Mei, however, called every mother Baby's Ma, and every infant Baby. It was simple that way, one set of clients easily replaced by the next.

"It's not for you to like," Auntie Mei asked. The soup had simmered all morning and had thickened to a milky white. She would never have touched it herself, but it was the best recipe for breastfeeding mothers. "You eat it for Baby."

"Why do I have to eat for him?" Chanel asked. She was skinny, though it had been only five days since the delivery.

"Why indeed," Auntie Mei said, laughing. "Where else do you think your milk comes from?"

"I'm not a cow."

I would rather you were a cow, Auntie Mei thought. But she merely threatened gently that there was always the option of formula. Auntie Mei wouldn't mind that, but most people hired her for her expertise in taking care of newborns and breastfeeding mothers.

The young woman started to sob. Really, Auntie Mei thought, she had never seen anyone so unfit to be a mother as this little creature.

"I think I have postpartum depression," Chanel said when her tears had stopped.

Some fancy term the young woman had picked up.

"My great-grandmother hanged herself when my grandfather was three days old. People said she'd fallen under the spell of some passing ghost, but this is what I think." Using her iPhone as a mirror, Chanel checked her face and pressed her puffy eyelids with a finger. "She had postpartum depression."

Auntie Mei stopped rocking and snuggled the infant closer. At once his head started bumping against her bosom. "Don't speak nonsense," she said sternly.

"I'm only explaining what postpartum depression is."

"Your problem is that you're not eating. Nobody would be happy if they were in your shoes."

"Nobody," Chanel said glumly, "could possibly be in my shoes. Do you know what I dreamed last night?"

"No."

"Take a guess."

"In our village, we say it's bad luck to guess someone

else's dreams," Auntie Mei said. Only ghosts entered and left people's minds freely.

"I dreamed that I flushed Baby down the toilet."

"Oh. I wouldn't have guessed that even if I'd tried."

"That's the problem. Nobody knows how I feel," Chanel said, and started to weep again.

Auntie Mei sniffed under the child's blanket, paying no heed to the fresh tears. "Baby needs a diaper change," she announced, knowing that, given some time, Chanel would acquiesce: a mother is a mother, even if she speaks of flushing her child down the drain.

■   ■   ■

Auntie Mei had worked as a live-in nanny for newborns and their mothers for eleven years. As a rule, she moved out of the family's house the day a baby turned a month old, unless—though this rarely happened—she was between jobs, which was never more than a few days. Many families would have been glad to pay her extra for another week or another month—some even offered a longer term—but Auntie Mei always declined: she worked as a first-month nanny, whose duties, toward both the mother and the infant, were different from those of a regular nanny. Once in a while, she was approached by previous employers to care for their second child. The thought of facing a child who had once been an infant in her arms led to lost sleep; she agreed only when there was no other option, and she treated the older children as though they were empty air.

Between bouts of sobbing, Chanel said she did not understand why her husband couldn't take a few days off. The previous day he had left for Shenzhen on a business trip.

"What right does he have to leave me alone with his son?"

Alone? Auntie Mei squinted at Baby's eyebrows, knitted so tight that the skin in between took on a tinge of yellow. *Your pa is working hard so your ma can stay home and call me nobody.* The Year of the Snake, an inauspicious one to give birth in, had been slow for Auntie Mei; otherwise, she would've had better options. She had not liked the couple when she met them: unlike most expectant parents, they both looked distracted, and asked few questions before offering her the position. They were about to entrust their baby to a stranger, Auntie Mei wanted to remind them, but neither seemed worried. Perhaps they had gathered enough references? Auntie Mei did have a reputation as a gold-medal nanny. Her employers were the lucky ones, to have had a good education in China and, later, America, and to have become professionals in the Bay Area: lawyers, doctors, VCs, engineers—no matter, they still needed an experienced Chinese nanny for their American-born babies. Many families lined her up months before their babies were born.

Baby, cleaned and swaddled, seemed satisfied, so Auntie Mei left him on the changing table and looked out the window, enjoying, as she always did, a view that did not belong to her. Between an azalea bush and a slate path, there was a man-made pond that hosted an assortment of goldfish and lily pads. Before he left, the husband had asked Auntie Mei to feed the fish and refill the pond. Eighteen hundred gallons a year, he informed her, calculating the expense. She would have refused the additional responsibilities if not for his readiness to pay her an extra twenty dollars each day.

A statue of an egret, balanced on one leg, stood in the water, its neck curved into a question mark. Auntie Mei thought about the man who had made the sculpture. Of course, it could have been a woman, but Auntie Mei refused to accept that possibility. She liked to believe that it was men who made beautiful and useless things like the egret. Let him be a lonely man, beyond the reach of any fiendish woman.

Baby started to wiggle. "Don't you stir before your ma finishes her soup," Auntie Mei warned in a whisper, though in vain. The egret, startled, took off with an unhurried elegance, its single squawk stunning Auntie Mei and then making her laugh. For sure, you're getting old and forgetful: there was no such statue yesterday. Auntie Mei picked up Baby and went into the yard. There were fewer goldfish now, but at least some had escaped the egret's raid. All the same, she would have to tell Chanel about the loss. You think you have a problem with postpartum depression? Think of the goldfish, living one day in a paradise pond and the next day going to heaven in the stomach of a passing egret.

■ ■ ■

Auntie Mei believed in strict routines for every baby and mother in her charge. For the first week, she fed the mother six meals a day, with three snacks in between; from the second week on, it was four meals and two snacks. The baby was to be nursed every two hours during the day and every three or four hours at night. She let the parents decide whether the crib was kept in their bedroom or in the nursery, but she would not allow it in her bedroom. No, this was not for her convenience, she explained to them; there was simply no reason for a baby to be close to someone who was there for only a month.

"But it's impossible to eat so much. People are different,"

Chanel said the next day. Less weepy at the moment, she was curled up on the sofa, a pair of heating pads on her chest: Auntie Mei had not been impressed with the young woman's milk production.

You can be as different as you want after I leave, Auntie Mei thought as she bathed Baby. *Your son can grow into a lopsided squash and I won't care a bit.* But no mother or baby could deviate just yet. The reason people hired a first-month nanny, Auntie Mei told Chanel, was to make sure that things went correctly, not differently.

"But did you follow this schedule when you had your children? I bet you didn't."

"As a matter of fact, I didn't, only because I didn't have children."

"Not even one?"

"You didn't specify a nanny who had her own children."

"But why would you . . . why did you choose this line of work?"

Why indeed. "Sometimes a job chooses you," Auntie Mei said. Ha, who knew she could be so profound?

"But you must love children, then?"

Oh, no, no, not this one or that one; not any of them. "Does a bricklayer love his bricks?" Auntie Mei asked. "Does the dishwasher repairman love the dishwashers?" That morning a man had come to look at Chanel's malfunctioning dishwasher. It had taken him only twenty minutes of poking, but the bill was a hundred dollars, as much as a whole day's wages for Auntie Mei.

"Auntie, that's not a good argument."

"My job doesn't require me to argue well. If I could argue, I'd have become a lawyer, like your husband, no?"

Chanel made a mirthless laughing sound. Despite her self-diagnosed depression, she seemed to enjoy talking with Auntie Mei more than most mothers, who talked to her about their babies and their breastfeeding but otherwise had little interest in her.

Auntie Mei put Baby on the sofa next to Chanel, who was unwilling to make room. "Now, let's look into this milk situation," Auntie Mei said, rubbing her hands until they were warm before removing the heating pads. Chanel cried out in pain.

"I haven't even touched you."

Look at your eyes, Auntie Mei wanted to say. *Not even a good plumber could fix such a leak.*

"I don't want to nurse this thing anymore," Chanel said.

This thing? "He's your son."

"His father's too. Why can't he be here to help?"

"Men don't make milk."

Chanel laughed, despite her tears. "No. The only thing they make is money."

"You're lucky to have found one who makes money. Not all of them do, you know."

Chanel dried her eyes carefully with the inside of her pajama sleeve. "Auntie, are you married?"

"Once," Auntie Mei said.

"What happened? Did you divorce him?"

"He died," Auntie Mei said. She had, every day of her marriage, wished that her husband would stop being part of her life, though not in so absolute a manner. Now, years later, she still felt responsible for his death, as though it had been she, and not a group of teenagers, who accosted him that night. *Why didn't you just let them take the money?* Sometimes

Auntie Mei scolded him when she tired of talking to herself. Thirty-five dollars for a life, three months short of fifty-two.

"Was he much older than you?"

"Older, yes, but not too old."

"My husband is twenty-eight years older than I am," Chanel said. "I bet you didn't guess that."

"No, I didn't."

"Is it that I look old or that he looks young?"

"You look like a good match."

"Still, he'll probably die before me, right? Women live longer than men, and he's had a head start."

So you, too, are eager to be freed. Let me tell you, it's bad enough when a wish like that doesn't come true, but if it ever does, that's when you know that living is a most disappointing business: the world is not a bright place to start with, but a senseless wish granted senselessly makes it much dimmer. "Don't speak nonsense," Auntie Mei said.

"I'm only stating the truth. How did your husband die? Was it a heart attack?"

"You could say that," Auntie Mei said, and before Chanel could ask more questions, Auntie Mei grabbed one of her erring breasts. Chanel gasped and then screamed. Auntie Mei did not let go until she'd given the breast a forceful massage. When she reached for the other breast, Chanel screamed louder but did not change her position—for fear of crushing Baby, perhaps.

Afterward, Auntie Mei brought a warm towel. "Go," Chanel said. "I don't want you here anymore."

"But who'll take care of you?"

"I don't need anyone to take care of me." Chanel stood up and belted her robe.

"And Baby?"

"Bad luck for him."

Chanel walked to the staircase, her back defiantly rigid. Auntie Mei picked up Baby, his weight as insignificant as the emotions—sadness, anger, or dismay—that she should feel on his behalf. Rather, Auntie Mei was in awe of the young woman. That is how, Auntie Mei said to herself, a mother orphans a child.

■ ■ ■

Baby, six days old that day, was weaned from his mother's breast. Auntie Mei was now the sole person to provide him with food and care and—this she did not want to admit even to herself—love. Chanel stayed in her bedroom and watched Chinese television dramas all afternoon. Once in a while she came downstairs for water and spoke to Auntie Mei as though the old woman and the infant were poor relations: there was the inconvenience of having them to stay, and yet there was relief that they did not have to be entertained.

The dishwasher repairman returned in the evening. He reminded Auntie Mei that his name was Paul—as though she were so old that she could forget it in a day, she thought. Earlier, she had told him about the thieving egret, and he had promised to come back and fix the problem.

"You're sure the bird won't be killed," Auntie Mei said as she watched Paul rig some wires above the pond.

"Try it yourself," Paul said, flipping the battery switch.

Auntie Mei placed her palm on the crisscrossed wires. "I feel nothing."

"Good. If you felt something, I'd be putting your life at risk. Then you could sue me."

"But how does it work?"

"Let's hope the egret is more sensitive than you are," Paul said. "Call me if it doesn't work. I won't charge you again."

Auntie Mei felt doubtful, but her questioning silence did not stop him from admiring his own invention. Nothing, he said, is too difficult for a thinking man. When he put away his tools he lingered on, and she could see that there was no reason for him to hurry home. He had grown up in Vietnam, he told Auntie Mei, and had come to America thirty-seven years ago. He was widowed, with three grown children, and none of them had given him a grandchild, or the hope of one. His two sisters, both living in New York and both younger, had beaten him at becoming grandparents.

The same old story: they all had to come from somewhere, and they all accumulated people along the way. Auntie Mei could see the unfolding of Paul's life: he'd work his days away till he was too old to be useful, then his children would deposit him in a facility and visit on his birthday and on holidays. Auntie Mei, herself an untethered woman, felt superior to him. She raised Baby's tiny fist as Paul was leaving. "Say bye-bye to Grandpa Paul."

Auntie Mei turned and looked up at the house. Chanel was leaning on the windowsill of her second-floor bedroom. "Is he going to electrocute the egret?" she called down.

"He said it would only zap the bird. To teach it a lesson."

"You know what I hate about people? They like to say, 'That will teach you a lesson.' But what's the point of a lesson? There's no makeup exam when you fail something in life."

It was October, and the evening air from the bay had a chill to it. Auntie Mei had nothing to say except to warn Chanel not to catch a cold.

"Who cares?"

"Maybe your parents do."

Chanel made a dismissive noise.

"Or your husband."

"Ha. He just e-mailed and told me he had to stay for another ten days," Chanel said. "You know what I think he's doing right now? Sleeping with a woman, or more than one."

Auntie Mei did not reply. It was her policy not to disparage an employer behind his back. But when she entered the house, Chanel was already in the living room. "I think you should know he's not the kind of person you thought he was."

"I don't think he's any kind of person at all," Auntie Mei said.

"You never say a bad word about him," Chanel said.

Not a good word, either.

"He had a wife and two children before."

You think a man, any man, would remain a bachelor until he meets you? Auntie Mei put the slip of paper with Paul's number in her pocket.

"Did that man leave you his number?" Chanel said. "Is he courting you?"

"Him? Half of him, if not more, is already in the coffin."

"Men chase after women until the last moment," Chanel said. "Auntie, don't fall for him. No man is to be trusted."

Auntie Mei sighed. "If Baby's Pa is not coming home, who's going to shop for groceries?"

■ ■ ■

The man of the house postponed his return; Chanel refused to have anything to do with Baby. Against her rules, Auntie

Mei moved his crib into her bedroom; against her rules, too, she took on the responsibility of grocery shopping.

"Do you suppose people will think we're the grandparents of this baby?" Paul asked after inching the car into a tight spot between two SUVs.

Could it be that he had agreed to drive and help with shopping for a reason other than the money Auntie Mei had promised him? "Nobody," she said, handing a list to Paul, "will think anything. Baby and I will wait here in the car."

"You're not coming in?"

"He's a brand-new baby. You think I would bring him into a store with a bunch of refrigerators?"

"You should've left him home, then."

With whom? Auntie Mei worried that, had she left Baby home, he would be gone from the world when she returned, though this fear she would not share with Paul. She explained that Baby's Ma suffered from postpartum depression and was in no shape to take care of him.

"You should've just given me the shopping list," Paul said.

What if you ran off with the money without delivering the groceries? she thought, though it was unfair of her. There were men she knew she could trust, including, even, her dead husband.

On the drive back, Paul asked if the egret had returned. She hadn't noticed, Auntie Mei replied. She wondered if she would have an opportunity to see the bird be taught its lesson: she had only twenty-two days left. Twenty-two days, and then the next family would pluck her out of here, egret or no egret. Auntie Mei turned to look at Baby, who was asleep in the car seat. "What will become of you then?" she said.

"Me?" Paul asked.

"Not you. Baby."

"Why do you worry? He'll have a good life. Better than mine. Better than yours, for sure."

"You don't know my life to say that," Auntie Mei said.

"I can imagine. You should find someone. This is not a good life for you, going from one house to another and never settling down."

"What's wrong with that? I don't pay rent. I don't have to buy my own food."

"What's the point of making money if you don't spend it?" Paul said. "I'm at least saving money for my future grandchildren."

"What I do with my money," Auntie Mei said, "is none of your business. Now, please pay attention to the road."

Paul, chastened into a rare silence, drove on, the slowest car on the freeway. Perhaps he'd meant well, but there were plenty of well-meaning men, and she was one of those women who made such men suffer. If Paul wanted to hear stories, she could tell him one or two and spare him any hope of winning her affection. But where would she start? With the man she had married without any intention of loving and had wished into an early grave, or with the father she had not met because her mother had made his absolute absence a condition of her birth? Or perhaps she should start with her grandmother, who vanished from her own daughter's crib side one day, only to show up twenty-five years later when her husband was dying from a wasting illness. The disappearance would have made sense had Auntie Mei's grandfather been a villain, but he had been a kind man, and had raised his daughter alone, clinging to the hope that his wife, having left without a word, would return.

Auntie Mei's grandmother had not gone far: all those years, she had stayed in the same village, living with another man, hiding in his attic during the day, sneaking out of the house in the middle of the night for a change of air. Nobody was able to understand why she had not gone on hiding until after her husband's death. She explained that it was her wifely duty to see her husband off properly.

Auntie Mei's mother, newly married and with a prospering business as a seamstress, was said to have accepted one parent's return and the other's death with equanimity, but the next year, pregnant with her first and only child, she made her husband leave by threatening to drink a bottle of DDT.

Auntie Mei had been raised by two mythic women. The villagers shunned the two women, but they welcomed the girl as one of them. Behind closed doors, they told her about her grandfather and her father, and in their eyes she saw their fearful disapproval of her elders: her pale-skinned grandmother, unused to daylight after years of darkness, carried on her nocturnal habits, cooking and knitting for her daughter and granddaughter in the middle of the night; her mother, eating barely enough, slowly starved herself to death, yet she never tired of watching, with an unblinking intensity, her daughter eat.

Auntie Mei had not thought of leaving home until the two women died, her mother first, and then her grandmother. They had been sheltered from worldly reproach by their peculiarities when alive; in death, they took with them their habitat and left nothing to anchor Auntie Mei. A marriage offer, arranged by the distant cousin of a man in Queens, New York, had been accepted without hesitation:

in a new country, her grandmother and her mother would cease to be legendary. Auntie Mei had not told her husband about them; he would not have been interested, in any case—silly good man, wanting only a hardworking woman to share a solid life. Auntie Mei turned to look at Paul. Perhaps he was not so different from her husband, her father, her grandfather, or even the man her grandmother had lived with for years but never returned to after the death of Auntie Mei's grandfather: ordinary happiness, uncomplicated by the women in their lives, was their due.

"You think, by any chance, you'll be free tomorrow afternoon?" Paul asked when he'd parked the car in front of Chanel's house.

"I work all day, as you know."

"You could bring Baby, like you did today."

"To where?"

Paul said that there was this man who played chess every Sunday afternoon at East-West Plaza Park. Paul wanted to take a walk with Auntie Mei and Baby nearby.

Auntie Mei laughed. "Why, so he'll get distracted and lose the game?"

"I want him to think I've done better than him."

Better how? With a borrowed lady friend pushing a borrowed grandson in a stroller? "Who is he?"

"Nobody important. I haven't talked to him for twenty-seven years."

He couldn't even lie well. "And you still think he'd fall for your trick?"

"I know him."

Auntie Mei wondered if knowing someone—a friend, an enemy—was like never letting that person out of one's sight.

Being known, then, must not be far from being imprisoned by someone else's thought. In that sense, her grandmother and her mother had been fortunate: no one could claim to have known them, not even Auntie Mei. When she was younger, she had seen no point in understanding them, as she had been told they were beyond apprehension. After their deaths, they had become abstract. Not knowing them, Auntie Mei, too, had the good fortune of not wanting to know anyone who came after: her husband; her coworkers at various Chinese restaurants during her yearlong migration from New York to San Francisco; the babies and the mothers she took care of, who had become only recorded names in her notebook. "I'd say let it go," Auntie Mei told Paul. "What kind of grudge is worthy of twenty-seven years?"

Paul sighed. "If I tell you the story, you'll understand."

"Please," Auntie Mei said. "Don't tell me any story."

■ ■ ■

From the second-floor landing, Chanel watched Paul put the groceries in the refrigerator and Auntie Mei warm up a bottle of formula. Only after he'd left did Chanel call down to ask how their date had gone. Auntie Mei held Baby in the rocking chair; the joy of watching him eat was enough compensation for his mother's being a nuisance.

Chanel came downstairs and sat on the sofa. "I saw you pull up. You stayed in the car for a long time," she said. "I didn't know an old man could be so romantic."

Auntie Mei thought of taking Baby into her bedroom, but this was not her house, and she knew that Chanel, in a mood to talk, would follow her. When Auntie Mei remained quiet, Chanel said that her husband had called earlier, and she had told him that his son had gone out to witness a couple carry on a *sunset affair*.

You should walk out right this minute, Auntie Mei said to herself, but her body settled into the rhythm of the rocking chair, back and forth, back and forth.

"Are you angry, Auntie?"

"What did your husband say?"

"He was upset, of course, and I told him that's what he gets for not coming home."

What's stopping you from leaving? Auntie Mei asked herself. *You want to believe you're staying for Baby, don't you?*

"You should be happy for me that he's upset," Chanel said. "Or at least happy for Baby, no?"

I'm happy that, like everyone else, you'll all become the past soon.

"Why are you so quiet, Auntie? I'm sorry I'm such a pain, but I don't have a friend here, and you've been nice to me. Would you please take care of me and Baby?"

"You're paying me," Auntie Mei said. "So of course I'll take care of you."

"Will you be able to stay on after this month?" Chanel asked. "I'll pay double."

"I don't work as a regular nanny."

"But what would we do without you, Auntie?"

Don't let this young woman's sweet voice deceive you, Auntie Mei warned herself. You're not irreplaceable—not for her, not for Baby, not for anyone. Still, Auntie Mei fancied for a moment that she could watch Baby grow—a few months, a year, two years. "When is Baby's Pa coming home?"

"He'll come home when he comes."

Auntie Mei cleaned Baby's face with the corner of a towel.

"I know what you're thinking—that I didn't choose the right man. Do you want to know how I came to marry someone so old and irresponsible?"

"I don't, as a matter of fact."

. . .

All the same, they told Auntie Mei stories, not heeding her protests. The man who played chess every Sunday afternoon came from the same village as Paul's wife, and had long ago been pointed out to him by her as a potentially better husband. Perhaps she had said it only once, out of an impulse to sting Paul, or perhaps she had tormented him for years with her approval of a former suitor. Paul did not say, and Auntie Mei did not ask. Instead, he measured his career against the man's: Paul had become a real professional; the man had stayed a laborer.

An enemy could be as eternally close as a friend; a feud could make two men brothers for life. Fortunate are those for whom everyone can be turned into a stranger, Auntie Mei thought, but this wisdom she did not share with Paul. He had wanted her only to listen, and she had obliged him.

Chanel, giving more details and making Auntie blush at times, was a better storyteller. She had slept with an older married man to punish her father, who had himself pursued a young woman, in this case one of Chanel's college classmates. The pregnancy was meant to punish her father, too, but also the man, who, like her father, had cheated on his wife. "He didn't know who I was at first. I made up a story so that he thought I was one of those girls he could sleep with and then pay off," Chanel had said. "But then he realized he had no choice but to marry me. My father has enough con-nections to destroy his business."

Had she not thought how this would make her mother feel? Auntie Mei asked. Why should she? Chanel replied. A woman who could not keep the heart of her man was not a good model for a daughter.

Auntie Mei did not understand their logic: Chanel's de-praved; Paul's unbending. What a world you've been born into, Auntie Mei said to Baby now. It was past midnight, the lamp in her bedroom turned off. The night-light of swim-ming ocean animals on the crib streaked Baby's face blue and orange. There must have been a time when her mother had sat with her by candlelight, or else her grandmother might have been there in the darkness. What kind of future had they wished for her? She had been brought up in two worlds: the world of her grandmother and her mother, and that of everyone else; each world had sheltered her from the other, and to lose one was to be turned, against her wish, into a permanent resident of the other.

Auntie Mei came from a line of women who could not understand themselves, and in not knowing themselves they had derailed their men and orphaned their children. At least Auntie Mei had had the sense not to have a child, though sometimes, during a sleepless night like this one, she entertained the thought of slipping away with a baby she could love. The world was vast; there had to be a place for a woman to raise a child as she wished.

The babies—a hundred and thirty-one of them—and their parents, trusting yet vigilant, had protected Auntie Mei from herself. But who was going to protect her now? Not this baby, who was as defenseless as the others, yet she must protect him. From whom, though: his parents, who had no place for him in their hearts, or Auntie Mei, who had begun to imagine his life beyond the one month allocated to her?

See, this is what you get for sitting up and muddling your head. Soon you'll become a tiresome oldster like Paul, or a lonely woman like Chanel, telling stories to any available ear. You can go on talking and thinking about your mother and your grandmother and all those women before them, but the problem is, you don't know them. If knowing someone makes that person stay with you forever, not knowing someone does the same trick: death does not take the dead away; it only makes them grow more deeply into you.

No one would be able to stop her if she picked up Baby and walked out the door. She could turn herself into her grandmother, for whom sleep had become optional in the end; she could turn herself into her mother, too, eating little because it was Baby who needed nourishment. She could become a fugitive from this world that had kept her for too long, but this urge, coming as it often did in waves, no longer frightened her, as it had years ago. She was getting older, more forgetful, yet she was also closer to comprehending the danger of being herself. She had, unlike her mother and her grandmother, talked herself into being a woman with an ordinary fate. When she moved on to the next place, she would leave no mystery or damage behind; no one in this world would be disturbed by having known her.

HIGH PURSUIT

Mitchell S. Jackson

BLOOD PULLS UP in a near-new new Caddie, heaven white, with flesh-colored guts and the white walls on his tires thick as rulers side by side. It's the kind of ride that hurts my feelings to look at but I can't keep from looking at it, from hawking him as he parks and cools out wearing a grass-green velour tracksuit—unzipped so you see he's shirtless—in reptile cowboy boots. He swaggers across the street and up the pathway, the same path that from the time I was a wee bit has been my chore to keep swept and weeded. Like in the few years since he night schooled his way to a diploma, dropped out of the only college for miles, and got booted out the house, he's become a grownass man who believes in himself so much you can't convince him not to. He stops just short of the porch and cheeses. I set my magazine (I stay in these custom car magazines) aside and stand.

What it is? he says.

Long time no see, I say.

You can whiff him from a distance. He smooths silky freshpressed strands that make it hard to tell we're brothers by the head. Aw, Maine, you know, he says. Been out here in high pursuit.

He fingers the thumbthick gold herringbone dressing his neck, peeps Moms' Plymouth in the driveway. He asks where she is, and I tell him in the house sleep 'cause she's fresh off a double and said she's ushering evening service. Blood asks what I'm into, if I'm down to roll, and since it's my day off, what the fuck am I supposed to say—no? No sooner than we pull off, he turns his 8-track low and gets to highsighting about his Brougham, about how much get-up the engine got, how smooth it drives on the freeway, about how he ain't yet decided what his custom plate will say. He runs his hand over the fur smothering his steering wheel, fiddles the handmade Playboy logo and forest of spanking-new Evergreen air fresheners hanging from his rearview.

Blood wheels over to the park in North East with the rose garden. Bloomed roses everymuthafuckinwhere and you can't not smell them if you try. We stride a couple laps in the garden catching up on the latest family business, Pops' latest appeal, Moms working a trillion double shifts to cover his legal fees, our sister's firstborn—a baby boy that Blood had yet to see.

Say, you still down there scrubbin them white folks' rides for a little bit of nothin? Blood says.

They say I'm bout to come up for a raise, I say. Plus, the tips is cool when the weather breaks.

Oh, I beg to differ, Maine. You know I know that elbow-and-ass work ain't never cool. He pulls out a bankroll that, no bullshit, would choke an Old Testament camel and peels off enough to make me good and envious. Check it, he says.

Give some to Mom and say it's from you. Give some to Sis and say it's from me. And the rest is fuckoff funds.

Before Blood second-guesses his largesse, I shove the bread in my jeans and tell him, Right on.

We stride another half-lap with him a half-step ahead and me thinking of them days when you used to couldn't tell me nothing about Blood. How it used to be that if you said something even halfway on its way to being sideways about my older brother to me, it was a prime cause for me going upside your head. How summers you used to couldn't find me and Blood apart for more than a few ticks: picking berries, building a tree house, stealing ten-speeds. When you saw him coming, you saw me fresh on his heels.

You can hear the hoop court's chain nets *ching* every so often, hear kids hollering and whooping on the playground, hear a hooptie in tragic need of a muffler stuttering up the street. Hold up, I say, and touch his shoulder. He swings so we're facing each other, and I crane so we're eye to eye. Allbullshitaside, I say. Is it really that sweet?

Aw, Maine, it's a toothache, he says. I tell you no lies.

■ ■ ■

Before visions of high-profile pimpin and flaunting, flaunting around North East in a Caddie, Blood pushed an AMC Pacer and worked graveyards at EastWest Janitorial. Can't tell you how many mornings he'd slump home smelling fetid as fuck with the whites of his eyes the color of industrial cleaner, then one morning—memorable even more for it being my first day at the car wash—he stomped into the attic room he and I shared, snatched the nametag off his work shirt, slammed it on the floor, and stomped that joint to shards. They can have this shit, Maine, he said. They can have this shit forever.

Quit bullshittin. You ain't quittin, is you? I said. What you gone do now?

What I shoulda been did, he said. What I was born to do, he said. Check it, a nigga done lived his everlast day on his knees.

The next evening Moms, who was weeks into ushering first *and* second Sunday services, called devotion, and Blood dawdled into the living room long after me and Sis stood smug over our circle.

Well, have a seat, Moms said.

With all due respect, Mama, not tonight, he said. Not tomorrow night neither. Matter fact, no more nights.

What? Moms said, and called him by his full name. What's this foolishness?

Foolishness? he said. Seem to me like foolishness is us down here every odd evening, praising the same God that let a white man put Pops in the penitentiary.

Moms, all the mirth sucked out her face, stood taller than I'd seen in life. So, I guess you got your heart set on being a heathen, huh? she said. God knows I can't stop you. But I tell you what: you won't do it livin here.

Blood tramped upstairs and made racket rummaging. He came back down an hour or so later, hefting a dingy duffel and a suitcase. He floated over and gave my shoulder a squeeze. He kissed Sis square in her forehead and went to hug Moms, but she crossed her arms, huffed, and gave him her back. He loaded his car alone in quiet, told us, Love is love, bid us a beauty contestant's wave, and eased the front door shut. Nam one of us saw him again till after the New Year flipped.

In retrospect, Blood's defiance was a declaration—to his damn self, to Moms, to the world, a stance that, truth be told, made him a hero to me, too, made me question whenif my nuts would ever swell that size, if I could summon the daring to seize from the world what I wanted, to proclaim who I am as this bitch keeps spinning.

■ ■ ■

Got the munchies something vicious, so I tramp down to the corner store on the corner of Union Ave and Failing. From a block or so off, I spy some broads standing against the wall, all of them in bikini tops, skirts cut so high you don't have to work to see their prize, and heels too tall for sure footing. See a car pull curbside and the girls scramble to the window and barter not more than a hot minute before one of them hops in, and the driver eases off as if what just went down was on the up and up. The unchosen totter back to the side of the building. This, mind you, is nothing I ain't witnessed under moonlight, but under a bright sun—well, that's something else. It's damn near stunning, and moreso when I behold who I'd trade a lung to *un*see—my ex, my one love. The best advice is to mind my motherfucking business, but see that's the thing about advice, though: we need somebody to give it to us. Ill-advised, I slug over to where she stands. She straightens her skirt and bra top, seeming about as happy to see me as she would be to see the police.

Nah, no, no, I say. Not you too. What you doin out here?!

She smacks her bright red kissing lips, waves a hand.

You out here like this? I say. How this happen?

She huffs. Just like you to be askin how, when what you need to be askin why, she says.

She's the one. Let me fingerfuck freshman year, pop her cherry—quiet as it's kept, popped mine too—when we was sophomores. The one that tutored me through a math class I wouldn't have passed in this life or the next without her. Was game for us wearing matching outfits to house parties. Was my date for homecomings and prom. We broke up last summer—I'd cheated her into tears for the last time; not too long after, I waltzed across the stage with my diploma in hand, and though I've heard rumors since, I ain't had the heart to ask. This close, I can see she's wearing a cheap wig, that there's a scar on her cheek that she's tried to mask with blush. C'mon, I say, and grab her by her bony wrist. We leavin.

She jerks free with strength, peers into my bony chest, and judges, as has been her gift, my percent of punk—too high. *We* ain't goin nowhere, she says. Unless *you* is payin.

■   ■   ■

While Moms pulls a swing shift, me and a couple of my patnas pass a J of homegrown and watch welterweights trade haymakers on the old console a crew of us moved upstairs once Pops began his bid. The blather champ among us gets to bickering with me about who's up on the scorecards, and in the midst of our back-and-forth, Blood flaunts upstairs wearing a silk shirt, slacks, reptile boots, a Cubanlink chain, and a fucking gold nugget watch.

What it is? he says.

Can't call it, I say.

He lazes on the couch beside me and asks if he can blow

with us. When the J reaches him on its circuit, he pulls deep, holds it and holds it, exhales a cloud, waits and waits, and shakes his head. Well, I'll be goddamned! Y'all down here puffin bunk, he says, and digs Zig-Zags and the fattest gram bag in all the world from a pocket. He opens it, tells me to smell, and I scent myself good and covetous. When it reaches him again, he rolls—Blood's a twisting phenom—a tumescent J on the shoebox top we keep near for the cause. He admires his handiwork from up close. He sucks a lungful and, beats later, coughs like he might got TB. Now that, he says. That right there's some killer.

He passes it to me, and I know in a pulse he ain't in the least bit overstating the truth. By the time the judges announce the fight's final scorecards, I'm high as dying stars and paranoid Moms will rush home early from her shift and, instead of, per her norm, calling from the base, will stomp upstairs, condemn my patnas into purgatory, and make me the latest and last of whom she bore bounced permanent out the house. Blood rolls another pregnant J, seeming oblivious about this prospect. But why shouldn't he be, when, as far as any of us can tell, he's making it happen?

Shit, I'm the one life's happening *to*.

One of my patnas asks to see Blood's watch, and he unclasps it and tosses it to him. My patna runs his fingers over the ridges, smashes it against his ear, measures the weight in his palm. What's this shit, solid gold or somethin? he says. This shit heavy as a motherfucka.

Pimp tools, Blood says. These hoes out here choosin.

We awe Blood's gold glory between us and back to him. He cuffs his sleeve and fastens it back on his wrist. Another patna asks how Blood got in the game and he mentions this old head he met at an after-hours spot, explains how the old head took a liking to him, said he was a natural, started putting him up on game.

What he tell you? my sycophantic patna asks. Yeah, what he say? another one chimes, because we're all, in our own way, waiting on a blueprint, or else a rescue plan.

Blood hops up and struts in front of the TV. He turns the sound almost mute. Say, Maine, this grade A is sold. Never pro bono, he says. So, if anyone of y'all so much as check a nickel, you owe me cents. He hits the J, breaths a troposphere, cough-sneezes, and knocks his fist against his chest. First off, it's rules to this shit, he says. And the first rule is ain't no such thing as halfhearted pimpin. Rule number two, ain't no love nowhere in it. When the game begins, friendship ends. Keep it purse first and ass last always, he says. Keep a ho in arrears and do it with this here, he says, and touches his temple. Keep it head down, hand out. And don't turn down nothin but your collar, he says. Earn a name in the game but don't black-eye it with that gorilla shit, he warns. Tell a ho, you're in high pursuit of a new prostitute. Tell her, let your next move be your best move. That you don't need her, you want her. That it ain't a force thing, it's a choice thing. Stay ten toes down and it's greater later. Say, Maine, it's rules to this shit, he says. Blood leans against the TV, flashes his pearl white voltage at us lackeys. Whatever you do, don't neva let it slip your mind that pimp is what you do *and* who you are.

You really believe that shit? I say.

Say, Maine, we believe what we want to, he says. Get it how you live.

■   ■   ■

It's the first dry day after days of rain, rain, rain, and cars are marathoning off the line, so if I play it right, I can bop home with a pocketful of singles at shift's end. This, though, depends on outhustling, by bounds, the white boy that, most days, no matter how tough I scrub, buff, simper, clocks a grip more tips than me. The belt conveys a Buick off the line and I hustle to it quick-fast, hedging that, since it's a latemodel, there's, forthcoming, a brag-worthy tip for a proper wipe and shine. Hopeful that is, until I see baldface, highbooty, feels-cursed-cause-he's-a-nigger type, gump over and linger beside it. He fiddles his belt turning his khakis to floods, straightens his geek glasses, crosses the arms of a button-down buttoned at his throat—in effect dashing all hope of more than a few coins for my effort. But I go at it with grit anyhow, because you never can be sure till you're done. Plus, I ain't trying to give the manager forever-threatening-to-suspend-me-for-petty-shit even a hint of just cause.

Once I finish, I turn my towel into a white flag and dude stalks a lap around his ride. His second go-round, he swings open a door and swipes the jamb and holds his finger close enough to me to, in most other circumstances, warrant me slapping his face clean the fuck off.

Is this what you call done? he says.

Sorry about that, sir, I say, and the next moment want to shove my fist in my mouth for sounding like a punkass lick-spittle. He hovers while I rewipe the jambs. How's that? I say.

How's what? he says. He ducks inside and plucks a phantom mote off his floor mat. The motherfucka complains of smudges on the paint, streaks on the windows, dust on the dash, dirt on the license plate, a pebble in his spokes, an ash tray that still smells faint of ashes.

Moms preaches a man who don't work is a washout, a burden, and since I'm loath to be her latest proof, I stoop to rub this and that and trail this low-octane sucka as he gestures at smashed bugs on his bumper and fender and tar on the car's underbelly that no amount of scrubbing will clean. He points to another complaint and I take a knee in the wet gravel and feel sharp pebbles gouge my skin. Sheesh, what do I have to do to get decent service around here? he says.

What would Moms say? I ask myself. What would Blood do? I ask myself, scramble upright, cock my head, and wrap the towel around my fist.

What you need to do is wash the shit yourself!

Dude retreats a step, goes rictus. Uh, excuse me? You're going to regret that, he says, and doublegumps for the office calling for the manager.

How am I gone explain to Moms that I lost my job? And where, now, will I get the bread to buy the Deuce and a Quarter I've had my heart set on buying and restoring since, shit, let there be light. Shit, how I'm supposed to live day to day when I got a grand sum of not one red cent saved?

Dude stomps out stabbing a finger at me, my punk manager devil-smirking behind him. But I can't give neither one of them the pleasure, so I yank off this cornyass workshirt and tell them both what they can kiss.

■ ■ ■

Sis's crib is a hike and a half from the carwash, but since bus fare at present seems a small ransom, I slink side streets past neighborhood girls doubledutching and hopscotching, an ashy-legged boy taking a wrench to a raggedy go-kart, a clique of grade-schoolers catching wheelies on ten-speeds, an oldhead ducked under the hood of a Glasshouse, Crazy Johnny dragging his frail Rottweiler—or maybe the dog's tugging him—on a leash made of clothes tied together.

Sis answers cradling her baby boy, my firstborn nephew.

Surprise, I say.

Surprise is right, she says. What brings you by?

Do I, I say, need a reason?

No, she says, you don't. But you almost always got one.

True, and I'm lookin at him right now, I say. Hey, nephew. It's your uncle. The handsome one.

My nephew makes a face as if he might agree. As if this young he knows how to speak with his eyes. His eyes are wonders like ours, though I hope they know more triumph than mine.

Sis leads me into the living room. She sits in the velvet love seat and kicks up her feet on a low table. Since there ain't another seat, I plunk on the floor beside a carpet stain the size of a toddler— it makes me feel poorer to see it—that wasn't here the last time I came by. Sis asks if I'm thirsty, hands me my nephew, shuffles into the kitchen, and returns with Big Gulp cups filled with something iced. I'd offer you somethin else, but all's I got is this and the baby's formula, she says.

Here, she says, and reaches for my nephew. Got to put him down or he'll be a terror tonight. She lowers Nephew in the bassinet I bought her for her baby shower. She forsakes the chair in favor of sitting cross-legged beside me. My nephew whimpers a bit and then goes quiet, and neither Sis nor I bother his gift for a good while. One thing about Sis, she knows how and when to let things be. The crumpled few dollars in tips I made I fish out my pocket, smooth them on the carpet, roll them into a tube, and hold the tube in my fist.

Look like somebody had a good work day, she says.

That what this look like? I say.

Moms kicked Sis out the day she told her she was pregnant. It was a Sunday, and Sis must've thought that the Sabbath was her best shot at grace. But Moms said, You won't be having no out-of-wedlock baby in this house, and made her hand a wall that ceased all talk. Sis had little choice but to move in with her boyfriend—a finger wave–sporting nigga who was an averageass hooper for my high school's archrival—and his mama until she finagled a way into this place.

Where's that wavy-headed man of yours? I ask.

Ain't seen him, she says. Since he came home loaded, claimed I tried to trap him with the baby, packed his stuff, and bounced.

Damn, I ain't even know. How come you didn't call me? I say, and in a blink, my troubles, by contrast, feel no bigger than a mustard seed.

Call who for what? she says. Boy, don't you stress over us. We gone be good. Got an appointment with the welfare folks this week and problem's solved.

Just like that? I say.

That's what they say, she says.

Sis, who's cordial with my ex, asks if I've seen her, if she and I are working on rekindling.

Not yet, I say.

But not yet is not never, she says.

Look at us, I say, and nod at the framed black-and-white picture of her, Blood, and me Easter before Pops caught his case. Yeah, better days, she says, and announces she heard Blood knocked one of her friends and has been ferrying her up to Sea-Tac to work a track. And I hope you got sense enough not to go that route, she says.

Sis, I say. Oh, how I wish I could tell as easy as you what make sense and what don't.

She draws a heart on my chest. You do, she says. Trust it.

We, per our usual, get around to chatting about Moms and Pops. Sis confesses she ain't sure ifwhen she'll let Nephew visit our father behind the walls, that she and Moms ain't spoke since the day she kicked her out. And I tell her how, mealtimes now, Moms is liable to recite the Ten Commandments, has also conceived of even more incontrovertible laws and Lords against me transgressing them, her having to boot her last child out the house and/or the specter of me worrying her into another stroke and/or my condemnation to hell on earth or eternal hellfire.

That woman gone keep believin life's a Bible till the rapture, Sis says, and snickers, but I remind her, in so many words, that Pops' case ordained Moms a zealot. No doubt, she be downright wrong sometimes, I say. But we've also doled her a fair share of disappointments. And who's to say what's her threshold?

Sis pulls at the nap of her carpet, recrosses her legs.

Enough about that for now. How about you tell me what's what with you? she says, and plies me with the eyes that, when I was young, when she was the one scooping me from grade school and quizzing me on my times tables and spelling words, would tug the truth right out of me.

Ain't nothin to spill, I say, flatten the little bit of nothing in my palm, consider giving it to Sis, think better of it, think better of my second mind, hand her most of it, feel richer for it.

What's this for? she says.

Wrong question, I say. Not for what. For who?

My nephew—the boy got lungs—rustles and starts wailing. Sis rises, fetches him, rests him on her shoulder, and strolls around the living room humming and patting him into a coo.

■ ■ ■

The invite said BYOB and smoke, and damn near everybody in this joint is rose-eyed saucy. Me and my greedy patnas post near a corner table loaded with near-empty bowls of chips and pretzels and a scant tray of crackers and cheese, and pass a jug of rotgut liquor. The DJ spins one funk jam, one disco. Songs later, my patnas cut out on prospecting missions, and I stagger through a touch-and-feel festival on a hunt for the toilet. Well, I'll be good and gotdamed, I see some sucka in a sharkskin sportcoat macking in the ear of my ex, my one love, as she leans against a wall wearing a dress so tight she might as well be buttass naked. Closer, I see he's the cat new to the neighborhood that my patnas have been envying for his rides: a ragtop Impala, a Cougar with a racing stripe, a Mustang with glass-packed dual exhausts. Call it the weed or the wine or wanting to save her—or wanting to save me, or wanting to save us, or—but, whatever it is, it throbs my heart near my headed-for-rot liver.

He fondles her hair—her natural hair, too, which is pulled into a bun—and her hand, and she titters and bats her eyes at him. It's how, moons ago, she'd fawn at me, a boon no other fool on earth but me should reap. He swanks

off through the crowd, peeking once over his shoulder with
the hubris of a nigga who's got more than a pittance in his
pocket. Then, steady as the liquor will let me, I bumble over
and catch her by the wrist.

Say. Let me holler at you.

Holler at me about what? she says.

About us, I say.

What don't you get? she says, and jerks free. There ain't
no us. There ain't been no us.

But it could be, I say. Let me make it right.

What you gone do for me that I can't do for me? she says.
What you gone do for me that the next man won't do for me?
she says. Shit, what you do for yourself?

The sharksuited sucker flaunts beside us holding a vodka
bottle by the neck and foam cups. He looks me a once over
and smirks as if, in an instant, he's done the math and figured he'd tip a scale.

Say, Baby Girl, who this? he says.

Who him? she says, and hooks her arm through his.
Nobody. Not no one we need to know.

■ ■ ■

Blood parks his newish Caddie off Grand Ave, and we foot
it halfway across the bridge and stop close enough to the
Made in Oregon sign to hear it buzzing, to see where some
of the bulbs have burned black. Called Blood and bummed
a few bucks because the peckerwoods at the carwash been
playing games with cutting my last check, and I can't—not
now or maybe ever—admit to Moms that I've lost my gig—a
confession sure to spike her systolic and have her on my
neck something terrible about my part of the bills. But we're

here even more so because, of late, I've been feeling like I've had enough, like I'm past that point—in plural.

Blood sweeps out his arm as if offering me the Willamette on bargain. Look, he says. What you see?

From up here, the river's a blue-black sheet twinkling the lights of the cityscape. Water, I say. What else is there?

Nah, Maine, he says. Blood explains how the river begins as streams in the mountains near Eugene and Springfield, how the stream cuts sharp around Newberg before splitting into channels around Sauvie Island, how the main stream flows into the Columbia and makes its way to a mouth of the Pacific.

Look again, he says.

And I shrug.

Current, Maine, he says. We got to stay in motion, you dig. 'Cause either we movin or we standin still. And if we standin still, well, shit, we may as well be at the bottom of that muthafucka. A car rumbles over the bridge, casts Blood in a halo, and flutters his silk. Say, check this out, he says. I don't mind spottin you a couple bucks every blue moon, but that ain't gone keep your head up day to day. So you gone hafta make a serious move.

Another car shakes the bridge underfoot, and I receive it as Godspeak.

For years I've dreamed of cruising a pristine Deuce and a Quarter up Union Ave with my windows dropped and an arm flung out, of wheeling by my old slave, ordering a deluxe in-and-out wash, and catching rubber on the favored white boys as I leave; of strolling into the park during the championship of a summer hoop tournament in a mean designer short set, gator loafers, and a watch and bracelet made of Pharaoh's gold; of catching my ex, the truest love, at an all-white affair and flashing a knot that would make her contrite. For years I've dreamed of being more than just another one of us.

Sometimes we got time, and sometimes we got to get to it while the getting's within reach, he says.

We tramp back to his ride, climb in, and bend corners. We stop in the Burger Barn, where a couple of old heads in zoot suits chomp jumbo chicken wings in a corner booth. We pop in the Social Club, where somebody's auntie grooves beside the jukebox. Blood wheels to an afterhours spot housed in somebody's basement—dice, spades, and poker games going full fledge. Everywhere we go, Blood greets the doorman like a long-lost patna, glides inside, knocks fists and slaps palms with the flashiest dudes in the site, chitchats with a couple of prime ones, and, just as suave as he came, gets ghost. He calls it campaigning.

Trust, they got to see you to feel you, he says.

We end up on the stroll in the wee hours. Blood points to a mile-legged white girl fretting the hem of a miniskirt. Over there. That one, he says. Knocked baby girl comin out a shelter. He drops his window, shouts and motions, and the white girl flits over. She leans inside the car on arms no more than nothing nothings. Hey, Daddy, she says. She's painted her face till the shit looks tribal and reeks of a discount scent.

What it look like? he says.

Slow, she says. But I'll hit my number before the night's up.

Correction, he says. We'll hit *our* number before the night's up. How many times I got to tell you, it ain't no me nor no you. It's us. It's us and us only—always.

He leans in his seat, regards the sparse traffic crawling the boulevard, the lot across the street that sells hoopties with a suspect warranty. In the distance, a pair of waifs totter into an all-night mini-mart advertised in flagrant neon. Closer, a squat broad in leggings parades past a ramshackle X-rated video store. Blood makes his hands into a pose that looks almost holy, and the white girl digs a fold of bills from the waist of her skirt and lays them in it.

He tosses the ends to me and asks me to count them, and I tab them once, twice, and call a figure that's less than I expected.

Blood frowns. What, you out here stashin or lettin somebody else outwork you? he says.

No, Daddy, that's all of it, she says. All of it for now. But don't worry, I'll have the rest by night's end.

Oh, I know you will, he says. 'Cause you got to. We don't fall short. We exceed.

Blood drives me home, hazards into the driveway, lowers an 8-track of Lenny wailing *'Cause I looooooove you* to a shush. Let's check your math, he says, and I hand him his slight harvest. He turns the bills same side up and smooths them on the dash. Say, Maine, he says, eyes unmoved from his task. We're born. That's a natural fact. So whatever's in me liable to be in you too. He folds the bills and stuffs them under his visor. He turns the ignition, and the Caddie sings a lullaby. He clamps my shoulder—what might be another revelation—and I get out and bop up the steps. From the porch, I watch Blood back onto the street, our street, behold his beams illume the dark, and turn most lucid the truth that, for all my days on earth, he's been out ahead of me—the beacon.

■ ■ ■

Armed with every copper cent of my last check, I bop into a boutique in the mall where Pops used to shop. The joint is scarce of customers, the kind of sparse that would've been a telltale work hazard those days me and my surreptitious patnas called ourselves boosting. A saleslady with a freeze of brunette curls and tweed work suit appears at my side and asks if I need help.

Yeah, that'd be nice, I say. I'm looking for a few dress shirts.

Then you've come to the right place, she says. We've got the nicest shirts in the whole mall. Follow me, she says, and leads me to shelves and spinning rack of dress shirts. She asks if I happen to know my neck and sleeve size.

Not off the top of my head, I say, and keep secret the fact that I ain't owned a new dress shirt since Moms copped me one for Pops' last parole hearing.

Well, don't you worry, she says. We'll get you fitted. What's the occasion? She picks a shirt off the rack and proffers it.

The fabric feels downright rich, like the least I should own in this life or the next. But I came for something silk, celestial—what flutters in a night breeze.

DO US PART

Nelly Rosario

ON THE THIRD night after our explosive fight, Tomás's snores killed so many of my dreams that I gathered my pillows and climbed the spiral stairs to the attic, because lying beside a husband who could rest in peace after such a blowup made me want to strangle him.

Him. The falsely modest man living inside my husband, the one always politicking in that quiet, humble way of his—a moon whose gravity had silently pulled at my sanity for decades. My blood reached high tide that Thursday, after he'd invited a crooked politician to our clinic for a photo op with the staff. And the staff. They were in deep waters with me, too, beginning with Negra the Pharmacist, who'd been secretly accepting samples from a Big Pharma rep in the face of our clinic's holistic approach.

Approaching Friday, I had the rest of the clinic household walking on eggshells—yes, the very ones, in fact, cracked by Amelia the Cook the moment I docked her a week's pay for stealing two dozen eggs from our Friday delivery (she was running a cake-making side business).

Busier still was Saturday, when I pounced wild-haired and red-eyed on staff talk about the sainthood of Tomás for putting up with a Gorgon wife like me, who "wants to turn Clínica Moya into a police state." I confiscated the doll a staff member had made from my own stockings, complete with red-button eyes and a shock of aluminum-foil hair. Pinned on its chest were new names for me: Doña Imbécil, the Warden, Lena la Leona, the Executioner.

"Executing orders without mercy all day, your damned wife," Berta the Nurse had been telling my husband when she looked up to see me, her superior, at the door of Tomás's office. Her face turned to stone.

Stone-cold, up in the attic. I was only able to sleep to a sixth dream (a snake digesting a staff) and was tossing and turning into a seventh (Tomás disrobed of his white coat), when a platinum light and an icy draft pricked me awake. The panes of the attic bay window shook. Sunrise? Impossible. The window faces west. And if this harsh light were true, my world was finally coming to its logical end. I wiped crust from my eyes. Then, slowly, it dawned on me: the new window of the building under repair across the street was reflecting the sun rising in the east.

Eastern sunrise in a house-turned-clinic. I stared in wonder at the upper quadrant of the attic window. It shook. Had our carrier pigeons returned, now flying into glass after so much time away? Another thump, too heavy and deliberate to be a pigeon. Through the glass, I caught a glimpse of work boots, the duct-taped ones I'd told Tomás countless times were unbecoming of a respectable doctor—of anyone. By now I was fully out of bed, sleep and eighth dream be damned. I broke a thumbnail to the quick trying to pry open the attic window, which Pedro the Janitor had sealed shut years ago, after a patient had tried to jump. By pressing my cheek against the glass, I was able make out the soles of those horrid boots as they struggled to get a footing on the awning above the attic window.

Win. Doe. *I do, my dear husband*. And right then, the platinum light blasting in my eyes eased up as the reflected sunrise drained from the windowpane across the street. The reflection was replaced by a vision that nearly ended my world a second time: the shadowy figure of my husband, balanced on the ledge of our brownstone. In the reflection of the bay window below his boots, I saw my own silhouette punctured by the gaze of Medusa.

Medusa. I was transfixed by our reflections, by how his back was turned to the street five stories below as if he intended to free-fall down to the pavement in perfect position to make a snow angel without snow. I willed gravity to invert. With my exhalation, his reflected feet found solid footing on the awning. Above me, I could hear him shift from left foot to right as if weighing whether to let go or to live.

Live! He would never jump. Not Tomás.

"No, Tomás! Stay—I'm going up to get you!" I banged on the glass, only for the reflected Tomás to turn his head up at the sky.

■ ■ ■

At the bottom of the ladder leading up to the roof, I made a sign of the cross, putting the Holy Spirit first and the Father last. Church has never been my strength. Neither has forgiving, nor forgetting. Fear of heights gripped me when the first rung bit into the thin soles of my slippers. Twelve rungs to go, and not a single apostle whispered in my ear. Like Peter at daybreak, I'd forsaken my husband. For three nights straight that week, we'd had our usual one-way. Rung two. Deaf-mute versus nag. I'd sent him to hell for playing Good Samaritan with the world while neglecting our heart health. Rung three. I'd enumerated every sin I believed he'd committed throughout our thirty-year marriage, his original sin being choosing me among all women. Rung four. I'd audited his lovemaking, a task he performed as efficiently as servicing an engine: oil change on time, never off-track, making scheduled stops on my lips, then exhaling a clean whistle on the finish. Rung five. Our marriage was coming to a dead end. There, I said it. Rung six. And Tomás had sat at his desk, taking notes without a word—rung six, no, seven—pausing every sixty seconds—rung eight—to relight his Siglo 21 cigar, which was put out by the glass of water I'd thrown in his face. At rung nine and a half, my left slipper dropped to the floor below, leaving me half-barefoot, half-slippered. And when Mia the Receptionist informed me that my own husband had started a patient file on his wife—rung ten—I told her that his left hand would be nothing without tracking me, his right. By rung eleven, I did not dare look at the depth below. The landing to the roof exit was now at my waist, and I could already hear the groan of the door to the roof as the icy morning wind repeatedly slammed it open and shut. The twelfth rung advanced me to the landing floor, where I remained on all fours to regain sensation in the soles of my feet and to catch my breath. God, I was getting too old for this shit.

Shit. I should have brought a blanket. The wind was brutal out on the roof. Near the pigeon coops, I found the old broom I'd brought with me from Santo Domingo and leaned on it for support. It used to sweep white-dust brujería deposited by neighbors from my porch. Back before I replaced witchcraft with science. All the same to a broom. Dust is dust is dust. Shit is manure is guano is dust. Our pigeon coops were still empty. Raising carrier pigeons to deliver prescriptions—bad idea from the start, I'd told Tomás. But I went along, as I had with all his birdbrained schemes. For years he'd also nursed plans to grow a rooftop garden. To install solar panels. Windmills. We should breed unicorns, too, I suggested to my Don Quixote, their milk surely a cure for delusions.

The delusion now was to face east, looking into a real sunrise, orange and milky and bittersweet as a cold glass of morir soñando as Tomás threatened to die behind his dreams. A slap of wind reoriented me westward, in the direction of the attic window and my husband.

Tomás, there he was—below me, but out of my sight. I could see only his ten fingers grasping the roof ledge, fingernails the dirtiest I'd ever seen on him. Normally square, the nail beds were round. When had I stopped noticing the toll time had taken on him? I feared getting too close to the ledge and swallowed waves of dizziness as I calmly addressed the fingers.

Me: "So this is your grand rebuttal, Tomás, to make me a widow."

Widow. A husband can respond to such a word only with silence. The beds of his nails alternated in color between white and dark pink. I tightened my robe against the infernal silence that always made my teeth chatter.

Chatter was always how I shamed him: "¡Sinverguenza!"

I hissed. "After all the CPR done. All the drug addicts re-habbed. The babies delivered." My voice rose like a vulture riding thermal winds. "At least be more discreet." He could have chosen to cross the street blindfolded. To fill the bath-tub and slit his wristwatch. To eat raw yucca, cyanide being the choice of poets, politicians, and revolutionaries. "In-stead, you hang out here like a flag of defeat."

Defeat in detail. To defeat the enemy by destroying small portions of his armies instead of engaging his entire strength. I'd have to tackle one of his fingers at a time, not the whole hand. "Details are always vulgar," I said, quoting Tomás quoting Oscar Wilde. And here I became acutely aware of the infinite grid of windows on the surrounding buildings, some already blinking awake with lamplight. There I was: embittered wife standing at her own precipice. Reason told me I should go downstairs and wake up a staff member. The staff has always had a soft spot for Tomás, who had an even softer spot for the staff.

Staff. Serpent. Which would swallow which? Were I to seek help, the staff would scorn me for leaving Tomás alone up here, for having put him in this predicament to begin with. Were I to stay, the staff would later question my efforts. A choiceless choice. Even the statistics had doomed him: one doctor a day attempts suicide, the rate of which among males nearly quadruples the national average. I'd ignored the article, certain that Tomás, who wrote didactic poems about the slow genocide of our body politic, would be the exception. No statistics on the doctor's wife in tattered robe extending broomstick over roof ledge, praying that the grip of her single slipper could outweigh the pull of her heavy marriage.

Marriage, a strong one, allows for the broomstick to sweep away past wrongs and scare away evil spirits, to accept the wife's renewed commitment to her husband and to their home-cum-clinic. When my broomstick grazed his knuckle, thumb folded under palm and index finger pointed at me. And I wanted to tell him—

"Tell me," he croaked like a frog hiding in the roof gutters, "what is the point where height . . . meets depth."

Depth perception was impossible for me, standing so high above the ground without my glasses or the courage to get closer to the ledge. "That point," I said carefully, "is where your left hand undoes everything done by our right."

Right? Consider the Hanging Gardens of Babylon he'd been dreaming about all these years. Was he going to throw all that away? Hadn't it been me who fed the carrier pigeons each morning, despite my fear of heights? To sketch out ideas for his kingdom of castles in the air? To plant organic vegetables around our chimney vents? To collect enough discarded X-ray plates to build the greenhouse of his dreams? All his confections, washed away in the endless brainstorming of his mind.

Mind him, today was Sunday, not Thursday—the beginning of a brand-new week, of a brand-new life. Our hands, our arms, were too compromised now to repeat Thursday's battle scene, that final brutal tableau of a long-standing civil war in which heart-hurt doctor relights his cigar after wife throws water in his eye.

"I . . . am . . . bli . . . chus . . ." The rest of his words were swallowed up by the roar of an airplane passing overhead.

Overhead, overheard, because by then I'd trained myself to hear when his deaf ear was listening and his good ear was choosing not to. We'd long abandoned our ritual of coming up to the roof early on Sunday mornings to watch the sunrise, Tomás supporting my hips as I trembled up the ladder carrying a thermos of coffee that bumped the rungs, and then us languishing on a plaid blanket with just two steaming mugs between us.

"Us," I said aloud, marveling at how so short a word can be so plural. "Did you catch the western sunrise this morning, Tomás?" Already I could hear his good ear softening. "Did our bedroom get the trick of light too?" Thumb peeked out of palm. "Just like you, Tomás, I woke up thinking my world was ending." Index finger stirred. "Then I looked out the window and, diablo, I saw the light and owned up to my error in judgment." I mustered the courage to lean over the ledge just so and caught glints of light on his sweat-beaded bald spot. Dios mío, how blinded I'd been not to notice the awful toll time had taken on him. I pulled away, shaken. "There I was, spooked by a multiplied blessing." A pause to wipe my eyes. "What I'm telling you, Tomás, is that from now on our home will have two sunrises, one in the east and another in the west."

■ ■ ■

Did he remember back in Santo Domingo, when we'd sworn to always luchar? *Luchar*, he'd said it himself, is one of those words that gets twisted in the ears of the un-Spanish as merely "to wrestle," "to struggle," "to fight," "to go to war." But to us luchar means "to survive." And to help others survive. Tomás and I, we love each other hardest when seeing the other give to others.

Others, didn't he remember? The new feeling of being

newly engaged to the other. Then the first big fight that dragged others into the fray. Blame me for starting our long journey together on the wrong foot. I was just joking when I called him stingy for not taking me out for seafood at Mello's. What was I thinking, demanding a farewell dinner at a fancy-wancy tourist hole the very week Tomás was to leave for Haiti on a vaccination campaign with the Jesuits? He wouldn't talk to me for days. A word like "stingy" hits square in the elbow when you're broker than a codfish. Especially when word gets around. Then, on the night before he left, it was as if Tomás had rubbed a genie out of his elbow. He gathered the neighborhood kids, whose mothers he'd asked to dress them in their Sunday best—ill-fitting shoes, starched shirts, and napefuls of talcum powder. My fiancé, he had the nerve to lead the poor little mice through the neighborhood en route to Mello's, making sure to parade them by Mamá's house that afternoon. And me, obedient daughter then, sweeping the porch in housedress and head wrap, stopping to lean on the broom, hand on hip and head cocked, to watch the ridiculous procession. Off they were, the fools, to gorge themselves on fried shrimp and french fries, best meal they'd ever had in their lives.

Live and let live. I went back inside the house, having my own fish to bread and fry for my parents' afternoon meal. I busied myself with sewing and other house chores, checking the window often for a glimpse of the pied piper on his way back from Mello's, but he must have taken the kids on a different route to their respective homes. The moon was bright and clear when I blew out the lantern and finally left the porch.

Porch movement at dawn the following day. I found the

mothers gathered at our door, complaining. Their children had spent the night vomiting. What, by the grace of Virgen de la Altagracia, was I to do about this misfortune? The man I was to marry was nowhere to be found, son of a motherson of a mother. I made coffee. As it brewed, the women listed their children's symptoms: chills, sweats, stomach cramps, fevers, hives. My diagnosis: food poisoning, seafood allergies, overeating, foolish pride.

Pride was the last thing on my mind. I agreed to clean up Tomás's mess. By now he had boarded the train out of town, leaving me to brew a large batch of ginger and anise tea, to pick up two buckets and a mop, and to follow the indignant mothers to their homes. All morning I spent working to atone for the man I would one day promise to love in sickness and in health. Once the two buckets were good and filled, I hung them on the ends of a broomstick and, with the load on my back, marched to Mello's later that afternoon.

"Afternoon," I said once inside the bar-restaurant. Of the two owners, only Dismas was sitting at the empty bar, his twin brother, Gestas, likely still tangled in bed with a tourist. Dismas I found sucking on imported beer, a fact he advertised as a greeting. The shutters of the bar were still closed, and all I could see in the darkness was the glint of his Rolex, a fact he advertised by reminding me that Mello's would open in precisely twelve minutes.

A dozen minutes, one of which I spent setting down the two buckets on the spotless floor of Mello's.

"Mello's served rotten shrimp to those poor kids yesterday," I said.

Just yesterday, Dismas had been a wretched kid himself,

the kind to turn his eyelids inside out to scare me, a chicken-hearted little girl in his mind. Now he turned to really look at me, eyelids heavy. "And you expect me to serve lobster to Les Misérables."

"You're a misérable. They were paying customers."

"Customers, not quite." He rubbed his eyes as if to remember. "Tomás was grateful for my donation to his cause. The carajitos even got dessert."

Dessert bile from the first bucket spilled at his feet. My aim was bad. But the second bucket drenched his head and shoulders in his own sliminess. With that, I reclaimed my buckets and left Dismas retching, just as a delegation of businessmen came into Mello's to seal some deal or another to suck our island dry.

Dried up—Mello's business was after that. Papá had to send me away to relatives in the campo until the scandal could blow over. Collective amnesia, too, stipulated I make myself scarce for a month or so. Two weeks into my exile, Tomás returned to town. He found tongues wagging about his commitment to marry this devil of a woman, whose temper had put a price on his head. Word was that Dismas Mello continued to reek of bile no matter how much he bathed, and that Gestas had vowed to avenge his brother. My parents advised Tomás to lay low. The Mello twins knew people in high and low places. Meanwhile, the mothers of the kids Tomás had taken to Mello's continued to hold a grudge, competing among themselves for the crown of Concerned Mother of the Month. My parents nevertheless stood by the side of their future son-in-law, who had been treating their cataracts and arthritis at no cost. They saw to it that Tomás board a motoconcho, a bus, and a donkey to the campo. He was to claim back their firebrand daughter, whom they worried had burned away any prospects of marriage.

Marriage. Ours really began as Tomás went knocking from door to door in that campo until the sound of screams led him to the house of a pastor's wife. There, he found me helping a midwife deliver a stillborn. We had no words when he entered the bedroom, a man uninvited. My look of abject defeat when our eyes locked compelled Tomás to roll up his sleeves without question, to wash his hands in the basin by the bed, and to work at keeping the mother stabilized. "Lucha," he growled at her, at me, at himself. "¡Lucha, carajo!"

■ ■ ■

Carajo, the roof of our long-ago commitment had serious leaks. Still, my husband's fingers would not grasp the broomstick I'd extended to the ledge. Many had been my failures.

"A failure, I am," he repeated and repeated, the first time I'd ever heard Tomás refer to himself in the singular.

In the singular was how I'd been existing for some time. A marriage surrounded by so many people inevitably gets lonely, a silent bubble in the noise of suffering. And I realized that this silence must have been worse for Tomás, who was already deaf in one ear. I suddenly understood the depth of his own loneliness and reminded him of what he once told a patient: "A damaged cochlea hears the word 'failure' as a logarithmic spiral."

Another spiral of words issued from his fingers: "Pointless, pointless, pointless . . ."

"*This* is pointless!" My patience was spent, my bare foot numb from the cold. "Open your goddamned eyes!" And I had to close my own to imagine what lay within his range of vision on the other side of the roof ledge.

Ledge, and four stories below it, yellow pumpkin flowers burst from the planter on the stoop of our brownstone.

And the other brownstone across the street to the west, the one we'd pressured the city to repair.

Repaired, and parked at the corner southwest, the ambulatory van gifted to the clinic by an anonymous donor.

Donated, too, was the mural on the corner lot to the south, depicting Saint Lazarus, painted as in-kind payment by the street artist whose father our clinic had saved.

Savior, walking due north, a youth volunteer on his way to our clinic for his Sunday-morning shift.

Shifting, I opened my eyes and saw four.

"Four right angles, Tomás. Even your failures form a perfect square."

Square into the ears on the back of my head, the sound of footsteps. Behind me, purposeful. I did not dare turn around, focused ahead on the fingers that were at last wrapping around the broomstick. Whoever the staff member standing behind me was had better get a good look at me saving a life and restore my good name.

"Lena, there you are."

This "you are" sounded more plural than singular, spoken by a familiar baritone, with its scent of coffee and spearmint and Siglo 21 cigar, made flesh by the feel of strong, warm fingers whose nail beds were square-shaped rather than round, with whistle-clean nails, hands that wrapped around mine on the broomstick. And then me and this unnamed apostle who whispered in my ear were pulling hard together in a tug of war between death and life, me laughing and crying from the realization that the man on the precipice had never been my husband but the man into whose chest I now leaned had always been, and we pulled and pulled together as if powered by a third rail, against a last stop, shifting gears under the screech of brakes, my slippers ripping and my body being propelled forward by a monstrous force broken only by the arms of the real Tomás wrapped around my ribs to keep my torso from being pulled over the ledge, where, trembling, I came face-to-face with the crossed eyes of a stranger.

■   ■   ■

Doctors spend a good part of their practice drowning to death in stories. Fail to listen patiently, and the story of the patient becomes the story of the doctor.

Doctors form the good habit of following their wives' orders to the letter. Tomás had only done what I'd asked of him and given away those horrid boots. The beneficiary happened to be the homeless man who liked to sit on our front stoop on Saturday nights nibbling on the pumpkin flowers. I of course forgave Tomás for the near-mortal scare inflicted on me by his doppelgänger. And Tomás forgave me "for underestimating our will to live and overestimating our will to die." But I could not forgive myself for inadvertently playing executioner by choosing to ignore what Tomás humbly called "the six differences" between my picture of him and that of the man whom the staff had fondly baptized the Doppelhanger.

The Doppelhanger we never saved. Nor did he ever fall.

He hung from our roof for forty days and forty nights, alive though not well.

"Well," said passersby, stopping to look up at the living gargoyle gracing the side of our brownstone, "I'll be god-damned." Some occasionally knocked on our door, convinced that they could talk the Doppelhanger into coming down from his perch. No one succeeded, and no one failed.

Failure would be to ignore the important function the Doppelhanger served in a community locked in the daily lucha of survival. We fed him. We clothed him in bad weather. The staff even built a tarp shelter for him. And soon our carrier pigeons began to return. As if paying their respects, each alighted on his shoulders before flying past him to fill our empty coops again. Whatever message they carried, they delivered only to his ear. And the only words he had been heard to utter were "I . . . am."

I'm much softer now. The staff was surprised to see me laughing with them when Tomás's twelve-year-old niece and new member of the household, Irma the Apprentice, said, "I want Doppel to hang out forever so I'll have me a wishing star." It was Irma the Apprentice who begged to sleep in the attic, suggesting that each Sunday at dawn, on the anniversary of Doppelhanger's coming to "die-live" in our household, the staff have coffee hour on the roof under a double sunrise.

Dawn wake-up, a tall order for our hardworking staff, but many were hungry for a new tradition.

Traditionally, Tomás and I had refrained from staff get-togethers. Nevertheless, we began to join the congregation for this unlikely Sunday Mass on the roof, presided over by the silent fingers at the ledge. A group of about twenty would sit on blankets, sharing coffee and donuts and telling stories that might keep the Doppelhanger's spirit alive and well. He never uttered anything besides his "I am"s.

I'm not sure why, but on what would be our last Sunday with the Doppelhanger, after much prodding from the staff, Tomás agreed to tell a story about his younger days for the first time ever at coffee hour. "When we were in medical school," he began, "a mule kicked us in the head and took away hearing from our left ear. It left us half-deaf but twice-hearing—"

Hearing a voice mid-story, Tomás stopped speaking and craned his neck in the direction of the ledge.

"Story is one . . ." croaked the voice from the western end of the roof. Tomás walked over to touch the fingers on the ledge as if to surrender his story. "I am . . . a thousand and one lives . . . in one man . . .

"One woman," continued the Doppelhanger, louder, as if drawing strength from the touch of the twenty people now also gathered around the ledge. With great labor, he began to tell us of the woman he'd once been. A learned woman who walked on foot all over the country, giving lectures on mathematics, literature, philosophy—on anything the people needed to hear.

Heard: On one of these trips, this learned woman falls terribly ill. Somehow she manages to get herself to a nearby bed-and-breakfast. She wants to check in, but when the owner asks for payment, the learned woman turns her pockets inside out and lowers her fevered head. The owner invites the learned woman to stay the night, putting her in the best room available. Days pass, and the learned woman's health takes a turn for the worse. The owner calls in a doctor, who charges the equivalent of two nights' stay, only to deliver a grim diagnosis. For a week, doctors and healers come and go, all delivering the same prognosis. The owner cares for the learned woman between shifts at the front desk. Certain that she will not make it through the month, the learned woman calls the owner. No, she does not want a doctor. She does not want water. She does not want pity. She asks for a wooden board, a brush, and ink. As the owner runs out to fulfill this wish, the learned woman has a last vision of a yellow pumpkin flower, perfect from petals to root. And when the owner returns with the wooden board, brush, and ink, the woman who has been learned in the School of Pythagoras draws a pentagram inside a circle. Her dying wish is for the owner to hang the wooden board out front, where all eyes can see it. And the owner is to pay special attention to the owners of the eyes that can read this sign. Those seers, she vows, will repay the owner the cost of the learned woman's care and thank the owner for the kindness. The owner promises to do as asked. Then the learned woman opens her eyes and dies. The owner pays for a small funeral attended by no one.

Days pass. Business grows slow. On the last day of the month, a traveler stops at the bed-and-breakfast and, while checking in, asks about the meaning of the sign out front. The owner has forgotten about the wooden board, whose symbol has faded under a heavy rain. The owner merely smiles and assigns the traveler the same room where the learned woman stayed. The traveler plans to stay the night, but during the first hour complains about the worn sheets and sudsless soap and cold coffee. The traveler leaves without so much as a tip for the many other services demanded. Days later, another traveler arrives at the bed-and-breakfast.

The traveler inquires about the sign out front. The owner merely smiles and offers the traveler the best room. The traveler politely declines any room at all for the night, but does have one request: Would the owner care to repaint the sign so that the true eye can better read it? The owner agrees to do so. And, asks the traveler, how had the sign found its way to this godforsaken place in the first place? In great detail, the owner relates the story of the learned woman. The traveler thanks the owner for the kindness and pays the owner five and twelve times over the cost incurred by the learned woman.

■   ■   ■

A woman's scream. Negra the Pharmacist was leaning over the ledge, her fingers gripping Doppelhanger's forearms. Shouting erupted. "Clear the sidewalk! Get a mattress!" someone yelled to the pedestrians below, while others begged Doppelhanger to hang on, for heaven's sake, because the torso of Negra the Pharmacist was beginning to disappear from view. Pedro the Janitor grabbed onto her thick waist, clamping his teeth into the material bunched at the small of her back. Then Berta the Nurse latched onto Pedro the Janitor's heavy leather tool belt, while Irma the Apprentice held tight to Berta the Nurse's knees, impelling Tomás to grip his niece by her small shoulders as I circled the breadth of my husband's chest with every inch of my arms, and so on, until our team of twenty, including one patient, had formed a chain anchored only by the door to the roof, which had just been replaced by Pedro the Janitor days earlier, after a windstorm had blown the old door off its hinges.

Unhinged, however, was Negra the Pharmacist when

she lost her grip on Doppelhanger. Gravity inverted. Our collective heart rose in our throats. Doppelhanger shot up to the sky in a vacuum of sound broken a second later by a peal of thunder. The roar scattered us apart, our bodies strewn across the tar as the first drops of rain stung our faces.

Facing me was Tomás, in whose eyes I saw a learned woman, in whose eyes he saw a learned man. Centuries passed in the minute it took for the two learned souls to help the other stand back up. We wrung out each other's white coats. We triaged the others. We helped fold blankets and collect coffee mugs. We opened the coops and freed the pigeons. We led the staff back inside, grateful that Doppelhanger's work with us had been done and that ours was just beginning.

MINE

Alexander Chee

I WAS VISITING my mom in the southern Maine town she lives in now, Saco, three towns over from where I grew up. We had gone to my father's grave, cleaned it, and had our version of the traditional Korean offering there, enduring the stares of the other visitors, and then she sent me on an errand to the local Hannaford grocery store to pick up a few things for dinner, including kimchi, and we'd disagreed about whether I could buy kimchi there. "It's not the same state you remember," she said when she insisted. Now as I stood in line for the checkout, holding the kimchi in my hand, knowing she had won, and amazed at being able to buy kimchi in this place I'd left behind so long ago, I noticed the man who came to stand behind me.

He looked familiar, though he was like all the kids I'd gone to school with—sunburned, blond, confident, or, if not confident, still capable of a good bluff. Things hadn't turned out quite the way he'd wanted, that was clear. He was like a slightly hurt version of who he used to be, but it was also clear he still believed things would go his way eventually. I suppose I was the same. In that one way, we were the closest we'd ever be to being like each other. And then I understood that I actually did know him.

He *was* from my high school—had been arrested for being a coke dealer, though I didn't know if he'd done time. I knew his sister better. She'd posed for her senior yearbook photo with her baby, which was more of a scandal for some reason than his arrest, or her actual pregnancy, as if the yearbook were something sacred you could spoil.

I figured, *Let's just begin what happens next,* and asked, "How's your sister?"

He blinked. "You knew my sister?"

"Yeah," I said. "I know your sister."

It sounded a little dirtier than I meant it—and, truth be told, it wasn't entirely innocent. His sister and I were not the most likely of friends at our high school, but we really had been friends, and had even drunkenly hooked up, exactly once. It was nothing I was prepared to tell her brother about, but it meant a lot to me. She was the one woman I'd ever had sex with before admitting to her, and then eventually to the rest of the world, that I was gay.

At the time, his sister Katie was well-liked, if not quite popular. She was never trying to get the approval of anyone. She seemed like a sweet baby-faced blonde who still wore her brother's boy jeans to school under pink knitted ponchos—jeans he'd long outgrown—but then she'd turn every so often, and her eyes let off a coolness, like she was older than most of us somehow. Even in that poncho. Do you know how hard it is to be cool in a pink poncho? She always looked like she'd just seen the makings of a very good joke walk by. That was the look she gave me when I walked in that first day and presented myself for training.

"Stanley Yu," she said as I walked behind the counter, clocked in, and pulled a name tag from my pocket. "Seriously."

"Yeah," I said.

"You're the one I'm training today."

"Yes, that is correct."

She bent over laughing, a sharp laugh that also somehow wasn't completely humiliating. "You won't last a week," she said as she stood up. "But we'll see if we can get you to Friday."

■   ■   ■

I had taken the job because a month previous I'd driven my mother's car through a stone wall while playing Assassin up at the school. This may have been why she laughed. It resulted in the game being banned from the school forever; my eternal humiliation, for being labeled the guy who took the game too far; and now this job, as I also needed to pay my mother back for the car damage, and the wall repair. As for the disgrace of being her only child, who had embarrassed her in front of the town, I could never pay that back.

I was a pariah back then anyway, a little too smart and unfriendly for my own good, and convinced that not only was I better than these people, I would always be better than them. And by "these people" I meant my whole town. We were the only Korean family—the only non-white family, for that matter; everyone else was white. Each time the kids at school called me a "chink" I would reply, contemptuously, "I'm not Chinese, I'm Korean," like I was telling them something that could matter to them. My arrogance was my fortress, built to keep me safe from even wanting these kids to like me. I think I still believed I was better than them, though I liked to think back then that I was just being fair when I hated them. But this was not the sort of position you launched a successful high school social life from—it was not even the plausible position of anyone who really was an intellectual superior. It was only a defense, the plan of someone with no intention of ever coming back.

On the morning of the accident, I walked outside of my house on my way to school just as the boy rumored to be winning Assassin pulled up in front. If you don't know the rules of the game, they are approximately as follows: everyone in the group—in this case, the senior class—is an assassin, and everyone has the name of one other person in the game. Once you "kill" the other person, you get the name of the person they were supposed to kill, and go on to your next target. In our game, the presence of two or more witnesses meant no kill was possible, and all classrooms were safe zones. He had a water gun—we all did—for the "shooting," and so, as a precaution, I jumped in my car for what quickly turned into a frantic car chase, and drove away.

I drove first at the top of the speed limit as we cruised past the school and were headed on our way out of town, but was soon doing about 65 in a 30; and as we turned the corner of a stretch of road called Devil's Elbow, because it had caused so many accidents, I could feel my mother's blue Oldsmobile station wagon slide into the oncoming lane. There I saw the headlights of a semi turning the corner and heading right for me.

I somehow remembered my driver's ed instructions—"When losing control, turn the wheel into the turn, not against it, because you can't fight the car"—and so I did. It worked. I went out of the lane and onto the shoulder, and then off it again, until I crashed through a stone wall and came to a direct stop a few feet from an ancient and very solid oak tree in the front yard of someone's beautiful home.

I stepped out of the car in total shock, which at that point felt like nothing, as if the fear of dying had seared all my nerve endings shut. I walked over and leaned on the very hard tree. From there I saw the boy I was trying to escape, Gerald Meany, pull up in his little Dodge Dart. He stood out of the car and pointed his water gun at me, and—to my stunned surprise—the jet of water he shot hit me in the forehead. I was done, out of the game.

"Alex Rule," I said to him. The name of my target, now his. He nodded. And then he drove away.

The owner of the house turned out to be the very pregnant ex-secretary of my mom's, someone I hadn't seen in years and who I certainly didn't want to frighten so badly, say, by smashing our Oldsmobile wagon through her old stone wall. The car itself was in pretty good shape, somehow—keep this in mind if you ever need to drive a car through a stone wall—but I was not. I wasn't injured, but I knew something terrible had happened, something unforgivable. I just didn't know what exactly. I managed to tell her the story of what had happened, and to my surprise she laughed as I described the water hitting my face. And soon everyone would laugh when I told the story, except my mother.

My mother had been on a boat off the coast of Portland when this happened, at a cocktail party, having what she thought of as a beautiful summer day. By the time I saw her, she was not so much cool to me as calm—a calm supplied, I think, by the knowledge of just how much punishment she was about to bring to bear.

Years later I would remember that my mom had taken a call about a car accident three years before this one, the one that took my father's life. I'd managed to replicate a call that had changed her life forever. History repeating, as they say, first as tragedy and then as comedy. For our purposes in the story, see me years afterward, knowing I had done a terrible, terrible thing, a thing I wished I could undo and also felt I could never undo, and that right then I didn't even understand enough to know what it was. In the meantime, I could go to the CVS and get this job, and I could do what I could to try and keep it.

* * *

My duties were not strenuous to the eye. I had to ring people up, sweep the floors, restock items and price them. Count out my register at the beginning and end of my shift. I got a discount and used it on a soda during my break. It was easy enough, but it was incredibly boring. The most strenuous part of the job was that you had to be there. That was what Katie meant about lasting, I understood, after some weeks had gone by. You had to withstand the boredom of it. And it was easier than enduring my mother's alternating silence and lectures back home.

And, to be honest, I lacked stamina. She wasn't wrong to think that. I had tried to get a job exactly once before this—a job I had for less than one day, at Burger King. I filled out the application, the manager interviewed me, he left me to watch the BKU (Burger King University, for the uninitiated) video, and then he gave me my uniform to try on in the bathroom. There, amid the thick scent of urinal cake, when I looked at myself in the bathroom mirror, in the brown and orange polyester, only then did I realize, with horror, not just what I looked like but what my future looked like. Yes, my hair, of which I was inordinately proud, with its Sun In sun streaks and waves, covered by the horrible visor, its brown polyester washing out my skin to a sallow color, my few freckles suddenly my only distinguishing factor except for my eyes, which were wide with fear. But the collar, the short sleeves, the sad weight of the shirt and the pants—I had a vision of myself behind the counter, the air slick with hamburger and fry grease slowly mixing into the fabric and from there into my being, until I became some new kind of fossil the world had never seen, there behind the counter. There would be exhibits of me, the amazing Korean kid who had turned into a single piece of hamburger-grease-soaked polyester.

I walked out of the bathroom that day, left the uniform hanging on the stall, and drove home. I never went back and they never called the house to find me. In my conversations with my mother about jobs I could get to pay her back, I never mentioned Burger King. When I got to the CVS and was handed the vest and pin, that seemed like very little to bear by comparison. The air-conditioning was a nice break from the damp summer, and the fluorescent light made it seem as if I'd died and woken up in an afterlife where I was forced to do things like count out cash register drawers.

Meanwhile, after the Assassin incident had made me the wrong kind of famous at school and the administration canceled all future games because of it, it was as if I'd gotten caught drunk in the fields around the town, where we all went to drink at night from spring through fall. Except much worse. I'd been considered an upstanding young citizen prior to that, the good Korean kid, the getter of good grades, if antisocial.

That was, of course, the right kind of famous at the school. But if there was anyone who knew about the wrong kind of famous, it was Katie. Or, she would. Just not yet.

■ ■ ■

After she was photographed with her baby for the yearbook, speculation as to the father of Katie's child settled on one of three different guys. There was her boyfriend at the time, Derrick. There was an ex of hers, Bob. And then there was Geoff, Derrick's best friend. She was, as I've said, not a notorious girl before this. She neither participated in the anorexia/bulimia weight-loss races the popular girls played with each other, which had them arriving at school looking a little like a line drawing, nor was she known as the sort of girl who would do anything for a ride home, a twelve-pack, or a handle of vodka. She was well-liked in part because she was so normal—not a prude, could roll a decent joint, would give you a cigarette and say hi.

Derrick, her boyfriend, loved her like it was a star-crossed romance, even though it had worked out. He seemed afraid of losing her even while in her arms. I think at first it seemed like passion to her, like this had to be love, it was so strong. But she grew tired of this intensity.

I know because we talked about it—a lot.

"I mean, when is he just going to get it?" she said. We were outside the CVS, having just finished a shift, smoking her cigarettes. It was Friday, and I'd made it, lasted out the week. The thing that matters to this story hadn't happened to her yet. She always smoked with her left arm across her chest, her right elbow balanced on her left hand so her arm went up at a right angle like a cigarette salute. Her hand gestures happened up there. She would swing her hand in, take a drag, and swing it back out, and the words would be full of smoke as she talked. "I love him. I really do. I'm not going anywhere. But it feels like all the love I have wouldn't make a difference to him. He'd still be there believing I was going to leave at any second."

I had no experience with this; I nodded, fascinated by the idea of how Derrick might lose her because he couldn't feel the love he said he wanted from her, and that she was offering. I wanted to hear more. It seemed like the worst thing in the world, too, if it happened. My only relationships were fantasies. Even being desired, much less loved, was a fantasy. I knew well enough to know I was "the gay" at the school, and that there might be others. I just didn't know them. Anytime I thought a boy liked me, I quickly decided it was just wishful thinking and pushed the thought out of my mind. And, of course, created extended fantasies that involved many of the boys in the high school, with each other but never me.

My fantasies back then never included me.

The lights were off inside the CVS, and the early summer dark was slow in coming down. Her hair in the sunlight seemed extra gold contrasted against the oak forest across the street behind her. She was my goddess right then.

A brown Camaro pulled up. "Geoff," she said to the driver. "Did Derrick send you?"

He grinned. "Yeah."

"So he's too shit-faced to come get me?" She said this with her voice rising on the "me." "And you're not?"

He nodded. "That's about the shape of it."

She tossed her cigarette down into the parking lot. "Well isn't *that* romantic." She crushed it out with her sneaker. "Good night," she said to me as she walked around the car, not looking, fishing in her purse. "See you tomorrow."

■ ■ ■

At work the next day she was quiet. When I asked her about how her night was, she just shrugged. Geoff didn't drink much, while Derrick drank more and more. And the more Derrick drank, the more Geoff seemed to like being Derrick's go-to guy. Katie's boyfriend was soon sending his best friend to pick her up most of the time. Katie, I think, at first felt special in a way, like Derrick had sent a car for her. Even if it was Geoff's pickup. Soon it was nothing unusual to see Geoff's truck in front of the CVS at closing time, waiting for her.

One night after work, Derrick had neither sent Geoff nor called. Katie and I were outside the closed CVS, smoking as the sun set.

"Fuck this," she said. "Stanley, your mother still let you drive?"

I laughed. "She does now. She doesn't want to have to drive me." The repaired station wagon sat outside a little glumly but looking fine. And I did feel better about driving it, knowing I could take it over a stone wall and live.

We went by her house, picked up some beers, and, with a few joints she had in her cigarette pack, drove out to the places we thought the boys would be. It was the eighties, before cell phones and texting. You had to drive around to look for someone. In our town, Cape Elizabeth, there were just a few known places: there was the cove, there was the Rock, there was a field, another field. The kids knew them and the cops knew them. It was a small town. The cove was starting to fill up with people—it was really the parking lot for the cove—and heads turned as I drove by with Katie looking stonily through the crowd for a sign of Derrick, her hair extra pale in the headlights of the other cars. The Rock, when we looked, was empty and it was a pain to check out: you had to park off the road and take a short hike up to the Rock, and when we got there, no one was around. By the time we stood in the first of the fields for drinking, as we thought about heading to the second one, she said, "You know what? *He* should be looking for *me*." She tapped a joint out of her cigarette pack and lit it swiftly, inhaling deeply. "Ain't that right?" she asked.

"Yes," I said.

"You got a man?"

I blinked.

"I know what's up. I've seen you checking out Derrick's ass when he comes in to see me. Hell, I don't blame you. It's a good ass, for now. Though if he keeps drinking like that, it won't be."

"No," I said. "I . . ."

"Besides the whole school, who knows you're gay?" She laughed and handed me the joint. Around us, fireflies had started up in the field. The tip of the joint glowed orange and then went gray as the ash covered it.

I lifted the joint to my mouth, and as I pulled in a deep draw, she said, "You do know you're gay, right?"

I just smiled. If I said nothing, I could wait a bit longer. Wait until I was really, really, really sure. I had never said anything to anyone. I didn't know how else to explain what I felt, though, and here she was, making it feel sort of easy and okay but also possibly not true.

"For all I know, Derrick could very well be your man next. He and Geoff certainly spend enough time together." She looked out into the distance to her left, back across the field toward the car, as if she could see through time and space to where they were. "You'd have to get him away from Geoff, though. God knows I can't."

"Next" was the operative word here. I felt a vague thrill at the idea of Derrick and Geoff intertwined somewhere in Geoff's truck.

"Do you really think—"

She cut me off. "I don't know what I think. I'm just not drunk and high enough, I guess, after a good day at the CVS." She rubbed out the roach of the joint on the bottom of her sneaker and stuck it back in her cigarettes. "So that's what I think. Not drunk enough, not high enough. Waste not, want not," she said merrily, tucking the pack away. "What do *you* think?"

"I think he ought to treat you better," I said.

"That's an easy thing to say," she said. "Come on, now, Stanley. I've taught you better than that, haven't I?" She pulled a beer up from where we'd set them on the ground and cracked the flip top as she balanced it against her hip. "It takes one to know one, right? Do you think Derrick is gay?"

I didn't want to answer this. Because the answer was yes, I did think what she did. Derrick and Geoff, seemed, well . . . Geoff had no reason to be Derrick's apparent servant. He had no reason to just drive her around like he was Derrick's slave. No reason, that is, unless he was desperately in love with Derrick. And it made sense, too, that maybe the reason Derrick drank so much was that, despite being with Katie, he was in love with Geoff also. That perhaps he feared losing her while he was in front of her because he couldn't feel anything for her, despite wanting to, or knew that if she knew he was gay, she'd leave him and he'd have to face being gay.

Yes, they could just be best buds. But there was something terrifically sad about it that made it seem like it wasn't just that. And a year later, after graduation, I would be back in the field for a party, overhearing Derrick drunkenly telling Geoff about two girls he had lined up for them, and Geoff balking. Which caused Derrick to say, "Tell me you're not gay, Geoff. Tell me you're not gay."

And then silence. And then: "Tell me you're not gay. Tell me you're not gay."

But for now I was here and that hadn't happened, not where I could hear it. "It's okay, you've been through enough," Katie said. "Don't answer that. Where the fuck is he?"

"Why do you think I'm gay?" I asked.

"Did I offend you?" she said, more of an assertion than a question.

"No," I said. "I just want to know."

"You're an awfully good-looking guy to just not have anyone around *doing* anything about it," she said. "I mean, you could be asexual. I understand that's a thing now in the wild eighties. But I think you're sexual. I just think you don't like the answer to the question yet."

I thought about this, but she was right.

"I bet there's people who like the answer, though," she said, after watching me say nothing for a little bit.

I have never been one to notice quickly when someone was interested in me.

I can tell you, after that night, I could no longer avoid that I was gay. Katie had, it's true, turned me on sufficiently that I did the deed, and, in my defense, I was seventeen. A lot could, then. I was already turned on by the thought of Geoff and Derrick. Also, I knew that it did mean something; it wasn't that it didn't mean anything, her and I. Quite the opposite. I did want to love her as I felt she deserved to be loved, and even had a fantasy about what that meant, her in the arms of a handsome fantasy lover that was not, of course, me. But I thought I could impersonate him.

After the deed was done, I was incredibly embarrassed, like I'd told the most incredible, well-received lie, thinking I'd performed admirably as a heterosexual. I hadn't, though, I understood, as Katie looked up at me with laughter.

"Well . . . now we know," Katie said. "Let's never do that again." I was so relieved, we just started to laugh, shaking until we stopped, there in the field, on the blanket I had pulled out from the back of the car.

Happier laughing than we had been during sex.

We left and went home. Geoff and Derrick were never found that night, and on the next shift I listened as Katie filled me in on the fight she had had with Derrick. As she did, I noticed we were closer now, but it was the closeness of a shared hurt, not the intimacy of love. But also, I had never had a friend who talked to me the way she did. Most of the kids in the town didn't treat me like a person, for being the one Korean kid. She was the only one there who had ever made this much time for me, and now, knowing I was gay, and accepting it, made her the only person who really knew me in the entire world.

We continued this way for the rest of my time there, and there was a lot to think about besides us, like just where Geoff and Derrick had been that night. Or how, a few days later, she and Derrick were fine. And then she wasn't feeling well, and then she was slipping the pregnancy test over the counter at me and I rang it up for her, and when she came in to work the next day, the answer was in her eyes.

By what I thought was an unspoken agreement, we put it out of our minds, what had happened between us. Or at least one of us did.

I always meant to write to her but I never did. This was true in regard to all my friends from back then. I was off at college in San Francisco, the California College of the Arts. I was finally meeting guys who would look me in the eye and ask me out while they twinkled at me. My ethnicity was not weird there and I had many friends who shared it. I was even at times really ordinary. I grew less bitter in the company of people I could be myself with, and writing home . . . well, it felt as if to reach back meant letting even a little of what I had left behind through the wall I had put up between my old life and my new one. And so I never did.

■   ■   ■

Later, when people thought it was maybe Geoff's baby, she rolled her eyes. "They would," Katie said. "They fucking would."

She looked at me for a minute. "Just because he let Geoff do the driving doesn't mean he let him do the driving." We laughed about that one pretty hard, and then harder, and then even harder, until soon we hid behind the counter, because we could not stop laughing.

"This is your fault," she said when she eventually ran to the bathroom to change her pants. It turns out when you are pregnant it is easy to have a little accident while laughing. By then we were like old friends. I was five months into the job. My checks were tiny, but I knew my mother felt better every time she watched me come in from work and put my blue and white CVS vest on the barstool in the kitchen. And I, I felt a different kind of pride for being on the inside of the biggest scandal at school, which was no longer me. Katie's pregnancy was interesting to me, a scandal partly because she not only announced it, she had no apparent shame about it: "What?" she said, of her decision to share the news. "Like you all weren't gonna know?" And then she said, "I'm keeping it, too." In her junior year photo for the yearbook, she even fought for the right to show how far along she was, though she lost. Derrick offered to marry her, but she turned him down and broke up with him.

I thought it was wrong of her to do, but I also thought it was beautiful. This confused me but also made it seem important. I was young, and it was my first time having that experience. I soon regretted thinking it was wrong. But I also graduated, and I never checked the next year's yearbook except after hearing she'd gotten her son into the photo. I opened it up to look at it once. She looked happy and proud, I remember. Her baby boy was cute, but also just a bump with hair, the smallest part of a small photo. That was about it.

. . .

Her brother didn't seem to know much about this at all. At the bar we found near Shaw's, we sat and talked amid several awkward silences. I worried that his sister was dead at one point—that I would find out in some way I couldn't bear. But instead he pulled out his wallet and showed me the picture she'd sent recently of her and her son.

"He's cute," I said.

"Yeah. He is. He looks like he's not quite white, right?"

I squinted. "Native American, maybe," I said.

"That's what I was thinking! But she won't say who the dad is, and honestly, my sister is like the Olympics: open to countries from around the world!" he said, making a welcoming gesture and then laughing like a maniac. I let it go for a moment and then, in a move that surprised both me and him, I sucker punched him, and it sent him flying off his stool.

I don't know if you know about how a sucker punch feels to set up and throw. It takes a certain kind of grudging anger and pretense. You have to act like you don't care, because if you flinch, if you emit the slightest signal, it is off. It's a cruel thing to do, though, as the victim never sees it coming, though usually the recipient deserves it. But again, to be clear, I lie to myself a lot so as to feel better about my life. I had waited for him and said nothing during his little joke, because out of something like scientific curiosity I wanted to hear what he would say next, and when he said it, my course of action was clear.

He shook his head, whipping blood from his nose around him, blinking in surprise. I was shaking my hand, because, well, it hurts to punch someone.

So, yes, her brother was a dick, but that wasn't why I

punched him. I punched him because I suddenly knew something, looking at the photo, something I hadn't let myself believe, not even once, not ever, this whole time. Maybe it was even what she meant when she said "This is your fault" as she ran to the back of the CVS, holding her belly, running to the bathroom. The boy in that photo, he looked like my dad. Like me. The kid was mine.

■ ■ ■

"You could have said something," I said.

"You could have asked," Katie said. She still held her cigarettes the same way. She noticed me noticing and said of it, "I only smoke while he's at school." We were waiting for him to come home. She smiled. She still worked at the CVS, but she was the pharmacist now. She'd done well for herself.

"And what was I to do, marry the town gay? No. No. It was never going to be like that." She flicked her ash. "You're high if you think otherwise."

I laughed at that against my will. Punching out Katie's brother hadn't been the greatest way to get her address, but once he understood, he'd given it to me and apologized. "You got a mean sucker punch for a faggot, I'll give you that," he said as we shook hands on it.

Now I was still trying to be mad at her, for not telling me, but I was also too happy to see her and too guilty, knowing what I knew.

"You were never going to stay here," she said. "And I wasn't going to make you. I'm glad you're here now, but understand, after what I learned about Derrick and Geoff, I never wanted to see any of you again." She pushed her cigarette out into an ashtray, then turned and walked into the house to run it under the sink and throw it away. I followed her.

She told me about how, after graduation, Derrick and Geoff left for California together, where they bought a condo with money they'd saved, and Derrick went to school while Geoff worked at a sporting goods shop and supported him. They eventually got married—the secret to Geoff's devotion and Derrick's hesitancy a secret no more.

I then told her about how I became a professional gay, as it were, working inside of gay businesses, for gay media, for my life since I went away. I had had boyfriends; finally, I had a man, and then I lost him. Had another, lost him too. Found another, still had him, as of the trip back home. She smoked on her stoop and filled me in on her and on the man she'd had and lost and had again; they had divorced and now were dating again.

All the while, I tried to imagine the call I was going to make later, to my mother, as well as my boyfriend. *Turns out I'm a dad* seemed like not quite the right tone to strike. My idea of my life going forward up until now had no room for a child, a son of my own. This was nothing I had planned for myself, and it all made me feel like I was barely able to take care of myself, much less anyone else. The bus stopped then, and as I waited for him to come into view, there was a silence in me into which everything I had been until then vanished.

I don't think there's any video of me from when I was his age, but I'm pretty sure that as he crossed the street I knew his walk. My fourteen-year-old son, the quiet, good-looking kid Katie had named Boomer, confident but with a slight sad streak of the kind that ran through me as well, the spitting image of me and my dad.

I am trying to think of how I can explain how it was to meet him. To stand in front of him and for Katie to say, "This is your father." Me thinking of how I wasn't ready to suffer his scrutiny of me, even as I found myself holding him in a sudden hug I knew he wasn't sure he liked.

But only when I walked into my mother's house with him and Katie and saw my mom's eyes, me with this old friend she'd had filling her prescriptions for all the years after I'd left for college, did I understand what I had done. I had told my mother to look for it, to prepare for it, but when she saw what I'd seen right away in Boomer, I could barely get the words out for introductions and then it didn't matter, my son being kind while a woman he didn't know wept on his shoulder, gently rocking him from side to side, speaking softly, in Korean, words I hadn't heard her say since I was a boy. And a new one for her: sonja. Grandson.

Katie was kind to her, and waited before quietly walking over so her son could see her. Our son? I don't think I knew until then what a family was or could be, despite having been in one all this time. That it was something you built to keep what you could of what you loved from the depredations of time and the world and how they would lead all you loved to ruin and death, no matter what. My mother had stayed here all this time, despite how alone she was. She and my father had been the only Korean couple in our town, and then she was without him. Just with me. And then I left. My father was buried there, and she had never remarried. She had accepted my being gay, and my decision not to have children. Somehow I had thought this meant we were okay, and yet all of this had obscured for me how the blunt and forcible separations caused by my father's death were not healed, maybe not even a little, in her or in me. I didn't know how much she still missed him. I often didn't let myself feel how much I did. As my mom wept on Boomer's shoulder, though, I knew I'd finally broken her heart the right way after breaking it the wrong way all those years ago. I had brought something into the world that neither of us was ever going to admit we needed, not until he was right in front of us.

There was a lot I didn't know and would come to know, about how Katie and I were going to manage this, or whether she would even let me do the three things I could probably do, or if she was ready for Boomer to have a grandmother, and one so close by, and my family in the bargain too. But just then, what stared out at me as I watched my mom let go of Boomer and turn to me, and smile, was that my punishment, my time at the CVS—this had never been about her anger at my accident and the damage to the car and the wall, or even her shame. It was all because . . . How could I be so careless, after she had lost my dad? How could I act like I could not die?

WISDOM

Nana Ekua Brew-Hammond

IT WAS LONG past the time of night when the prostitutes on Lagos Avenue shouted "Ah-way!" at any car that dared slow without intent to purchase. The kebab, waakye, roast pork, and guinea fowl sellers had packed up. The drinking spots were closed. Only armed robbers, avuvis, taxi drivers, and prayer warriors were awake, and maybe watchmen, if they were good.

Of the sleepless, Yao was among the first group, if you counted the two clothes hangers he had unraveled and joined to create a long, wiry accomplice. He inserted it now through a torn window net and the space between missing louvers, moving the hooked extension past two bodies rising and falling in the surrender of sleep on two mattresses joined together on the floor.

He directed the wire to the red dot of a charging cell phone, bypassing the green light of a charged laptop for the former's easier mobility. He wiggled his wrist like he was turning a key, unlocking the house he peered inside of. When his hook fastened onto an edge of the phone, Yao took advantage of the faint magnetic connection, yanking his booty with ginger determination, slowly dragging it along the ground, past the dreaming owners, up the inside wall, and out.

The mobile lit up and trembled in his hands just as he clasped it, an alarm surprising him. Yao juggled the phone in reflex, almost dropping the device and his wiry extension as he simultaneously noted the reminder accompanying the alert—"*Exams.*" He jabbed the power button and scrambled toward the section of wall he had hopped over, past the window he had first looked into, finding nothing but a naked old woman sleeping next to a rotating fan.

A light switched on.

Now straddling the pillow he had used to smother the jutting shards of glass affixed along the top of the wall for security, Yao looked back momentarily. A man poked his head through the absent louvers and fraying net, heaving with the anger of interrupted sleep and the shock of violation.

"Heh! Djulɔ! Djulɔ! Djulɔ!"

He repeated the thievery charge in firing squad succession, shedding more grogginess with each declaration as he became increasingly infuriated. His rising decibel was a call to arms, a desperate rallying cry to his neighbors and the watchmen that manned the mix of modest bungalows and code-flouting mansions that dwarfed the domicile Yao had picked because it had no guardhouse or dogs. A distant Doberman barked, but no one emerged from the adjacent watchhouses or visitor gates.

It was two hours before dawn, when sleep most resembles death—the time night security snore in peace. It was also the part of East Legon that had managed to maintain its quiet neighborhood aspirations, even after Boundary Road was paved to connect it to the motorway, and a spree of new construction had changed the area's topography.

Shiashie had become a sprawling grid of mansions and newly built town houses, complete with companion sign-boards advertising US dollar asking prices, and protected by a firewall of amenities for expats. International schools, corner provision shops, and passion project clothing boutiques hid and hemmed the movements of the shantytown Shiashie had taken its name from, and the residents that predated the gentrification.

Lagos Avenue, with its bars, outdoor eateries, ATMs, and nearby mall was a minutes-long drive from Shiashie—a long enough walk that it kept revelers, riffraff, and the prostitutes' patrons out, unless they were coming home. This was why Yao had gone in.

Now on the street side of the wall, the mobile in his pocket, adrenaline lacing his blood, Yao sprinted away, his extended hanger and punctured pillow in tow. Somewhere between the French Embassy Lycée and A&C Mall, he started laughing.

The mirth-cum-bravado of relief escaped him in dog-throated guffaws, pooling in his eyes. He moved the pillow to the hand that held the deformed wire and felt for the phone, his spontaneous howls ebbing to intermittent wheezing and gulping sounds as he recalled the naked old woman he had spied.

The abiriwa's legs had been spread and twisted like his hanger, stuffed and misshapen like his pillow. He had watched her roll over, the moonlight illuminating breasts with the loose heft of fufu as they slid into her armpits, before he remembered his mission and moved to the next window in search of a valuable left out that could be easily pocketed. Now Yao shook with a renewed stream of cynical giggles at the thought of making the grandmother munch her pillow as he drilled himself inside her, her rotating fan their only witness.

A hissing sound interrupted his brutal reverie.

The serpentine call had come from a woman sitting on the steps of the closed mall, the light from the adjacent filling station and an overhead security beam making an eerily frizzy halo of her wig. The short hairs had the plastic pluck and ambition of a storefront boutique mannequin. Her outfit was as elegantly garish—a T-shirt bearing the bedazzled noun-verb "Flirt," and similarly spangled jeans that tapered above platform stiletto sandals.

Prostitute, he decided with a mix of condemnation and arousal. He stopped to look her over from his position across the street, and yanked the waistband of her jeans to her shoes in his mind. His penis stirred at the thought, pushing against the zipper of his shorts. He waited for a taxi to pass before padding over to her, still clutching the pillow and extended hanger.

The girl sat as stoic as the Kwame Nkrumah statue in the new "Dubai" park near Circle, dubbed so, Yao assumed, because the United Arab Emirates city was also awash in blue floodlights. Only her eyes darted, from the rectangle in his pocket to the burglar's accessories he carried.

"You've come to sleep or to clear a drain?" she asked when he stood in front of her. "What do you have in your pocket?"

Smiling, Yao rehearsed a line of dialogue he had heard

on *A Traição*, a Brazilian soap opera that always seemed to be on at the salon next to the construction site he shared a room in. "Something big for you."

"That's for me to find out," the girl replied. She had apparently watched the same episode, her accent morphing to match the baby-pitched English of the actors who voiced over the Portuguese-speaking talent.

He brought himself closer, dropping the pillow and hanger. She stood, slighter than she had looked sitting with her knees grazing her breasts, and shorter, even in her platform stilts. Her wig at his chest, he fixated on the fake patch of scalp the hairs radiated around as her hand reached for his bulge.

"Ahshhh!"

Yao tore away from her in pain, but she had let go first, skipping away into the taxi that had passed moments before, taking the rectangle in his pocket with her.

Shame lit through his body as he watched the yellow flanks of the cab turn the corner. He looked around wildly, helplessly for witnesses. The only ones who had seen were two ginger-haired dogs, uninterested as they trotted across the empty street.

Yao wandered now, fists curled up like weights at his side. He didn't want to go home, where the mosquitoes that nightly besieged the half-built building he squatted in would have him for supper. And he didn't want to be alone. He was always alone.

His roommate was ever occupied with work or a party. His many neighbors—also squatters paying the architect overseeing the house's construction for some Ghanaians in Germany—were always around, but not with him. They offered polite greetings when they passed him in the back of the house when he looked for a private spot to bathe, or when he passed them as they scrubbed their clothes and hung them to dry. But that was the extent of their connection.

He thought of the man whose phone he had taken in Shiashie, and envied him the one who slept on the adjoining mattress as well as the old woman in the next room. If not for Elinam's accusation, he would be home in Tafi with his people too.

Unlike his closest friend, Kofi, who dreamed of leaving their hometown for the capital, Yao had been content to man his mother's banana stand opposite the Tafi Atome Monkey Sanctuary. It wasn't that he didn't realize that there was far more to experience outside his small town; he just appreciated the experiences he had right there in Tafi. He relished chatting with the visitors who stopped to buy enough of the crescent-shaped fruits to entice the bearded primates from their homes deep in the grove. He missed peering from his perch outside the sanctuary, watching them pose for tremble-selfies when the mona monkeys hopped on their arms, carefully peeling the fruit for themselves.

Yao longed to amble Tafi's wide streets again, strike up a conversation with a woman stooped over a sudsy bucket, or simply perch near the visitor center with Kofi and watch the stream of passersby. People came to Tafi from across Ghana and the globe to connect with the monkeys, the people, and a part of themselves. In Accra, there was no time for connection unless it could lead to profit. No one wanted anything to do with anyone unless they had something in their pocket the other could spend. Especially the girls.

He vibrated with new anger at the memory of Elinam's

charge, and the aftermath, replaying the incident that had ultimately driven him to Accra.

As he had once before, Yao had gone with Elinam, his mate since primary school, into a part of the sanctuary forbidden to all but the priests. Deep in the thicket of mahogany and ficus trees, he had taken off her top and his shorts. She had knelt to take him in her mouth, but when he moved to join them at the hip, she pulled away. He was already inside of her, had already been inside of her, but this time she ran from him wailing.

He had accepted her histrionics as part of the maddening game of virginal pretension girls were raised to play to prove the masculinity of their pursuers. Their first time, he had played along, gently unfolding her crossed arms, prying apart her shut thighs as he coaxed her in the drowsy octave of desire to give in to her own wanting.

Days after their negotiation of limbs and longing, Elinam performed a routine of contrition. What else could it be but an act, Yao wondered, when his old friend began turning her head when they encountered each other in town?

"She says it was rape," Kofi reported back after Yao had sent him as an emissary to find out why Elinam had abruptly gone cold.

"Nonsense," he replied, fear, confusion, and anger behind the defensive swallow that followed.

"I know you have to be sorry about what we did," he said, confronting her at the Tafi Abuife Development Youth Association Celebration Week Game Day. The TADYA pickup truck roared by, packed with, and trailed by, revelers dancing to the jams DJ One Touch blasted from the tent that housed his turntables. Yao leaned in to tell Elinam, "I am not sorry."

Elinam's head jerked at his statement.

"You were begging me. Pressuring me. You forced my hands to touch you," she said.

"Heh! Did I force you?"

"There are more ways to force than by force." She folded her arms under her breasts now, her words seeming to give her courage as her tone became firmer. "You continued to coerce me, even after I resisted. I told you I didn't want to, but you wouldn't stop." She shook her head.

"Do you mean to tell me you vex," he said, slipping into a hybrid of pidgin and English, "because I was able to persuade you?"

"Because you wouldn't stop until I did what you wanted."

He studied her tightly wound arms now, remembering how he had detangled them. "But you gave me head."

"That was all I wanted to do. Full stop."

Her friend Ana had been watching them from the edge of the crowded street, as had Kofi from the opposite side of the road. Now Ana strode over.

"O le okay?" she asked Elinam, mixing English and Ewe.

He almost laughed as he swallowed again. Watching Ana rub circles of comfort on Elinam's back as they walked away, his certainty that he had done nothing wrong gave way.

■　■　■

Now Yao stalked futilely in the direction of the long-gone taxi, his anger at Elinam and the prostitute becoming one. As he walked along Lagos Avenue, the streetlamps went black. *Dumsor.* He sucked his teeth at the latest in a string of intermittent power outages, and the feeling that the ground had dropped out from underneath him again.

The white rubber capping the toes of his sneakers slowly reappeared as his eyes adjusted and he decided what to do. He had planned to liquidate the phone at the electronics repair shop near American House Junction. He needed to get money some other way for the two trɔtrɔs he would have to take to reach the room he shared in Oyarifa. His alternative was a two-hour walk home.

Yao picked up his pace now, focused on beating morning's first light, resolving in that moment to return to Shiashie for the money. By the time he passed the American International School, he had broken into a trot.

Breathing hard from the risk, he stopped in front of the house he had burgled earlier. He could chance another home, but this one had no snarling dogs or gateman to elude. And he knew they had a laptop. It wouldn't be as easy to take as the phone, but the residents of the house were likely sleeping again, he told himself, the humiliation of violation giving in to their respective circadian rhythms. They would never expect him to come back. No one expected the same misfortune to strike twice in one night.

He advanced to the wall, suddenly remembering he had left his pillow and wire at the mall steps. Hastily, he removed his shirt and shorts and folded them into a padded cushion before placing them over whatever glass it could cover. When he pat tested it, he could feel the jagged grooves through the fabric. He inhaled, resigned to the pain that would come as he gingerly twisted his left hand to place it along a glass-free space before gently pressing his second palm into the material and hopping up.

In his briefs, he couldn't sit into his straddle and gain the balance to jump. He fell into an awkward heap on the other side. Ignoring the pain shooting through the arm he had landed on, Yao furiously rubbed the scratch on his inner thigh. Relieved to find the skin wasn't broken, he lay still for the seconds that followed, listening for movement inside the house. The sleeping silence unbroken, he rose to his sneakers, bravado beginning to numb him again.

Yao left the folded clothes on the wall so he could make a quick escape and sidled up to the first window for his momentary amusement. The old lady was still lying in the buff, the rotating fan muffling her snores. He felt his penis stir. Without the added barrier of his shorts zipper, it strained the thin cotton of his briefs, embarrassing and titillating him.

Was he so lonely that he was seriously entertaining this old body? Was he still so inflamed at Elinam's equivocation of persuasion and force that he would use this abiriwa to settle the matter once and for all? Was he really willing to risk going to counterback again?

He turned to the sky. Still black as night. With dawn an hour or so away, he decided he had time to fuck her if he moved quickly. Unlike the window that looked into the young man's room, all the metal frames bordering both sides of her window were empty of louvers. Yao gripped an edge of the net pane and yanked it toward himself, grinning with relief when it came apart neatly and quietly.

Discounting the logistical fact that he could not have sex with her, take the laptop, and get away, he convinced himself this would end well: that the old lady wouldn't scream, that the young man and his roommate next door wouldn't burst in to save her, that he could fuck her and find wherever she hid her money without being caught before night yielded to light.

He hoisted himself into the bedroom with the arm that wasn't in pain, the intimate scent of sweat and perfume instantly filling his nose. He tugged at his erect penis, his heart beating in his ears as his eyes adjusted.

Yao advanced to the bed, stepping out of his briefs when the old woman abruptly sat up. He stopped as she moved past him and pulled open a door in the wall, leaving it slightly ajar as she sank onto a toilet. In the fog of sleep she hadn't seen him.

He sighed at himself, remembering the morning the CID officers had come to his home, luring him to the Golokwati Police Station. They had come under the guise of being from Strategic Foods, looking to sell surplus bananas behind their boss's back. He could still smell the putrid cell behind the police station reception counter, his room for the night after Elinam identified him. Sense flooding back to his brain, Yao bent to collect his underwear. He had not belonged in that cell, and he did not belong here.

He would dart out of the room before the old lady returned to her bed, and leave the way he came. He would beg a trɔtrɔ mate at American House to let him ride to Madina Market free, and do the same at Madina for the ride home to Oyarifa.

He started to move, but the abiriwa's voice suddenly arrested him. Instead of the trickling or plunking sounds of toilet relief, she began to sing in tongues. Yao could not speak the heavenly language, but he recognized its repetitive cadence instantly. There was no one in Ghana who did not know the sound of tongues, diverse as they were. Many a night was pierced with the projectile shouts launched from open-air and open-plan church buildings.

The old lady wove Ga and English into her prayer. "Oye-wa'dɔ, Nyɔngmo. Thank you, Jesus."

Still clutching his briefs, Yao started to move again, but he smacked into a wall. The prayer paused with the sound of listening.

Yao was scrambling off the floor when the light switched on. The old lady emerged, childlike plaits on her head, the stretch-marked and folded flesh of age telling the short story of life. She gasped, noticing his nakedness and hers, before she began to scream.

"In the name of Jesus, Foul Spirit of Rape, I bind you. You are not welcome in my home. You will not shame me, and you will not shame this boy."

On his feet now, with the aid of the light, Yao ran out, but the young man who had seen him leave with his mobile hours earlier stood at the door. He looked to be about Yao's age, twenty, and he was a twin, as there were two of him blocking Yao's escape.

One of them bent to take off his left chalewote and slam it across Yao's cheek. The thong of the rubber shower slipper snapped out of its socket.

"Leave him," the old woman commanded, her voice hoarse from shouting or because the blow was ringing in Yao's ear.

"Grandm—"

"I said leave him!" The abiriwa sank to the edge of her bed and gathered her bedsheet around herself. "The devil is already tormenting him."

She exhaled with the weariness of age and broken sleep. "Look at you. Fine boy. A young man hoping to rape an old woman. You see how the devil is making a fool of you?" The woman closed her eyes now. "Satan, you will not shame this boy. You will not waste his life. Take your hands off him. Release him, in the name of Jesus."

Satisfied her order was heard, she opened her eyes and readjusted the bedsheet, looping it under her armpit again.

"Give him some of the kenkey," she directed the twins.

Yao turned to the young men for confirmation of what he was hearing.

"Grandma, we should take him to the police station."

"So he can sit in a jail cell not knowing his right from his left? First, he must be arrested in the Spirit."

"But, Gra—"

"I said get this boy some kenkey! And fish!" She sucked her teeth as one of the boys retreated, annoyed she had had to repeat herself.

Yao moved to leave.

"Where are you going?"

"*Ahshhh!*" Yao folded, felled by the pain that inflamed the arm he had fallen on as she reached out to yank him to stay.

"They are bringing you kenkey. Put on your pants." She shook her head. "Where are your clothes? Derek, go and bring him something of yours to—"

"Madam, my clothes are on your wall." He grimaced as he massaged his shoulder.

"Ahh," she said, verbalizing the breath of exhaled judgment. "Derek, go and bring his clothes."

"Madam, I am—"

"Do you know it's a demon?" she asked him. "The Spirit of Lust and Theft. You have let them both in. You have given them rest." She threw her hands up now, exasperated.

As Yao stepped into his briefs, Grandma continued.

"Foul Spirits, I dismiss you in the name of Jesus. This home is sealed in the blood of Jesus. At my Lord's name, you have to flee." She paused to call her grandsons—"Derek! Eric!"—before turning to him again.

"Where are you from?"

He ignored her, assessing whether he could overpower her grandsons with his pained arm and escape.

"I said where are you from?"

"Tafi," he said finally, ashamed of the tears that suddenly brimmed in his eyes.

"O de suku-ah?" she asked him in Ewe, knowing now he was from the Volta Region.

"'Vegbetɔ?" He swiped a tear at the sound of his language, comforted by this little piece of home.

"I am not, but my former husband was a proud Guan." She rolled her eyes at the memory. "He grew up in Volta and we lived there for some time."

"I completed BECE," he answered her earlier question, proving it by returning to the English he had passed in the Basic Education Certificate Examination.

"Then how did you end up here?"

Yao inhaled as Derek and Eric entered the room with his shorts and T-shirt and a plate of food. He eyed the meal with suspicion, but hunger overtook his trepidation.

The plate was crowded with kenkey slices, the midsection of a fried tilapia, ground green micro chilies, and a lump of black shitɔ. Saliva instantly pooled in his mouth, the fragrance of the fermented corn dough mingling with the blackened pepper, dried fish and tomato condiment, and seasoned tilapia. He hadn't eaten since seven that night, the small waakye and two five-hundred-milliliter sachets of Special Ice pure water long burned away with the night's action.

A cock crowed outside, the official announcement of morning. Soon the sky would show it.

"Eh-heh, I'm listening."

The boys hovered, and Grandma folded her hands on her lap as Yao bent to put the plate on the ground and step into his clothes. When he was dressed, he picked the plate up again in silence.

"Have you attempted rape or burglary before?" Grandma asked. "Because you were emboldened to come into this house naked, though Jehovah had other plans for you and me, and us." She turned to her grandsons. "Go on. You were saying?"

Yao sighed, pinching a piece of kenkey from the ball, dipping it in the pepper as he decided whether to tell the old lady the truth. A small part of him was curious how someone who didn't know him or Elinam would read the situation.

"I was falsely accused."

"Of rape?" Grandma leapt.

"But I didn—"

"Did you ask permission? Did she tell you she wanted you?" Grandma pummeled Yao with questions. "Or did you come into her chamber like you did mine, naked and full of a lustful, lying spirit?"

"She was my girlfriend." He overstated his friendship with Elinam for the sake of simplicity and brevity. It had taken years of flirtation and missed opportunities to get her in that sanctuary.

"And so what? Does that give you the right to take what she didn't want to give?"

He inhaled with fresh anger. "Excuse me to say, but she went down on me of her own accord. She admitted she did."

Grandma turned to her grandsons quizzically. "'Went down'?"

"She sucked my penis."

He waited for the old lady to get his point that Elinam was no angel, that she had indeed wanted to fuck, but Grandma twisted her head again.

"The devil has made a fool of you, but do you know Wisdom is at work too?"

Annoyed, he handed the plate to a twin and moved to leave.

The young man's eyes narrowed with knowing as Yao tried to move past. "You are the one who took my phone! Grandma—"

Grandma stopped him, sucking her teeth. "The phone I told you not to buy to save money for your visa? 'Wisdom cries aloud in the street,'" she told them all, pointing to the wall behind Yao. He turned to see she was reading from a paper taped above his head labeled "Proverbs 1:20."

"In the markets she raises her voice," she continued, "at the head of the noisy streets she cries out; at the entrance of the city gates she speaks: 'How long, O simple ones, will you love being simple?'"

Derek and Eric scowled.

"I spent the night in counterback because my girl regretted her own decision," Yao cried to the old woman. "The officers of the CID call themselves Criminal Investigation Department, but there was no investigation."

He snorted. "They trick me into accompanying them to the police station before revealing their true identity and telling me if I say anything to them, it can be used against me in court!"

Yao sliced the air with his hands to punctuate the officers' next order. "They force me to go inside the station. I see Elinam standing there with her father. They ask her 'Is he the one?'"—he jabbed his pointer finger in accusation—"without asking me anything! And when she says 'Yes,' they take me behind the counter, take my shirt and trousers, and lock me in the cell with three others, all of us in just our boxer shorts."

His hands instinctively gathered in a fist in front of his crotch. "If not for one kind officer who let me use her phone to call my mother, and provided food to sustain me, I don't know how I would have survived that night. My mother had to go all the way to Ofankor to get her cousin to sign for my bail—ten million cedis." Yao shook his head now and paused to let the sum sink in. "Now I can't stay in Tafi, because everyone was separating themselves from me and my family. No one was buying our bananas, so I had to take my uncle's job offer in Ofankor."

His explanation didn't replace the judgment in Grandma's eyes. Spent from the memory and the rush of anger and shame he now felt, Yao turned toward the window net he had torn. "I have to go."

"You can go out by the door," Grandma told him. "Derek, show him. And," she preempted, "don't ask him about any phone."

Yao followed his angry leader, trailed by his angrier twin. They walked through a narrow terrazzo hallway, past a sitting room fat with ornate stuffed chairs. More Bible verses were taped in magnified print along the walls. He exhaled when he was finally standing outside, morning's hazy first light flooding his eyes. He waited with restless fidgets as one of the twins fumbled with the lock at the gate.

"If you don't go and bring Eric's phone—" Derek whispered.

"Young man!" Grandma's voice sliced through the twin's threat. The three men turned to find the old woman filling her doorway. "Are you working?"

"I—yes, madam," Yao lied, exhaling again as Eric finally pulled the rusted gate from its mooring in the ground, freeing him from this house and night.

"Doing what? Stealing and raping are not professions."

He rolled his eyes as Eric laughed at him now.

"I was a seller. In Tafi."

"Well, I need security," she said. "As you know. We need someone to be in the house with us day and night to deter armed robbers and help us keep the compound neat. I'll pay you 200 Ghana a month, plus food and accommodation here. Use Wisdom," she said before turning away.

Yao backed out of the gate and heard it lock as he walked off. He inhaled relief that the old woman hadn't turned him in to the East Legon Police Station, even as he regretted the meal he had left half-eaten.

He walked down to the end of the block, turned the corner, and followed the road to Lagos Avenue. It was just after six a.m., but the thoroughfare was already busy with koko and bofrot sellers setting up respective stands for the porridge and fried sweet dough breakfast staples.

The road that fed Lagos Avenue to George Bush Highway was beginning to fill with peddlers hawking P.K. chewing gum, pure water, MTN and Airtel phone credit, car floor

mats, and the daily newspapers. Cars and trɔtrɔs were starting to pile up, the hawkers taking advantage of the captive
consumer traffic.

With rush hour beginning, Yao doubted a mate would let
him ride to Oyarifa for free, so he walked. Past A&C Mall,
along the dirt that skirted Adjiringanor Road, he passed
former president Rawlings's mansion, the luxury housing
development Trasacco Valley, and Cahaya Lounge. When
he reached the Allied Oil filling station, hunger taunted his
decision to abandon the kenkey Grandma had served him.

He detoured at the sight of the convenience grocery store
beyond the petrol pumps, walking into the air-conditioned
cool of the empty supermarket. His mouth went dry from
the artificial blast and sudden thirst. He had no food at
home. He would have to steal something to eat, and a bottle
of water.

Yao wandered the aisles, blinking in exhaustion from the
multitude of choices. Whole milk. Skim milk. Almond milk.
Coconut milk. *Ah!*

He wanted an egg. How he wanted an egg. But he couldn't
take just one. If he stole a carton, he would have to pay his
roommate both to use his stovetop and for space in his refrigerator. Everything was a transaction in Accra, an extraction of
the little someone could take, yet he was the supposed djulɔ.

Bread was the only thing that made sense to take. Yao
swiped a small bar of butter and pushed it into his pocket.
Where would he hide the bread, though? He sighed, stag-
gering out of the store breadless and squinting for a corner
provisions shop. He could taste the fresh-baked sweet bread
delivered every morning across the city.

He continued down the increasingly crowded street, giving way to parents and uniformed schoolkids, workers, and cars, the sun blistering his path with rising intensity. By the time he reached Halima's Breadbasket and Provisions, the pain in the arm he had fallen on throbbed in his feet too. He was too tired to plot.

"Auntie, I don't have money." He must have said it so pitifully, because the proprietress handed him two loaves without question or comment.

He cradled them in gratitude before tearing the plastic casing from the end of one and ripping a piece to eat. The soft flour was like blades in his dry throat, but his gag reflex quickly followed with just enough moisture to lubricate his swallow. He ate half of the loaf in the short distance between Halima's and his home.

The gate that hedged his house materialized ahead of him, shimmer-floating like an oasis. He walked up to the structure of exposed beams and rods, past the hills of silvery gravel, stacked cement bags, and planks of wood, to the back, where six rooms were finished.

He shared a room with one Titus Benyarko. Though Titus would charge him to use his fridge or stovetop, he would happily eat Yao's bread if he left it on the box at the head of Titus's bed. Yao buried the whole and half loaf in his suitcase before unfurling his sleeping mat.

■ ■ ■

"My guy! You for get phone!" Titus woke Yao to tell him. "I find some job give you, but I no fit give them your number. They already take give someone else," he continued. "You for buy phone."

Yao inhaled and rolled over. When he woke up again,

Titus was gone and the room was hot with the flatulence of sleep.

He sat up, strength returning to his body, noticing a blot seeping through his shorts. He sucked his teeth, remembering the butter.

He scanned for his bucket in Titus's corner, where it usually lay, but it wasn't to be found. *Fucking Titus.* He walked out to see if any of his neighbors were home to borrow one of theirs. Unusually, they were all out and he remembered vaguely now that one of them had mentioned a death in the family—that they would all be journeying to their village for the funeral.

Perhaps, instead of stealing in Shiashie, Yao mused, he should take what he could from his housemates. He had lived there a month without incident. No one would suspect him. He tried a doorknob absently, knowing it would be locked, but thinking of what he could use to jimmy the door quickly.

Sucking his teeth, he abandoned the door for now, and took his towel and Titus's shower caddy to the tap at the back of the house. Squatting naked under the nozzle, he lathered with Titus's fragrant soaps, sounding out the French labels to himself as *A Traição* floated in surround sound. "*Silvia, you have to tell him what your father made you do!*"

The soap opera came on at 10:30 a.m. It was still early enough to make something of the day.

Back in the room, Yao pulled out his suitcase and retrieved a shirt, trousers, and an iron. As he waited for the appliance to heat up, he oiled his skin, ate some more bread, and psyched himself up for what he had to do: beg his uncle for his old job.

When he had stepped off the orange Metro Mass Transit

Tata bus in Kaneshie Station, with only the 100 Ghana his mother had sent him with in his pocket, he had had employment. His mother's cousin, the one who had bailed him out of counterback, owned a commercial photo and digital printing shop in Ofankor.

It had been a relatively painless gig. Most of their customers were local churches and businesses in Accra proper seeking cheaper printing services than they'd find closer to home. All Yao really had to do was take the orders they phoned in and pass them on to the men who manned the industrial printer and cut the flyers, photos, and signboards to size in the back of the shop. But the resentment and embarrassment he had felt having to leave Tafi under a cloud of shame, and the rage he felt at Elinam—coupled with the tiresome four-hour commute: two hours in and out, day after day—gathered into a storm. Impulsively, he quit. Just stopped going to the shop one day and directed his neighbors to say he wasn't home when his uncle came, twice, to look for him.

But the signs posted on the electric poles in his neighborhood advertising for garden boys and watchmen had not yielded work in the wake of his abrupt decision. The 100 Ghana evaporated along with the 80 Ghana his uncle had paid him for the two weeks he had helped man the shop.

His living arrangement with Titus had been predicated on the fact that it would be temporary. Titus, the grandson of a family friend in Tafi, had agreed to let Yao sleep on the floor of his room for 20 Ghana a week until he found something better, though he would have to hide from the landlord.

Yao tugged the iron's plug from the wall and dressed quickly before rifling through Titus's pockets for the change he needed to pay the 2.30 GHS fare from Oyarifa to Circle, and the 1.80 from Circle to Ofankor. He took only 5 Ghana, hoping his restraint would elicit Fortune's leniency in the form of his uncle restoring his job and sending him back home with the return fare.

Slipping into his hard-soled black shoes, Yao stepped out into the searing Accra morning. Almost immediately, circles of sweat drenched the armpits of his white shirt as he moved briskly to the trɔtrɔ stop, passing faded election ads along the way.

After an hour-long ride sitting knee to chest in the now afternoon traffic, Yao stumbled off the trɔtrɔ and wove through the dense foot traffic, passing hawkers peddling all manner of goods from the silver pans on their heads, and men with satchels and backpacks whispering black market exchange rates: "I get dollar, pound, euro."

In the trɔtrɔ to Ofankor, Yao tapped his foot as the driver waited for the cab to fill. Trying to suppress the impatience and frustration that had caused him to abandon his job without a fallback, he looked for a view of nearby "Dubai."

In the daytime, without the aquarium-blue lights, the new structures circling Kwame Nkrumah's statue looked a cluttered mess. Former president Mahama had billed it as a "flyover destination," a landmark for people to identify Accra when they were in the air. He had seen photos of the over-head view online. The monument to Ghana's first president, nestled in the center of the newly built, overlapping road interchange, was indeed impressive from that vantage point. But most Ghanaians were only able to see it from the ground.

When the cab filled, the mate who managed the collection of fares slammed the top of the vehicle through his open window, indication they were ready to leave. Yao dozed in his window seat, waking up intermittently to obfuscated views of bumpers and hawkers, before finally alighting in Ofankor.

It was nearly two p.m. when he strode with gulping breath to the printed poster of the pop star Beyoncé and her newborn twins in the window, miniature versions of the image arranged underneath it like an old-school filmstrip.

He saw a young woman standing at the computer behind the counter where he had hunched a little over three weeks before.

"Is Uncle Edem in?"

Everyone called him Uncle Edem, so the girl didn't register respect at his familial connection. "Who may I tell him is here?"

"Yao."

"Your surname?" she asked when she emerged from the door that led to the workroom in the back.

"Denu."

When she returned with his uncle, Yao swallowed nervously. Uncle Edem did not return his searching smile.

"Uncle—"

The older man raised his hand to stop him. "When Adwoa told me a Yao Denu was here, I was sure she was mistaken. I thought, 'It could not be the same Yao Denu who, after I had bailed him from counterback and given him a job, left me without so much as a word.'"

Yao's eyes darted to and away from the girl, who had returned to her post, shame and defiance battling within him at the mention of his encounter at counterback.

"'It could not be the same boy,'" Uncle Edem continued, "'who pretended not to be home when I came looking for him out of fear some danger had befallen my sister's only son, out of guilt for not insisting he stay with me and my daughters in my home.'"

Yao bowed his head in performance of humility, banking on the sibling-like closeness between his mother and her cousin. He hoped, too, that the 10 Ghana note he had left behind in Titus's pocket would grant him karmic clemency.

"But, behold, it is. The same Yao Denu."

"Uncle, I am so sorry," he said. "I was still in shock from the false accusation." His eyes skipped to the girl with his emphasis of "false." She stared intently at the computer screen. "But I am ready to—"

"Ready to do what?"

"Ready to help you in any way that I can. I am ready to forget about going back to Tafi and work for you here."

Uncle Edem laughed through a closed mouth, the cynical sound escaping his nose. "My friend, I am not ready."

Yao watched his uncle disappear behind the workroom door, leaving only him and Adwoa in the shop. Beyoncé and her twins hovered with their backs to him. Adwoa looked up at him now as he searched around, regretting his haste in quitting even more. The job hadn't paid well, but it was easy enough, and his uncle had provided lunch.

He backed out into the sunshine, inhaling to preempt the impatience he already felt just thinking about the trek home and the dread that dripped in his stomach as he wondered how he would pay Titus rent next week and the week after. He boarded the trotro bound for Circle, his mind made up to pass by Shiashie before he went home to Oyarifa. The old woman had made him an offer he would be foolish to refuse now.

The mate directed the woman sitting next to him to tap him. "Your fare."

He pretended to rummage in his pockets, knowing he had spent all but ninety pesewas of the five Ghana he had taken from Titus's jeans pocket. When the mate didn't tell him to forget it, he rolled his eyes and gripped the back of the seat in front of him to hoist himself up. His seatmate tapped him again, this time handing him four fifty-pesewa coins. He returned one of the coins, digging in his pocket for the remaining thirty pesewas.

■   ■   ■

At the sound of the gate bell, Yao looked up from his stooped stance. He twisted the gathered reeds he had been sweeping the compound with and moved to open the door of the visitor gate. Peering through the hole in the rusted metal, he saw a woman in dark glasses.

Grandma had told him her granddaughter was coming from Holland. He retrieved his key to loosen the padlock, then dragged the side latch and pulled the metal stopper that moored it to the ground. When she was on the other side of the gate, she looked him up and down, from chale-wotes to haircut and back again, as she stretched her hand in greeting.

"Where are Derek and Eric?"

"They've gone for exams."

She nodded. "Is Grandma here?"

"Of course, I am."

The younger woman squealed as she ripped off her glasses.

"Atuuu!" Grandma cooed the parlance that accompanied hugs, stretching out her arms where she stood, waiting as her granddaughter ran to her.

"Wisdom!" She called Yao by the nickname she had christened him, disentangling from the embrace. "Come and meet my grandgirl, Stephanie."

Yao placed the broom gingerly on the floor.

"It's a pleasure to meet you, Wisdom. Have you just started working for Grandma?"

He nodded even as Grandma shook her head. "What 'working for'? This is my grandson!"

Stephanie smirked at the old lady, unsurprised by this presentation of a new relative.

"Isn't it so, Wisdom?"

Yao shyly basked in her embrace of him as family, even as the reason it had come to be taunted him. He averted his eyes from the granddaughter, who was staring at him now, hoping the old lady would dismiss him to return to the solitude of sweeping. Instead, she clasped his hand and dragged him into the sitting room.

"Come. Sit," she said, patting an old brocade chair. "I want you to tell Stephanie how you came to be part of the family."

BOY/GAMIN

Brandon Taylor

les lézards et les fourmis

Jackson is five, small, and blue-eyed, and he is stepping outside for the first time that day. The heat has not broken yet, but the humidity is receding to the river's edge four streets over. He lives in a small corner house made of brick painted white. Colors are easy for him; he knows blue, yellow, green, purple, red, brown, black, white, and orange. His box of crayons sticks out of his left pocket, and he has a rolled-up piece of paper in his right hand. All day, he has been begging Mama to let him color on the front porch. It is June and already too hot to spit, she says. He does not like it when it is too hot to spit. Too hot to spit means he can't go outside to color.

Mama is tall and blond; her eyes are not blue. He does not know what color they are. He doesn't have that crayon. She has yellow hair and red lips and white skin with red splotches on her arms when she folds them across her chest. She finally said, "Okay, Jack. Go color. Don't get mad when your crayons melt." They weren't going to melt. The front porch is small and cramped. It is made of concrete. There is a little walkway running to the cracked sidewalk, and a mailbox leaning to the right. Jackson crouches and rolls out his picture. It is a picture of a dog with a big smile and a collar too big for its neck. He balances, rocking back and forth on his feet as he pulls out his box of crayons and, with the wavering inconsistency of a left-hander, begins to color his dog bright orange. He wants an orange dog.

Daddy's hair is orange. Daddy comes around on Wednesdays. Jackson knows his days now. He wants to show Daddy with the calendar the way he showed Mama the other day. He climbed on her lap and pointed at each day with his finger, saying in a loud, certain voice, "Sunday. Monday. Tuesday. Wednesday. Thursday. Friday. Saturday." Sunday is first and Saturday is last, and they are next to each other like brothers. It is weird to him that the start and the end are next to each other, but he is happy that he knows his days, and he wants to show Daddy, but today is not Wednesday. It is Thursday, and it will be a whole Friday, Saturday, Sunday, Monday, and Tuesday before it is Wednesday again.

Jackson colors his dog, feeling the crayon scratch over rocks and uneven grit on the porch. It makes his orange streaks bumpy. He colors crouching on bare white feet with his body leaned down between his legs, breathing in a watery rattle. Cars rush by and the air they leave behind brushes up against the porch. He stops, looks out, and goes back to coloring. There are four houses next to his on the right. There are five across the street, and another set off to the other side. Some houses have screened enclosures. His has a tall pole that droops wires against the side of it. They get electricity from the poles. The wires hum and drone. It is familiar, like the sounds of the cars and the barking dogs across the street, and the cats that dart through the tall grass.

He wipes at his nose when it starts to drip. Coloring for ten minutes, the heat from the cement bakes his feet, but he loves being outside on the porch instead of in the dark house, lying around with his mama, who smells like milk and sweat through her skin. A black man walks by in a green shirt down to his knees and black pants; his skin is creased at the corners of his mouth but smooth like purple pen ink everywhere else. The color is oily and full of lots of colors. He glances at Jackson. Jackson's body goes cold and prickles everywhere. The man's eyes are white with big black missing spaces in the middle. He smiles, waves with a pale palm in a slow swipe. Jackson waves back, watching him go, trying to make himself smaller the way he does sometimes when the men don't walk by and instead hop-walk up the three steps to knock on the screen door. They disappear inside with his mama, and he sits outside like a good boy because his mama told him that if he was good, he could get new crayons and a new coloring book. He was always good when his mama had company. He behaved and colored by himself on the porch.

A long string of ants marches by the end of his paper. He stares down at them in the shadow his body makes. They are the only pets he keeps. He leaves dead bugs for them on the porch. Sometimes he catches grasshoppers in his hands and leaves them for the ants. It doesn't matter where he leaves the bugs, the ants always find them. Once, he followed the ants, all the way down the side of the porch and around the house. The heat wasn't so bad earlier in the year. He got to go outside more. Walking barefoot on the spongy grass, he walked until a warm smell came up to his nose and made him want to go home. He had followed the ants to a dead baby bird. They swarmed its tiny blue body. There were no eyes in its head, just more ants. Ants are finders. They are keepers. They find everything and anything that is hidden.

There is a lizard living on their porch too. He has seen it. Its colors are yellow, orange, and blue. Its tail flicks across the cement. The lizard is not alone. There are lizards everywhere in Montgomery, Alabama. Daddy killed one. Jackson sat and watched while his daddy stepped on the lizard that had come out of the corner of their bedroom.

It is summer, and in Alabama, that means lizards and ants.

les garçons de la rivière

Montgomery, Alabama, has a rail yard next to the state docks. The slope that separates the two is made of blue crushed gravel out of which scraggly ferns and beginning cedars sprout. Jackson is twelve, and he sneaks out of his house to slide down this gravel slope to the banks of the river, but first he stops in the graveyard that is the rail yard. He stands on loose rocks that in the high summer moon glow white and hot from baking in the sun. There are old train cars pushed onto their sides, rusted from the inside out and painted in streaks of gray and gold: gray and gold are the most prominent colors of spray paint sold in Alabama. They must be. He never sees any other color scrawled on the sides of the deserted railcars. Trains still blast through here sometimes. You can hear them from his house. The rails are red-rust metal winding through all the gravel into the tunnel, emerging on the clay bluffs that slope up and into the distance, toward the bridges that take the trains out of state. He does not know what is shipped through Montgomery these days except for cotton. The cotton fields are on the outskirts of town and in West Montgomery. He has seen them. He knows people who work in the fields all summer for money; people turn to sharecroppers to feed their families because the welfare isn't enough for everything.

Standing in the rail yards, Jackson waits to become a riverboy. That is what he and his four friends call themselves and each other. They sneak out from their homes and slide down the embankment to the river's edge. They know better than to go near the buildings. They, instead, move through the brush, rocks slipping under their feet and weight, until they're at the impromptu jumping block they've built from old barrels, blocks, and boards stolen from the abandoned wharf shack.

There is Tim, James, Eric, and Ben. Eric is the only black one in the bunch. They're from the projects. At the end of the summer, they are all going to different schools. This is the end of the years they have spent leaping into the river and swimming close to shore. They kick at the loose clay and silt. Minnows spin around their feet and kiss their stomachs. Then they drag their bodies out of the water and lie on the warm gravel, staring at the clear sky. Montgomery has no ambient lighting near the water. The cicadas and night birds sing in the wide water oaks and wispy willow trees; there is the creak and groan of the boats tethered nearby, and the cars that rush by on the overpass. But they swim in the black channels underneath, hidden and laughing together, all bare and slim-bodied.

Tomorrow there will only be two weeks before school starts. Tomorrow they will be another day closer to never talking again. Jackson stares at the hollow mouth of a railcar, trying to imagine what it was in another life. His thoughts intersect with the memory of Daddy, who is still orange-haired and skinny, but now he lives with them again. He and Mama fight a lot. Jackson lies curled up on a small bed in the back, covering his ears, trying to hear something other than their voices mixing higher and higher in the night. There are the sounds of cars on the road, and police sirens spin around in the dark outside of his bedroom window.

When he is out with the riverboys, he is not listening to Daddy. The railroad makes him think of his daddy, though, of the life he lived before he came back to them. Jackson stares at the railcar and tries to imagine who Daddy was in that other life. A pair of cats howl from the reeds, and he glances that way. The silence of the rail yard echoes with the sounds of the cats fucking, mating like beasts in the dark. Jackson turns and pulls his white shirt over his shoulders and away from his body. He walks with crunching steps toward the shimmering green-tinted black water. His friends are not here yet, but he wants to feel the water against his skin. He wants a few minutes to himself, weightless and free of time and space.

Jackson slips into the water and walks until his waist barely rises above the water line. He stands on sucking clay. Two summers ago a boy drowned when the clay sucked him under. Jackson imagines what it is like to drown. Pulled under until the water rushes into your mouth and throat, tasting brackish like the exhalation of water oak roots into the river. If you are not careful, it is easy to die; but they are riverboys, and soon they will be five bodies floating on the river, staring at the sky and the bridge, watching the world drag above them.

For now, Jackson is alone and twelve, letting the water stick his hair to his head and press some bits of pine straw to his side. He closes his eyes, water drops on his nose, and he listens to the hushed echoic sounds of water worlds. For a second he imagines he can feel Eric's fingers on his stomach. His eyes open, blue and cross-eyed staring at the galaxy of overlapping stars in the sky; he sees Eric's face, long and angular like a dog's, black skin everywhere, green eyes staring over thick eyelashes. He's beautiful and skinny and Jackson wants to punch him in the nose to make him ugly. He wants to punch him because he doesn't want to feel anything for somebody who is going to leave him again.

The voices of his friends carry through the graveyard stillness of the rail yard. They're nearby, and he is a naked body floating on the water. He doesn't care. He lets the water fill his ears.

Their loss is already a distant hurt in his chest.

la même bouche

French is the last class of the day. Madame Gray points at the whiteboard with her fingers spread and her hand pushed up; he remembers using that same gesture to play Itsy Bitsy Spider with his mother. Madame's bangles clang, and she looks around with slightly bugged blue eyes at them, trying to make it clear that passé composé avec avoir does not apply to reflexive verbs. Jackson knows that the way that he knows colors and days of the week; it is probably a distinction too simple and insulting of French's abstract complexity, he thinks with a bored smile, but it is one he made months ago when he started French II. Être is for verbs of movement and verbs that reflect and rebound to the speaker; avoir is for the external, non-self verbs. He told himself to remember it, and he has remembered it for the most part. He looks down at his desk. His passé composé test has no red marks, just black checks next to the fifty regular verbs he has conjugated into the past tense. French makes sense to him. The patterns, conjugations, order, and strictures of the language are not always easy to understand, but it triggers something in his mind like memories of things he has never experienced.

A second-string running back sits next to him, his back against the wall, with his broad thighs spread, watching from under his wide brow with a bored look. Madame makes no sense to him. He nudges at Jackson's leg, and Jackson looks at him. He is dark-haired, brown-eyed, and tan skin peeks from the collar of his Polo shirt. There's a ghost of a scar in the little indent of his upper lip, curled like a lizard's tail. He smells like Old Spice. There is something grinding and burning in the air, and Jackson can feel it. It makes him want to throw up. He doesn't. He cuts his eyes away. Jackson is fourteen and tall but skinny. His shoulders are getting broader and his stomach firmer every day, but he can't seem to put on weight. Not enough to try out for a team. He doesn't want to, anyway, he says to Daddy, who teases him every night about not playing sports. He wouldn't be good at it. He isn't a sissy, just clumsy.

They play video games, and he watches all the lights zip up and down the outside of the machines. He is poor, but a lot of the kids in his high school are poor, from the projects. The running back's name is Davis Howell. He's a confident but shy guy of sixteen who hangs out with his friends in the mall. He is the son of a local news anchor. He is good at math. They have math together, too, and Davis talks to him sometimes. They exchange bored smiles and laugh. Davis has warm eyes, but he gets into trouble. He's always looking around, chatting up the people closest to him. He is good at making people like him. Jackson likes him. Something gets between them and keeps them apart, though. It feels like a force field. Some tense force holding them at a distance like two magnets with the same charge.

Davis nudges his leg again and motions with a helpless flap of his hand toward his test paper. He mouths *Help* and laughs. Madame catches it, sends a glare their way. Her eyes are puffy underneath. She slaps the board, saying through her nose with a tinge of Southern accent, "Darling, you need to pay attention." They are all Darling or Chou. They go by French names in class. Davis is Cédric and Jackson is Jacques. Davis picked his name out for him. They had French I last semester. Davis leaned over and pointed at it on the paper; Jackson can still feel the warm breath on the back of his neck, and the way his fingers twitched on the page. Davis gives him a sad look, a faked sad look, and then smiles. Something remains of the sadness, though. Jackson can feel it, or thinks he can. Some deep sadness. Davis gets straight As, but in French only Cs or Ds. Jackson writes in an even, left-handed scrawl on the end of his paper, *7 the gully*. He rips this corner off of his paper and tosses it at Davis, his insides twisting. He doesn't look at Davis to see if it's a yes or a no.

Davis nudges his leg again, and they remain that way, magnetic rubbing against the field of their like charge.

At seven, Jackson waits in what everyone calls the gully; it is not a gully, just a place near an old bridge with no river. It's an overpass now. It's deserted, except for the few people who spill into the bottom of the echoing cement tunnels for shelter or to sell drugs. The homeless people sleep there sometimes, but not in March. The sky is heavy and dark for seven, but it is not too cold. It is a mild winter day, and the wide sky hangs between the old brick buildings. Jackson waits for Davis on a cement ledge, staring down at the open belly of the cement tube. If he dropped down there, he would die. He contemplates dying. He doesn't want to go home yet. Mama is probably cooking instant ramen again, and Daddy is sitting on the couch, watching reruns of *Sanford and Son*. His daddy is pale and red-faced, with a green-ink tattoo of twisted vines going down his left hand. His mother is wispy and frail, her body constantly shaking as if cold or scared. Jackson stares at the bottom of the gray pipe where a river used to run, imagining what it would have been like to slip away and die a hard, echoing death. The air between them is always ready to erupt into war cries. The yips of chaos dogs bay in the distance as he thinks of his parents. More cars. He leans forward on the railing. He hears crunching. He feels Davis. Davis walks with a wide swing of his legs and his hands stuffed in his pockets, always.

Jackson looks back at him and feels his stomach clench. Davis sits next to him on the rail and puts his chin up on the cold bar. Their breath turns to gray ash between them.

They're sitting close enough to touch, and for a moment they do just that, sit with their hips touching, their blood dragging between sensitized planes of skin. It's enough to sit next to Davis. Davis is wearing a blue flannel shirt under a gray jacket, and it makes his skin look dark. He smiles. The braces are gone and have left a wide, beautiful smile. His legs shake. Davis is sixteen. Older than him. He brushes a shoulder against Jackson. Jackson hangs his weight against the bar. It feels like comedy, but no one is talking. Davis leans closer. Jackson retreats, but Davis just laughs at the corner of his mouth and leans closer anyway. It's dark and gray all at once.

Their mouths touch.

Jackson's breath shudders in his throat, and he thinks about Daphne Christianson, who he kissed at a party when he was thirteen. He thinks about her skin under his hands, and the fear, wild and hectic, racing through him everywhere. He thinks about how she smelled, the press of her body, and how they fumbled through the experience. Kissing Davis is not like that. Davis is an expert, and his mouth is not shy. It is assertive and warm, verging on overheating. He makes a deep, gritty sound in the back of his throat, and Jackson feels something warm give way inside of him. Davis slides his fingers against Jackson's skin, leaving behind a sensation like a bone-deep thirst. Jackson grips the end of Davis's jacket.

Their lips slide apart, and Davis pants with a broad grin. Jackson can't look up; he stares down, his body thumping. Davis's hand slides over the back of his neck, and Jackson coughs, finally laughing. Davis is good at math, and Jackson knows that this is some calculated move on his part, but he can't help it. He likes the way Davis talks and moves and walks and hangs his hands on his pockets. He likes the way Davis's clothes always seem just right, the way their colors are bright and well-kept, not dull. He likes the angles of his hips just below his stomach, and the way he catches then runs, even if he's not that fast. He doesn't mind that Davis is second-string. He likes Davis. For all the squinting and laughing and getting into trouble, Davis has so much energy that he seems always on the brink of snapping.

They sit for a while together, mouths grazing and fingers pulling along the solid ridges of their denim jeans. They're getting to know each other's edges. Davis kisses him and asks if they can meet again. Jackson nods, then shrugs. He doesn't want to seem to want it. He doesn't want to want it. Davis gets up and walks backward, grinning at him. When he is gone he licks his lips. They are raw from Davis's teeth. His fingertips hum from the rasp of having touched Davis's jaw. His body feels scraped and abraded. He is hard and the sensation of wanting but not having is familiar to him. He glances at the imprint of his erection.

To get hard. Which auxiliary does that take in the past?

nouveau et ancien

The wrestling team has a 100 percent acceptance policy, and because Jackson is human, he qualifies for a spot on the junior varsity team. He is sixteen, and after four months of working out and practicing, his body is strong and firm. He is no longer tall for his age, and has evened into a healthy six feet no inches. He is taller than Daddy, who is only five-ten, but Daddy is stronger than him, though not by a lot. Jackson works out every day after school for two hours. Working out is lifting weights and running laps, trying to put weight on and turn it into lean muscle. His arms are muscular and taut, his stomach is even, and he can see the beginning of muscles peeking through the skin. He is not a good wrestler, but he likes the long bus rides to wrestling meets. He likes getting to see the river slide under the bridges; he likes the way the light in the trees spills into the quiet of the long rows of pine and oak that line the roads. He likes stepping off the bus into new places. At each school, he strips down and lets them weigh him. He then stands around listening to the sounds of bodies thumping mats and shouts ripping through the air in terse barks of command.

He wrestles at the 165 class. He handles his weight okay, but the other boys are faster and stronger than he is; their hearts are in it. He would rather be somewhere watching the sun track across the tops of buildings or reading. He writes in energetic bursts on the backs of napkins from fast-food restaurants when he gets spare moments. These he crams into the side of his backpack. The other boys don't write. They stand with their hands on their hips, staring under their eyes at their opponents across the gym and chewing thick wads of gum to limber up their mouths. They are dark-skinned and curly-haired.

There is a pair of Italian brothers with English last names from their daddy's side, Southern through and through. Their names bring cheers. They are known throughout the state. They are gifted athletes, and watching them is thrilling. The older one, Justin, has English with Jackson. He sits in the back with his head down. He has diabetes, and has a wire sticking from under his shirt. His arms are thick, his body tight, and everywhere there is muscle, no fat. He walks with a shuffle-footed swagger, smelling like sweat and something like cinnamon. His body makes Jackson's hands itch. He has warm skin. He is always pulling Jackson into a headlock and farting in his face when he walks by. Justin is loud and eager for a fight.

The younger one is Heath, and his hair is very dark and shorter than Justin's, but curly. His body is not as heavy as his brother's, but he moves with the same shuffle-footed walk. He is shy and picks at his shirt when he talks. His voice is still cracking from the change. He is fifteen, and he has the same birthday as Jackson. Heath and Jackson sit together sometimes on the buses, slumped down next to one another. He asks Jackson if he wants to come over and swim, but Jackson always says no. He is embarrassed because he does not have swimming clothes. He is more embarrassed that he does not want to be around the boys with better bodies all throwing each other into the body. He does not want to go because he does want to go and does not want to want to go.

The last time he wanted, the wanting turned to long nights sweating on top of his sheets, waiting for Davis to answer his text message. Or waiting to see him the next day. He wasn't built for that kind of wanting. He isn't now. Heath makes him uneasy, but he likes the way Heath laughs, in that raspy, breathy way that is barely getting air inside and outside. He likes the way Heath does not insist or beg for company, but seems to want it the same way he does. It is nice.

■ ■ ■

Jackson is sitting outside of the school on a bench at the end of the school day. There is no practice today, so he sits and writes in a notebook so that he does not have to go home to Mama throwing Daddy out again. She has already thrown him out four times this week, and it is only Wednesday. He can't keep up with their ripping and raring. Their change is too fast, too sudden, too much for him to keep inside of his head; it makes him dizzy. So he sits and leans over his notebook, writing nonsense lines of poetry about the winding crack in the brick outside of his window. He has been writing poetry since Madame Gray suggested it to him. Writing to him is not so much relaxing as it is an erratic and fast-breathing attempt to scratch out something true. His heart is beating faster, because he still does not understand what to do about Heath, and his sideways script turns from sidewalk to Heath and he writes in loose French: Je ne sais pas.

A shadow sticks across the edge of his book. Heath stands above him, looking down at his notebook. Jackson pulls it away, out of breath and afraid that something showed even though he knows it didn't. Heath smiles in a confused, small way, and he drops down on the bench. They're sitting together when Davis walks by across the pavilion. Jackson's eyes sting, but he shrugs and drops his notebook into his backpack. Davis stops and stares at them. Heath speaks quietly, his voice deep and wobbling between pitches. He wants to know if Jackson wants to go hang out. Come this time, he says with an exasperated look. Jackson can feel Davis's eyes on the back of his neck. Heath's eyes are olive green. How did he get eyes like that? He reaches out and puts his hand on Jackson's knee, and Jackson turns red-faced.

"Okay," Jackson says. Heath grins and slaps his knee.

He stands and hangs his backpack on his shoulder, and Davis, who has watched all of this, frowns and walks away. Jackson watches him go. He will have to do something about that, he thinks later. There will come a time when he and Davis must talk about the time when they were together last, rolling around in Davis's room, pulling at shirts and their bodies against one another. It never went further than that. Davis kept pressing, touching him, and Jackson wasn't sure he was ready for more than what they were already doing. He stopped talking. Stopped coming around. Stopped leaving notes in his locker. The hurt in Jackson's chest flexes and cuts deeper, coils around something like fear, a hard little knot of want. Davis, Jackson thinks. Heath reaches for him, grips his shoulder, and Jackson's head jerks toward him.

"Where'd you go, space cadet? Earth to Jackson."

"I'm here," Jackson says. "I'm here."

"Let's go, then," Heath says, and Jackson nods again, but he's thinking still about Davis, the pressure of his body, the solidity of it on the bed, how they'd lain there together, touching, close. The wet sound of Davis's breathing. His thick eyelashes. He'd fallen asleep there next to Davis, and had gone home late at night, climbed in through the window and gotten into his own bed, still feeling Davis's warmth around him. And then the next day, the great silence, dropping down all around them. Not a word. Not a sound. Just quiet. But when Davis is ready for words again, Jackson will be too. When Davis is ready to say something to him, Jackson will be too. Waiting—he hates it, the terrible beat, the awful rhythm, how waiting is so full of quiet. But he thinks, watching Heath's curly hair bounce as they walk, that waiting, for Davis, could be worth it. Is that what love is?

Waiting despite how much it hurts you to wait? Being silent no matter how much you want to speak? How strange that language seems to him. How odd. But this is a language he can master as readily as French.

He walks behind Heath, and the other students empty out of the courtyard, leaving only the gray shadows of later afternoon in early fall.

THE KONTRABIDA

Mia Alvar

MY MOTHER WAS waiting in front of our house when I rode up in a taxi. "There you are," she said, as if we'd simply lost each other for an hour or two at a party. I only half embraced her, afraid she might break if I held too tight. She hadn't been able to collect me from the airport herself. Years ago my father had forbidden her to drive, though I supposed he could do little to prevent it now.

"Let me," she said, reaching for my suitcase. I waved her away. I would no sooner allow my mother to carry my suitcase than allow her to carry me. "Oh, Steve," she protested. "You don't know my strength!" She dropped her arms, flattening the palms against her lap, a habit I remembered well. Throughout my childhood she often looked to be drying her hands on an apron, whether or not she was wearing one.

In the decade since I left she hadn't aged, exactly. To my eyes she seemed not older but *more*. More frail; more tired; softer-spoken; her dark, teaspoon-shaped face cast farther down. Every feature I remembered had settled in her and been more deeply confirmed.

My parents still lived in Mabini Heights, a suburb of Manila and a monument to a time when they belonged to the middle class. My father had called himself an import-export businessman before sliding, through the years, down a spiral of unrelated jobs, each more menial than the last, and harder for him to keep. And my mother had been a nurse before he banned her from working outside the house altogether. But if they'd come down in the world, so had Mabini Heights. Ever since my childhood in the seventies, when so much of that middle class fled Marcos and martial law, houses had been left unfinished or carved up for different uses. Squatters set up camp amid the scaffolding and roofless rooms. Families took in boarders or relatives. Our house had changed too: on its right, a gray, unpainted cinder-block cell had been added, taking up what used to be a yard. My parents had cemented over the grass and built this sari-sari store five years earlier, selling snacks and other odds and ends through a sliding wicket to people on the street. The sari-sari compromised what I imagine was the dream of my parents, who grew up poor: a green buffer between the world and *their* world.

The addition seemed to shrink the main house to a toy, its windows tiny and its clay roof something storybook elves might have built. Next to it, I felt gigantic. I hunched my shoulders as I followed my mother inside. I was convinced, walking behind her, that the dishes on the shelves were rattling.

"Papa's in here," said my mother, opening the door to my old bedroom. The blast of cold came as a shock, then a relief. There was an air conditioner now, in the window under which I used to sleep as a child, and my old bed, where my

father lay, was pushed into a corner. I saw, from the straw
mat rolled up beside him, that my mother had been sleeping
on the floor at night. Otherwise the room was clean and bare
and quiet as I remembered—same white cinder-block walls,
same wood-tiled floors, same smell of mothballs from the
same chest of drawers—if all faded a little, like an old photograph. My mother kept a tidy house—a trait we shared—and
things probably lasted longer in her care.

Two oxygen tanks stood beside my father's bed. He
breathed through a tube. The sight of him brought me back
to New York, where I lived, and to the hospital where I
worked as a clinical pharmacist. My father no longer resembled me. The short boxer's physique, a bullish muscularity
I'd always detested sharing with him, was gone. In fact he no
longer resembled anyone in the family; he belonged now to
that transnational tribe of the sick and the dying. Without
the dentures he'd worn most of his adult life, my father's
mouth was a pit, a wrinkled open wound below the nose.
What I could see of his eyes, under lids that were three-
quarters closed, did not appear to see me back. He looked
not only thin but vacuum-dried, desiccated—less a human
than the prehistoric remains of one.

He groaned, a low and heavy sound.

"All right, Papa. All right." My mother took a brown
dropper bottle from a chair next to the bed. "This used to
hold him for a while," she said. "But lately he's complaining
round the clock." Steadying his chin, she released a dose of
liquid morphine into his mouth, with the dainty caution of
a woman ladling hot soup or lighting a church candle. He
let out another groan. "Shhh." She stroked the sides of his
face. Even bedridden and in pain, my father had managed

to preserve their old arrangement: when he called, she was there to wait on him.

I'd predicted this, and how much I would hate to watch. In my suitcase, I carried an answer. Succorol was the newest therapy for chronic pain on the market in America. White and square, the size of movie ticket stubs, Succorol patches adhered to the skin, releasing opiates much stronger than morphine. Doctors had just started prescribing them to terminal patients in New York. Succorol could take years to reach the Philippines, a country whose premier pharmacy chain boasted LAGING BAGO ANG GAMOT DITO! (WE DO NOT SELL EXPIRED DRUGS HERE!) as its tagline. Still, something kept me from unpacking the patches right then. I did not want my mother to see my hands shaking—to know what I had done to bring them here in the first place, let alone the price I'd pay if anyone found out.

"Is that better, Papa?" My mother returned the morphine to the chair next to a rosary, a spiral notebook, a folded white hand fan. She logged the dose in the notebook like the nurse she'd once been. I picked up the fan and opened it, rib by wooden rib. Its lace edge had frayed, but the linen pleats remained bright and clean. I remembered sitting in her lap as a child during Sunday Mass, as she flicked her wrist back and forth to cool me with it.

She'd brought my father to the doctor eight months before, when he had trouble breathing and couldn't finish a meal without hunching over in pain. His belly had grown to the size of a watermelon and, from the veins straining against the skin, nearly as green. When my mother called me in New York and said "liver cancer," I imagined my parents as clearly as if I'd been sitting in the free clinic with them. I saw my father shrug or grunt each time the doctor addressed him, as proud and stubbornly tongue-tied as he always became around people with titles and offices. I saw my mother frown in concentration and move her lips in time with the doctor's, as if that would help her understand. I saw her dab the corners of my father's mouth with the white handkerchief she always carried in her purse.

Because of his age and his refusal, even after this diagnosis, to stop drinking, he never qualified for a transplant. At my mother's request, I wired money into a Philippine National Bank account that I kept open for the family. Whenever someone needed rent or medicine or tuition back home, I sent what I could, having no wife or children of my own to support. In my father's case, I thought about refusing. But it occurred to me a relative might say he could get better care in America. His coming to New York for treatment and staying with me—or, worse, in the hospital where I made my living—was something I'd have wired any sum to avoid.

When chemotherapy did not stop the cancer's spread to his lungs, when radiation did not shrink the masses, my father's doctor began to speak in a code we both understood: *pain management* instead of *treatment*; not *recovery* but *comfort in his last days*. My money turned from doxorubicin and radiotherapy to oxygen tanks, air-conditioning, the dark-brown bottle of morphine. Still, I expected my father to survive. For all the years I'd spent wishing him dead, it was my mother's role in the family drama, not his, to suffer. *Esteban has got some heavy hands*, the family always said. *Loretta is a saint.* When she called to tell me *end-stage*, my mother may as well have said we'd never lived under a clay roof in Mabini Heights, that I remembered my entire childhood wrong.

■ ■ ■

I insisted on seeing the inside of the sari-sari store before lunch. "Corporate headquarters," said my mother. She pulled aside the screen door that once led from the kitchen onto grass.

Once more, I felt like an ogre in a dollhouse. The vast and open yard of my childhood amounted now to just ten feet from the screen door to the wicket, and barely six across. Sacks of rice, tanks of soy sauce, and bricks of dry glass noodles, stacked against the walls, narrowed it even more. Candy in glass jars, each with its own metal scoop, sat in rows upon the shelves above. Reels of shampoo and detergent hung from the ceiling, dispensing Palmolive or Tide in single-use packets. I thought of the thin, sealed sleeves of Succorol, flanked by dental floss and blister-packed vitamins, in a side pocket of the toiletry bag lodged between my socks and shirts. A complete amateur's attempt at smuggling, which nearly froze my heart nonetheless as I sent my luggage down the airport X-ray belt.

I closed my eyes and tried to breathe. *Sari-sari* meant "assorted" or "sundry," and so the store smelled: like a heady mix of bubble gum and vinegar, salt and soap, floor wax and cologne. My mother switched on a ceiling fan that hung between the fluorescent striplight and the wheels of Tide and Palmolive.

"We should get you another air conditioner," I said. "There's a lot that could melt or spoil in here."

I walked to the far end of the store and ran my palm along

the wooden counter. Receipts were impaled on a spike next to a calculator with a roll of printing tape. Behind the scratched Plexiglas wicket, my mother had placed a call bell and a RING FOR SERVICE sign. They'd opened the sari-sari five years back, after my father was fired from another job, this time for stealing a crate of Tanduay rum from the restaurant where he'd been waiting tables. "He isn't built to work *under* someone," my mother had said. "It's just not his nature, answering to another man." I said nothing, just sent the money they needed to start. The sari-sari gave her a loophole, at least, in his law against her working outside the house.

At the time I hadn't minded so much about the money, which I never expected to see again. But I knew I'd miss the yard, my refuge in the years before I could stand up to my father. When he called my mother a dog or a whore or a foul little cunt who'd ruined his life, she sent me outside. When he seized her by the hair and asked, *What did you say? What did you just say to me?* she sent me outside. When he struck her face with the underside of our telephone until she wept and begged, first for forgiveness and then for mercy, she sent me outside, into the grass of the yard, where twigs from the acacia tree would have fallen overnight.

■ ■ ■

In the kitchen, my mother set the table for two. Then she planted a baby monitor at the third chair and tuned it to a grainy black-and-white broadcast of my father snoring. "This thing saved me," she said. "Now I can keep an eye on him while I work. Or while you and I sit and eat together."

But she hardly sat or ate at all. Throughout lunch she alternated between serving him and serving me. She stood to answer a groan from the sickroom, then heaped my plate with fried rice and beef. She uncapped a bottle of San Miguel for me, then went to feed him a bowl of broth. I spent most of the meal alone with him: my father's screen image and me, facing off across the table.

At this time three days earlier, I was in the hospital, taking inventory of the narcotics cabinet. As I unloaded the most recent shipment of Succorol, I found six more boxes than were counted on the packing slip, a surplus as unlikely as it was expensive. And immediately I imagined my mother, titrating morphine into his mouth by hand, as I recounted the boxes and rechecked my number against the invoice. I thought of my mother, running back and forth between the sari-sari and the sickroom, as I typed the lower figure into the inventory log. I thought of her, crying or praying after morphine had ceased to comfort him, as I wheeled the Pyxis in front of the surveillance camera and slipped a month's supply of Succorol into the pockets of my lab coat.

"Bed or bath?" she asked, returning to the kitchen. A pail of water was filled and waiting for me in the bathroom; on the master bed, new sheets. Which did I want first? All that was missing was the "sir."

The baby monitor groaned on the table. The call bell dinged in the store. My mother glanced from one to the other, torn.

"I've got the store," I volunteered. "You take care of him." Her eyebrows rose, but I said, "What is there to know? I saw price tags on your jars and a cashbox under the counter. I'll print receipts from the calculator if people want them."

As it turned out, I was no help at all. My first customer wanted shampoo. I pulled too hard on the Palmolive, unspooling hundreds of packets to the floor. My mother had to climb a stepladder to reel them back in. Another customer asked for detergent. I ripped a packet of Tide down the middle, sending a flurry of blue-flecked snow everywhere. My mother swept up after me with a broom. The women barely spoke above a whisper, sometimes covering their mouths to hide bad teeth. "Ano?" I asked, over and over. The louder I asked, the softer they answered. The farther they retreated from the wicket, the closer I stooped to read their faces, feeling more like a bully than a shop clerk.

My father's groans, on the other hand, I heard perfectly well. In her trips back and forth from the sari-sari to the sickroom, my mother moved the baby monitor to the freezer case, rushing from the store as soon as he called or stirred on-screen. While she was gone, a teenage girl asked me for Sarsi cola. Relieved to understand, I handed her a bottle from the freezer. She giggled, staring, and said something else behind her hands. ". . . plastik" was all I heard. Remembering the jar of plastic straws on the counter and the bottle opener underneath, I uncapped the bottle and added a straw. She giggled and shook her head, asking again for "plastik." I wondered if she meant a plastic shopping bag and searched the store, finding one crumpled on a shelf. Now she was giggling too hard to speak. I felt as confused as in my earliest days as a clinical pharmacy resident in New York—a beginner desperate to impress my superiors, bungling even the basics.

When my mother returned, she spoke to the girl and poured the Sarsi cola into a plastic sleeve, thin as a layer of onionskin. She stored the bottle in a crate that would go back to the factory. How had I forgotten? I'd drunk sodas from plastic sleeves up until the age of twenty-five. And yet the liquid bag I handed over made me think not of my childhood but of some dark, alien version of the waste pouches and IV fluids I'd see at the hospital. "Relax, anak." Dragging a stool to the center of the store, my mother invited me to sit under the ceiling fan. "You're sweating." She handed me a mango Popsicle from the freezer case. The jaw-cramping sweetness of each bite felt vaguely humiliating as I sat and watched her work.

Unlike me, she had no trouble hearing her customers. No sooner had a face appeared at the wicket than she was reaching for the shoe polish or cooking oil. Her right hand could pop open a bottle cap while her left tore a foil packet from the shampoo reel. To the voice of a young boy, so small I couldn't see him through the wicket, she sold three sheets, for ten centavos apiece, of the grainy, wide-ruled paper on which I'd learned to spell in grade school. It was a way of shopping I had completely forgotten: egg by egg, cigarette by cigarette, people spending what they earned in a day to buy what they would use in the next.

■ ■ ■

That night I lay in my parents' bedroom. Jet lag and the whir of an electric fan kept me awake. Somewhere above me a gecko made its loud clicking noise, and I was no longer used to the Manila heat. But I refused to sleep any closer to my father, even if it meant losing out on the AC.

Down the hall, he groaned nonstop, as if to say, unless he slept, no one would.

Growing up in this house, I used to hear other noises from him at night. I must have been four or five years old, lying where he did now, the first time a lowing through the wall made me sit up. Until it had echoed once or twice, I didn't know the voice was his. My father sounded more like a flagellant on Good Friday, parading through the streets of Tondo. I thought my mother had found a way to strike back: that he was the one, this time, suffering and forced to beg.

I rushed to the door they'd forgotten to close, and detected my parents' shapes in the dark. He was sitting on the edge of the bed. Naked, but hidden from the waist down by my mother. She knelt, a sheet around her shoulders, wiping the floor with a washcloth. And though she was at his feet, though her shadow rose and fell as she cleaned, as if bowing to a king, my father did not look to be in charge at all. He peeled the lids off his eyes, unsticking his tongue from the roof of his mouth. His skin was waxen with sweat. Stripped and drained, limp and compromised—he could not have hit her, in this state.

Then he saw me in the doorway. "What now?" he said, alert again, his fists starting to lock.

My mother startled. "Anak!" She pointed past me, the wet washcloth covering her hand like a bandage. "Get out!"

I ran out to the yard. Not to escape him, but because I knew he'd punish her for every second of my presence there.

This was before I'd learned much about sex; I was too young to be disgusted by it. For a while after that, whenever I heard him groan in the darkness, I didn't know enough to pull my pillow over my ears or run outside in embarrassment. Instead my father's baying, and his stupor afterward, put me under a kind of spell. I'd listen through the cinderblock wall, believing he had fallen out of power, was in pain. Whatever else he might do to my mother, at any other hour, during this shimmering nighttime transaction *he* was the conquered one.

■ ■ ■

A swarm of aunts, uncles, cousins, and cousins' children descended on the house early the next morning. I passed out all my pasalubong, or homecoming gifts: handheld digital games, pencil-and-stationery sets, duty-free liquor, nuts and chocolates I'd stockpiled on layovers in Honolulu and Tokyo. A balikbayan knew better than to show up empty-handed.

After the gifts came the inquisition. How cold was it in America? How often did it snow? I kept my lines brief. I had a role to perform: the balikbayan, who worked hard and missed home but didn't complain, who'd moved up in New York but wasn't down on Manila. "You get used to the winters," I said. I didn't tell them I loved the snow, was built for the American cold, and felt, upon entering my first job in a thermostat-controlled pharmacy, that I'd come home. What did I miss most about the Philippines? "The food, and Filipinos," I said. "Good thing the nurses always bring me lumpia and let me tag along to Sunday Mass." But my days in New York never involved Mass or lumpia: outside of work, I spent my free time exercising at the gym, or cleaning my apartment on the twenty-eighth floor of a building made of steel and glass. What about women—was there someone? An American? "The hospital keeps me busy," I said. "No one special enough yet to meet you." I didn't describe the women who sometimes spent the night with me, how they chattered nonstop, intimidated by the tidy home I kept. "Is this an apartment or a lab? " said one, glancing at my countertops. "Are we getting laid here, or embalmed?" asked another, under the tightly tucked bedspread. In every case, I found a reason to stop calling: false modesty, too loud a voice, careless toothpaste spatters around the bathroom sink. Any time a woman opened her mouth and I could imagine myself clapping a hand over it, pinning her to the bed, I knew that my father still breathed somewhere inside of me. I couldn't risk repeating his life.

The questions ended when the karaoke began. Bebot, my cousin's son, had hooked the monitor of my old Commodore computer, outgrown since I first bought it in New York, to a DVD player. When he fed it a karaoke disc, song lyrics and video footage of couples on the beach appeared in green screen. I took on "Kawawang Cowboy" ("Pathetic Cowboy"), a Tagalog satire of "Rhinestone Cowboy," to show I remembered my Tagalog and to cover my lack of singing talent with silliness. "*A pathetic cowboy*," I sang. "*I wish I could afford some bubble gum / Instead of dried-up salty Chinese plum. . . .*" The family roared. In New York, the nurses would have shooed us out of any hospital. But here no one worried about disturbing my father, who loved karaoke and had a gift for it. In a voice like wine and honey, he used to croon everything from Elvis Presley to classic Tagalog love songs. Even I had to admit that, back then, his signature "Fly Me to the Moon" was charming.

My mother scuttled through our living room reunion like a servant, pulled in opposite directions by sick groans and the sari-sari bell. I thought again of the Succorol but stayed in my seat. Twice—first in Tagalog, then in English—I had taken a pharmacist's oath to tell the truth and uphold the law. People lost jobs and licenses for less. If our suppliers discovered their mistake, called all their clients, and somehow—between timestamps, shift schedules, signatures, and security footage—found me out, I could land in jail, to say nothing of the damage to my name with colleagues and the department head who'd trusted me with inventory to begin with. Deceit of any kind was a foreign country to me. As a child, I'd never so much as shoplifted a comic book, or lied to a teacher, or cheated at a game of cards. This discipline earned me perfect grades in high school, scholarships through college, my first job at a Manila drugstore, a doctor of pharmacy degree from my school's brother university in New York, fast promotions at the hospital. Whenever I saw classmates copy each other's homework or make faces behind the priests' backs, I thought of my father and how he, too, must have started small on the path to worse.

I considered hiring a live-in nurse, but my mother was the kind of woman who waited on even the people she'd paid to serve us, back when we could afford them: the laundress, the gardener, the yaya who watched me before I started school. Now she did the same for relatives who covered sari-sari shifts and friends who visited them. They all ate at our table and helped themselves to free snacks and sodas from the store. A paid nurse would only give her another plate to wash, another chair to pull out.

The next time the bell rang, I followed my mother into the kitchen and through the screen door. Away from my family's relentless yammering, the sari-sari felt like a sanctuary again: in but not of the house, and cooler than the crowded living room. My mother helped a customer, then gazed at the baby monitor, perched up on a shelf between jars of Spanish shortbread and tamarind candy.

"I've got a gun without a bullet and a pocket without

money," she turned to me and sang, off-key. "You inherited my singing voice, anak. Sorry."

"Apologize to your family," I said. "They had to listen to it." From the shelf I picked one of her favorites: pastillas de leche, soft mini-logs made with sugar and carabao's milk. My mother had a sweet tooth that didn't match her frame. I set the yellow box on the counter and reached into my pocket.

"Oh, no you don't," she said. "This is on the house."

"Absolutely not," I said.

"We're a Filipino store; we don't accept American dollars."

"Nice try. I exchanged my money at the airport."

"Your money's no good here."

"Stop giving things away for free." I unwrapped one of the pastillas, knowing she wouldn't start ahead of me. "That's no way to keep a business afloat. There's my first piece of advice for you."

"It's your second," she said. "Yesterday you said it was too hot in here." She pointed at the whirling blades on the ceiling. "People pay all kinds of money for good business advice, don't they? So I'm not giving anything away for free." She frowned as she bit into a pastilla, as if eating required all her concentration.

I took my hand from my pocket, and we crunched for a while without speaking.

"If I ever leave the hospital and open my own pharmacy," I said, "it will be a lot like this." I walked her through my rather old-fashioned vision: tinctures and powders in rows, a mortar and pestle here, a pill counter and weighing scale there.

"Oh, anak." I'd become her young son again, pointing

at a mansion in Forbes Park or a gown in a shop window, luxuries I vowed to provide her in the future. My mother's eyes filled with tears. "Your pharmacy will be fancier than this. And you could have built it years ago, if you hadn't been busy helping us."

That settled it. Nothing disturbed me more than the sight of her crying. It was time to end her call-button servitude once and for all. "Ma," I began, "I've given everyone their pasalubong, except you."

The baby monitor groaned, bringing her to her feet. "You've given me so much already." She wiped her eyes. "Pastillas, free advice . . ." Setting down the call bell and the SERVICE sign, she rushed out, again, to attend to him.

I dropped five hundred pesos into the cashbox and brought the rest of the candy to my relatives in the living room. Once they'd emptied the box, I took it to my room and filled it with the patches of Succorol, then went to the sickroom and closed the door behind me.

My mother was pressing a washcloth to his forehead. "You're a CEO, not a slave," I said. "No more scurrying around. You've got a business to run." I showed her the Succorol and how to use it, peeling a square from its adhesive backing and pressing it to my father's side. "Remove this and apply a new one at the same time tomorrow," I said. "On his back, or arm—anywhere there isn't hair. Rotate or you'll irritate the skin." In my mother's notebook I started a new page and recorded the dose. "So we don't double up," I said. "This isn't Tylenol, if you know what I mean."

We stayed until my father quieted and slept. I closed the yellow box, now full of Succorol, and placed it in the top drawer of the dresser. Before we left the sickroom, she touched my cheek.

"You're home," she said. "All the pasalubong I need."

In the living room the family had switched from karaoke to a Tagalog movie. Even in green it looked familiar, observing the rules of every melodrama I'd grown up watching: a bida, or hero, fought a kontrabida, or villain, for the love of a beautiful woman. The oldest films would even cast a pale, fair-haired American as the bida and a dusky, slick-mustachioed Spaniard as the kontrabida. Between them, the woman spent her time batting her eyelashes or being swept off her feet; peeking out from behind lace fans; fainting or weeping; clutching a handkerchief to her heart or dangling it from the window as a signal; being abducted at night, or rescued from a tower, or carried away on a horse. My relatives talked back to the screen as it played. *Kiss! Kiss!* they insisted, not with any delight or romantic excitement but in a nearly hostile way, heckling the protagonists and the plot to quit stalling and hurry along to the payoff. Even I joined the chorus. When, at last, the bida won the woman, we cheered and whistled, again not out of joy so much as a malicious sort of triumph. The script had succumbed, in the end, to our demands.

■　■　■

For three days my father dozed peacefully, waking only when my mother fed him or shifted a bedpan under his haunches. With the Succorol, he never groaned again. At first she ran to check his breathing throughout breakfast and lunch, but by the second day she trusted the baby monitor to show the rise and fall of his chest, his mouth dilating and shrinking. Seeing her relax, I slept better too.

Meanwhile the heat climbed to ninety-three degrees. I

woke on my fourth night in the country feeling stained by my own sweat. Next door the air conditioner was humming, and I craved the cold rush that first greeted me there. If I could just stand in that doorway a moment, I might feel better and fall back asleep. I found my way through the dark living room, running my fingertips along the cinder block. The door creaked on my push. I stepped forward into the chill but didn't enjoy it for long.

My mother turned with a gasp, her eyes wide. Moonlight through the window fell onto the bed, and, for the second time in my life, the silhouette of my father, bare-chested, the sheet pulled down to his waist. Her back, bent over him in a ministering pose, straightened up. "Anak, don't!" She raised her hand to stop me, mittened by a white washcloth, her body twisting to cover his.

I shut my eyes and the door. My stomach turned. I couldn't go back to their bed now, the place where I'd first walked in on them. Like a child once again, I ran through the living room and kitchen for escape.

The screen door to the sari-sari was locked. I shook it, panicked, before remembering the loop hook above the handle. My fingers searched the wall to switch on the light and ceiling fan. I headed for the wicket as if I could flee through it, then climbed and sat on the counter. A mouse darted across the floor to its hiding place behind the freezer. Moths buzzed around the fluorescent strip above me, and another gecko made its clicking sound. It seemed that all the secret forms of life and movement that took place in this house at night had decided to expose themselves to me, and by the time I forced myself back to bed, the sweat on my neck and face had turned cold.

. . .

In the morning I heard a man's voice through the wall. I startled, thinking at first that my father had recovered. Then I recognized it, from long-distance phone calls in New York. The doctor. My father was dead.

At his bedside the doctor was removing the buds of a stethoscope from his ears. He gave me a collegial nod. My mother paced across the room. Pins from her hair had scattered at the foot of the bed. ". . . peacefully," Dr. Ramos was saying. "In his sleep." But my father looked far from peaceful. In death his face had gone thuggish again, the underbite and squashed nose giving him as aggressive and paranoid a look as ever. In forty, fifty, sixty years this was how I might die: with my worst impulses petrified on my face.

My mother had stopped pacing but kept rubbing her hands flat against her lap, as if this time she couldn't get them clean. "Loretta?" Dr. Ramos said. Only when he called her name a second time did I notice her head rolling backward, her eyes to their whites. I caught her just before she fainted to the floor.

"I'm sorry" were her first words upon coming to. Her eyes bounced from me to the doctor to my father.

"You're in shock," said Dr. Ramos. "Happens all the time."

I opened the fan on the nightstand and waved it over her face. "Nothing to be sorry about," I said.

And there wasn't. The doctor assumed that my father had passed in a morphine-softened sleep, but now I wondered if he'd gone into cardiac arrest while my mother satisfied some dying wish. Perhaps this would haunt her in the days to come. The hair she usually pinned back hung loose around her face. But I felt calmer than I had the night before; there was no mystery. She'd served him to the end. I should have known she would.

•   ▪   ▪

In the basement of the Immaculate Conception Funeral Home, the mortician curved a sponge between his fingers, spackling my father's face with brown grease. An American parlor would never have allowed me downstairs. But Manila wasn't so strict, and I liked to keep a close eye on everyone I paid. The mortician had gone darker than my father's current skin tone, closer to the shade he was before the illness. I wondered if my mother had shown him a photograph.

The funeral directors led us to their Holy Family room. "We asked for the penthouse," I said. They apologized; a service was running long in their Epiphany suite. "Then tell them it's time to leave." My father had relatives coming from all over the archipelago to pay their respects, I explained— from all over the world, in fact. Again they were sorry, throwing in a *sir*: the funeral taking place in Epiphany was a child's. "Did the child pay you in American dollars?" I asked. Doing business in Manila hardened something in me, the same muscle I'd observed in men who stood up in hospital rooms and did all the talking for their families. I focused on the French doors of the penthouse as we skated my father past the displaced mourners and their four-foot coffin.

Our family brought in plates of fried rice, barbecued chicken, pineapple salad in condensed milk, sandwich halves stacked in pyramids. Only the corpse, really, distinguished the wake from any other party. People kissed and caught up. Bebot fiddled with the green Commodore computer. My uncles set up speakers beside the guestbook and blew into the microphones: "Testing, testing, one two three."

"Loretta, please eat," an aunt was saying. "Next time we see you, you'll be invisible."

My mother accepted a cheese pimiento sandwich. Then the room started to fill with the family's insistent clamor, and I longed for another escape. She looked like she could use that, too. My sandwich-pushing aunt noticed the bare platform around the coffin. "They call this a 'full-service' funeral parlor," she said to me, "but apparently that does not include flowers."

I saw my chance. "The flowers aren't going to buy themselves," I said, approaching my mother's chair. "Shall we?"

She abandoned the sandwich and took my arm. We stepped out onto Araneta Avenue, Manila's funeral district, walking past the parlor, stonemasons, chapels, coffin shops, and rent-a-hearse garages: one after another, like beads on a grim rosary. A rough and glittery dust filled the air, as if crematory ashes had mingled with fumes from the traffic.

We stopped at a flower stand outside the parlor. "How much?" I asked the vendor, pointing at a white spray of carnations and roses that my mother liked. I didn't know what flowers cost. I never bought them in New York—not for promoted colleagues or sick friends, certainly not for women. Flowers reminded me of my father and the hangdog contrition that followed his nights of drinking: the swooping, romantic gestures that came after he'd blackened an eye or broken a bone.

"Five thousand pesos," said the vendor, "plus fifty per letter on the banner."

FONDEST REMEMBRANCES, the display models said. IN LOVING MEMORY.

"I can do two thousand," I said, "banner included."

The vendor shook his head. "This is difficult lettering, sir. The roses are imported."

"That's a pity." I took my mother's arm and headed for the next kiosk.

"Twenty-five hundred with banner," the vendor shouted after us.

I walked on, to keep him guessing for a few paces, before doubling us back. I couldn't have cared less about the cost of flowers. I simply wanted every peddler in the city to know he didn't stand a chance against me.

None of the things I wished to say to my father were printable, so I took my mother's suggestion: REST IN PEACE, YOUR LOVING FAMILY. We strolled the avenue waiting for our banner. "Don't let anyone try that on the sari-sari," I said.

"I don't think anyone could," she said. "You still haggle like the best of them."

"What choice do I have? They can read balikbayan written on my forehead."

"Ah, no—it's too long to fit there." Her words hung in the air a moment before I realized I should smile. Ten years before, I had arrived in New York with ideas of what I'd miss most about my mother: her cooking, her voice, the smell of rice and detergent in her skin and hair. I did not expect to miss her humor, the small wisecracks that escaped her mouth sometimes, often from behind her fingers, hard to hear.

When we returned for the flowers, my mother reached out as if to carry them. I waved her away as I paid. "This thing is nearly twice your size."

"You underestimate me," she said, pretending to flex her muscles.

■ ■ ■

After the memorial service, my uncles offered to stay with the body overnight. The last of our relatives were expected in the morning. We would bury my father in the afternoon.

Back in Mabini Heights, my old bedroom was mine again. The air conditioner seemed louder now that I was alone in the room, but I slept easily. I dreamed of winter in New York, walking alone in snow, pulling my collar up against the cold.

I woke in a sweat again. The AC had stopped. I turned the dial, but the vents stayed silent. I flipped the wall switch and got no light.

A brownout. My first since returning to Manila.

Moonlight from the window told me only a few hours had passed. A muffled sound, like crying, came through the wall. I stood, ready to console my mother on the sofa or at the kitchen table. But the living room was empty, the kitchen dark. The only light I saw flickered weakly from the sari-sari. Approaching the screen door, I saw a candle burning on the counter. Was she keeping vigil? Praying? I squinted in the shadows.

She certainly wasn't crying. In fact, she was laughing—a strange, sleepy laugh that dominoed through the sari-sari. She reached along the counter and picked up a white square. Succorol. I watched her slide it through the wicket. Then she was repeating my instructions, in my accent.

"This isn't Tylenol, if you know what I mean." She drawled the words, like a cowboy trying to speak Tagalog, as if I'd lived in Texas, not New York, for the past ten years. She reached toward the wicket and came back with a fistful of cash.

I turned from the screen to the darkness, as if a film projector behind me had faltered. Her laughter followed me through the living room as I tripped against the furniture and nearly missed the sickroom doorway in the dark. I opened the drawer where we'd stored the yellow box. Six Succorol patches left, of the thirty I'd brought. Five days had passed since I'd arrived, four since I'd given them to her.

My skin itched with the humidity. I grabbed the fan beside my father's bed and flapped it at myself, then felt ridiculous and snapped it shut. Nothing about my mother— not her voice, soft as a lullaby, when I could hear it; not her hands, drying themselves on her lap; not her posture, a constant curtsy—squared with the woman in the sari-sari. I had to erase that strange laughter from my mind, the tongue that wet her thumb before it counted out the money.

Returning to the dresser, I fingered the box of Succorol. Would the world end if I indulged this once, crossed another boundary, broke one more rule?

I glanced again over my shoulder before peeling a patch from its backing. I pressed it to my chest as if saluting a flag or anthem. My heart raced under my hand. In the distance, my mother's laughter rose and fell. But nothing changed as I lay back on the cot. It seemed as if the years of virtue had made a fortress of me, a barricade that human appetites and weakness couldn't breach.

Then my bones began to melt. Things happened too quickly, at first, to feel good. The rosary, the notebook, and the fan, unfolding pleat by pleat, rose from the chair and hovered over my father's bed. The doors swayed. I gripped the edges of the cot, feeling control slip from me inch by inch. Only when the melting reached my fingers, loosening their hold, did I begin to enjoy it. Patches flew out of the box and lined up like a filmstrip in the air, each one a panel with a picture in it, and from there every square inside the house became a screen: song lyrics in the baby monitor; my father's face in the green computer. Even the windows and the wicket came alive with scenes of bida, kontrabida, and the woman they both claimed. My body sailed up and out of the room like a streamer: through the corridor, the kitchen, the sari-sari. Walls and ceilings yielded to me as they would to a ghost. I heard my mother laughing and my father singing "Fly Me to the Moon," the sounds and words escaping through the roof into the stars.

■　■　■

I woke the next morning to find my bedsheets balled on the sickroom floor, the Succorol patch still on my chest. Tearing it off, I wondered if my mother had checked in on me and seen it. In the bathroom I tried to soap off the patch's square footprint, but the adhesive was stubborn. I needed a washcloth to work at the residue.

Rubbing away the evidence, I looked down. As if I'd never seen my own hand before. I stretched my arm out and stared at the white cloth wrapped around my fingers like a mitten. A bandage.

I rushed from the sink to the doorway of the sickroom, thinking back to the night he died. Here was where the moonlight had shone over the bed. Here was the step I took before seeing them. Here was where she gasped, stopping me in my tracks, and bent to hide his body. My mind shuffled through the kinds of scenes you saw in those trashy Tagalog melodramas: on-screen villains polishing their guns and planting their poisons; my mother, not ministering to him as she had when I was four years old, but instead waiting for me to fall asleep, kneeling at my father's bedside, removing his shirt, and applying a patch to his chest. I pictured her adding another patch and then another, a week's worth, her fingertips blanching his skin briefly at each point of pressure. I could see her laying an ear to his chest. After midnight, when his breath and heartbeat stopped, she must have peeled off the patches, soaked the washcloth, and tackled the sticky residue just as I opened the door for some cold air.

Now I opened the candy box and counted again: five. Only three should have gone to my father on my second, third, and fourth days home; one to me. I'd seen my mother sell one. Of the other twenty that were missing, how many had she sold? Had she sold some in the nights before as well, while I slept? How many would it take to finish off a dying man?

I must have known a drug so powerful could end his life. So what? Didn't I want him gone, hadn't I always? My mother was better off. But at what cost? I had to ask myself. If she had killed him, I had handed her the weapon. If I'd kept track, a closer eye on the supply, I might have caught it all sooner. What kind of pharmacist lets days go by without taking inventory? Someone incompetent as well as criminal. Like him, in other words.

■　■　■

In spite of what I'd told the staff, my father did not have a vast global fan club traveling to see him. No need to drag the wake on for days, as other Filipino families might for more beloved men: we would bury him later that second day. At the cemetery, a block of earth had been hollowed out for the grave. My aunts cooled themselves with lace fans, or brochures they'd lifted from the funeral parlor and folded into pleats. A priest read from his small black Bible. *The Lord is my shepherd, I shall not want.* In this kind of heat the valley of the shadow of death sounded inviting.

My cousins' children broke flowers from the bouquet set on the coffin. Before the lid was closed and locked for good, I looked for the last time at my father's face, under its sheet of viewing glass. The mortician had not only restored the color but buoyed up the flesh itself, faking fullness in the hollows and droop. I could almost imagine that face moving again, the mouth stretching backward to spit. Nearby a headstone waited, even simpler than the banner on his flowers: ESTEBAN SANDOVAL, SR. 1935–1998. SON · BROTHER · HUSBAND · FATHER. My head ached, and my mouth felt dry; there was a grit behind my eyelids I couldn't blink away.

Now, at his grave, my mother wept into her white handkerchief. She still looked frail, the woman who cleared platters and pulled out chairs, who knelt at my father's feet and mopped up after him. Her tears affected me the way they always had. I swore to stop them; I'd do anything. I reached for her, then froze—afraid, for the first time in all my years consoling her, that I might cry myself. For years there'd been no question of how much she leaned on me, like any mother on her overseas son. It never dawned on me how much I'd leaned on her: to play her part, stick to the script. Her saintliness was an idea I loved more than

I had ever hated him. I put my arms around her, making vow after silent vow. I'd never cut corners again, no matter what the value, who the victim; I would never violate any code, professional or otherwise. I would take her with me to New York. I would never leave her again. I'd bury the patches somewhere no one would find them, so long as she could always remain the mother I knew, not some stranger laughing in the dark.

My uncles turned a crank to lower their brother into the ground. They picked up shovels and began to bury him scoop by scoop. My mother passed her fan to me, then her handkerchief. It felt damp in my palm, the cloth worn thin and soft from all its time in the wash. She stepped forward to join her in-laws, struggling with the shovel's weight.

A smell of grass and earth took me back to the yard that once existed in Mabini Heights, and I half expected an aca-cia tree to appear beside me, or my mother's voice to call me to dinner through the kitchen screen. I remembered how I used to climb that tree and sling a branch onto my shoulder, aiming sniper-style at the place in the house where my father might be standing. Another time I stabbed a fallen twig into the grass and twisted it, imagining his blood. But I'd fought tooth and nail to rise above that yard. Even in return for all the harm he'd done my mother, to harm him, to be *capable* of harm to him, was to honor what was in my blood. His blood. I trained myself into his opposite: competent, restrained. The hero in an old Tagalog movie did not win by stooping to revenge; there was a pristine, fundamental goodness in his soul that radiated out to crush the villain. Character and destiny—I believed in all of that, I guess. My mother raised her foot and staked the spade into the ground. She heaved the dirt into the plot and made a noise, almost a grunt. *You don't know my strength!* Through all the melodramas that my family and I had seen over the years, in which the bida and the kontrabida crossed their swords over a woman, I never guessed that *she* might be the one to watch.

THE AFRICAN-AMERICAN SPECIAL

Jason Reynolds

"SEE?"

"See, what?" I asked Fortune, snatching the soggy dollar off the bar and dropping it into the tip jar. I wished it required more effort, more than a drop as if dollar were coin, but instead needed to be finagled—stuffed—into a crowded cash pit. But that wasn't the case. This was the first tip of the night. And it hadn't come from Fortune. Fortune never tipped.

"That white man left you a tip," Fortune said, pointing at the door as if the man he was referring to could be seen through the wall.

"So."

"So, he didn't have to, and he did." Fortune shrugged.

"He left me a dingy-ass dollar on a twenty-dollar tab." I cleaned the spot where the single tipper sat, wetting the wood, folding the rag, wiping it dry. "They'll take whatever they can. He could've left two. Ten percent is at least a tithe, and you know better than most that this place might as well be a church."

"Oh, is that right? And who you 'posed to be, Jesus?" A smile crossed Fortune's face. "'Cause I ain't *never* known Jesus to cry about not being praised enough. See, that's what's wrong with us now. We think they owe us something."

Fortune adjusted his weight on the stool, his body curved like the handle of an umbrella, leaning into the walnut like a plant to sunlight. He sat on the same stool he'd been sitting on for well over a decade. The keys that always dangled from his belt loop had scraped scratches into the right half of the seat, a marking, a coded inscription that this stool was reserved for the one and only Frank Fortune. Half-man, half-mash, whole mess.

"Like, just the other day," Fortune continued, "somebody was giving me some bullshit 'bout white people this and that, white people that and this. All this 'bout white people taking over everything. And I'm like, *Taking over what?*" Fortune scowled and patted himself as if he was looking for a lighter in his chest pocket, which he couldn't have been, because he knows it ain't no smoking in my bar, and further-more, his shirt didn't have a chest pocket.

"Yep, still me." He smirked. "They ain't take over me yet. Some young boy talking this smack. What's his name? You know him, too, 'cause he come in here all the time getting on about how he can barely afford his rent, and it's getting higher and higher, crying pity in his pint glass. See, that's the problem. That's the damn problem right there. We coddled these kids, and now they weak. We done mommy'd they asses to death. Now they don't got the . . . the . . . the gumption to figure some shit out without blaming everybody else for they problems. What's his name?" Fortune ticked tongue to teeth. "Lord. I'll tell you what, getting old ain't no fun, but if you ask me, being young these days is a damn disability in and of itself. Their brains broke. I swear. These young'uns got broke brains thinking somebody coming to take something from them."

"That's not from having broken brains," I shot back. "That's from having broken hearts. A lot of these kids know what it feels like to get a dollar tip on a twenty-dollar tab." I leaned against the counter, folded my arms. "Trust me, I know. Like a four-year education, a fifty-thousand-dollar debt, all for a job that'll barely afford them"—I caught the metaphor—"a couple of fish and a few loaves. Meanwhile, the white kids they go to school with, their daddies own the damn bread factory, and . . . you already know they got boats!" I slapped the bar, shook my head, murmured, "And even if they don't, they do. Yeah . . . a dollar tip."

I turned around to make Fortune another drink. I know better than to respond to him. Usually I just keep his tab open and let him rip till he's ripped, then I ease him off the stool and walk him back to my office—the only place in the bar that don't smell like sixteen-year-old hormone and sixty-year-old hardship—where he can lie down on the couch and sleep it off. Every night. Same thing. But tonight . . . I don't know. I just couldn't resist the banter. The white guy who had just left, who hadn't really done anything wrong, for some reason was like a shot. Not quite a gunshot, though maybe that too. But I mean a shot as in a swallow of something harsh. An overproofed, overpriced moonshine shoved down my throat, burning all the way to my belly, and now my opinion—which I usually keep to myself—was belching out of me.

"Anyway, this is pint number three," I announced, setting Fortune's drink down in front of him.

His drink—his concoction—is a simple one, and he's the *only* person who drinks it. Kentucky bourbon mixed with a strong Nigerian lager I get sent over here by my wife's folks. Been doing it for years. All kinds of international beer and spirits before it was a thing. Now people call it *craft*. Back in the day, I just called it options. Always felt like the folks in my neighborhood deserved the same things as everybody else. Why not have some Nigerian beer? Or maybe something from Trinidad. I don't know. Let's mix it up—which, by the way, has always been Fortune's favorite thing to do.

"You ain't gotta tell me what number drink it is. I know what the hell number it is. I can count. I can see. I can do all that. It ain't me you need to be checking up on, anyway. I don't care what you say, it's these young folks like that one I was just talkin' 'bout. What's his name? His mama used to run that little fish place 'round the corner. How 'bout that for *boats*. You know the one. The one with no menu. Just come in and say 'Plate' or 'Sandwich' and walk out with a little bit of heaven in a big piece of Styrofoam. You know the joint I'm talkin' 'bout? Right 'round the corner, over where, um, what's in there now? Shit, I don't know. Something else in there now, but that woman who used to own the fish spot—it might've even been called 'Round the Corner—it's her son that I saw the other day going on and on about white people. This fool done grew up with a mama who was a businesswoman, and got the nerve to tell me white people buying up property and making it hard for folks 'round here. And you know what I told him? I said, 'Maybe if we would've bought more fish plates, you wouldn't be whining like this.' I told him maybe if his mama had them gates up on Sundays, and if they'd figured out how to do breakfast, and stayed open past ten o'clock so that I could slide through there and put some grease over top of the best damn drink on earth, the *African-American Special*"—Fortune lifted his glass, toasted no one, took a big swig, then continued—"maybe we wouldn't be having this stupid-ass conversation."

"And what he say to that?" I asked.

"He said his mama died." Fortune set his glass down. "And to that, I said, well . . . *damn*. Told him I was sorry to hear it. But as soon as I said I was sorry, you know this chump tore right back into the hides of whites, and I had to stop him again and ask him if he took over the business, 'cause it seemed like the natural follow-up."

"And?"

"And he said he did. Then I asked him what the problem was, 'cause as far as I know, white folks love themselves some fish just as much as we do. And I doubt they were coming in there complaining about not getting their grouper on *ciabatta* bread or whatever the hell it is, so I don't wanna hear this bullshit about them taking from us. Not now."

Fortune lifted his glass again, took a few more gulps, wiped his mouth, and trapped a burp behind puckered lips. "Now, if we talkin' 'bout history, then okay, I'll hear you out. Shit, ain't no doubt about that. They've taken and taken from us in the past. I mean, we built this whole damn place and ain't get a damn thing for it. I'm old enough to remember some of the things these kids read about in school. Old enough to know what it means to *really* be taken from. My daddy was murdered by a white man in Georgia, which is how I ended up in DC in the first place. Me and my mama was on the damn run, chased from the red clay by the white sheets. I was at the march." Fortune pointed at the bar. At the bottles lined along the wall like holy figurines, backlit for effect. He wasn't actually pointing at the booze, but rather in the direction of the National Mall. Then he continued, "*And* the riot." He now pointed in the opposite direction.

"I joined the Army and got stationed down in Virginia. I remember not being able to be served a beer, and if I was, having to worry about who might've done spat in it. I fought in Vietnam, lost my friends, seen their insides on the outsides of their bodies, seen the life disappear from their eyes like their spirits being sucked down a dark hallway, and came home to a parade, a protest, and a warm plate at the fucking back door of a restaurant." The one hand that was free, the one not clutching the glass, was balled into a fist, Fortune digging his fingers into his own palm, gripping his own hand so tightly that the veins in his wrist pressed lightning patterns through his skin.

"And I seen the inside of an iron box too," he stammered on, his eyes wild and distant. Looking at me but seeing something else. "Served years for some bullshit, trumped-up charge, wrong place, wrong time, caught up in a drug sweep in the late eighties. Some shit I ain't have nothing to do with but couldn't afford a lawyer to get out of." And then he was back. I could tell Fortune was talking to me—to *me*—again. I had seen him take this trip before. "So if you wanna talk about that—*history*—then maybe I'll listen. But that's fact. That's what I *know* is true. That's *real*, not a bunch of crying and whining about white people moving into the damn neighborhood. I owned property here, too, so . . . miss me with the nonsense." He pounded back the last bit of his pint and slammed it down on the bar. "One more 'fore I hit the road."

But I knew there was no road to hit. Not for Fortune. That the house he'd owned around here was gone. Long gone. Foreclosed on after he went to prison. But he had this bar. He had this drink—his drink—the *African-American Special*, a four-count antidote that would lead to his inability to venture out into the street in search of a home that was no longer his. He wore his memory and his anger like a top hat, and that stool, scraped and cut by keys that led to doorless locks, was his stage. This bar, a whiskey-soaked slab of wood, his lectern. The old couch in the back, a post-show respite. And me, though often frustrated by the performance, his biggest fan.

I made his final drink and set it down in front of him, the foam from the lager oozing down the sides of the glass. And as he dipped his top lip in so that the head foam could make a frothy blond mustache, he mumbled, "White folks these days can't take nothing we don't give 'em."

LONG ENOUGH TO DROWN

Glendaliz Camacho

BRANDON IS A war buff. A few months ago, I joined him on a work trip to Omaha. We drove an hour to a Civil War museum in Nebraska City. We spent the afternoon staring at Springfield rifles encased in glass. A bullet a soldier chewed for lack of anesthesia. Faded draft exemptions. Means of death and ways to cheat it. Nothing makes Brandon feel as alive as picking up what people who died left behind.

Brandon was engrossed in a conversation about Pickett's Charge with the museum tour guide, who sounded like David Letterman. I stood in front of a mannequin that wore a Confederate soldier's uniform. Slouch hat, butternut wool shell jacket, matching trousers. A pink quilt slung diagonally across his chest. The information card on the wall explained that female kin made the soldiers' quilts. They didn't just serve as bedding, but as emotional support too. Something to give men the will to come home.

I stopped short of feeling sympathy for a Confederate soldier, but it is unfair what we march people through. Unrealistic what we expect them to come back from.

Back at our hotel, Brandon made love to me. That's what he calls it. Making love. It's too sickly sweet a term for me. I prefer sex. Sounds sly. Fitting for what we're doing. I wouldn't take offense if he said "fuck." Deployed under the right circumstances, the word itself becomes a third party to the act. Brandon would never use words like "sex" or "fuck" to describe what we do.

In the middle of packing our suitcases to fly to New York in the morning, Brandon held up a toy submarine he bought at the museum.

—Did you hear the story that guide told? About the *H. L. Hunley*?

—The what?

—The submarine.

—No, must've missed it.

—There was this legend about a lieutenant. His girlfriend gives him a coin for good luck before he leaves for the war. He keeps it in his pocket. In the middle of a battle, he gets shot and—

—Let me guess.

—the bullet gets embedded in the coin.

—What does that have to do with the submarine?

—Well, he went on to command the *Hunley* after that. In the mid-nineties, they recover it from the ocean—

—Wait. It sank?

—Twice. The third time with the lieutenant and the entire crew, but a researcher found the gold coin near his body.

Brandon rushed through the sinking as if it were a minor detail.

—The lieutenant's initials and the date of the battle were

engraved in the coin. Forensics found he had a healed injury to his hip. From the bullet. The legend was true. Amazing, right?

—Not much of a lucky coin.

—It saved his life.

—He drowned.

—He got to go home to his sweetheart before he did.

Only Brandon would use a word like "sweetheart."

—Maybe he needed to do things. In the two years between the battle and the *Hunley*. You know, affect things.

I let it rest. Brandon needed that fairy tale more than I did.

■   ■   ■

Brandon lives by himself in the three-bedroom, two-bath house he grew up in. He bought it from his parents at their first mention of retiring to a condo farther down the Jersey Shore. Sometimes, I get up while Brandon's asleep and sit in his brother Davey's old bedroom. Everything redecorated with sale items from Target. Changed and unlived in. A battlefield where grass grows again, as if that proves anything.

Not long after Nebraska City, a US Postal Service box appeared on the dresser. Something Brandon must've bought while we were there and arranged to have shipped. The return address belonged to a fiber artist's shop in Omaha. The tape sealing the box had been sliced apart. I reached in and felt something soft. Cloth. Folded and thick. I slid my hands between the softness and the cardboard sides of the box and pulled, delivering it into the room. A white quilt. I unfolded it to reveal a yellow-skinned Xipe Totec stitched in the center. An Aztec life-death-life god. He wore a scowl and a red headdress that resembled a bird, the beak serving as the brim of his helmet. He gripped a red staff in one hand, a white shield in the other.

Brandon's brother, Davey, used to collect action figures. Eighties wrestlers, cartoons, soldiers. He kept one in his coat pocket to fiddle with when he felt anxious. Davey was always between jobs, so he fiddled a lot. I would assure him he'd find something soon. Tell him that we're all between something, always beginning and ending. A platitude offered with genuine belief from the safety of my stable life. What did I know, really know, about existing in that space between an ending and a beginning?

Davey finally got a kitchen job in a restaurant. One night after his shift, he came over to my place and pulled a box out of his Carhartt coat pocket. He nudged it across the coffee table toward me. I opened the box to find an angry action figure wearing a headdress.

—Xipe Totec. The cape is supposed to be flayed human skin.

—How romantic.

—Shut up. I'm not explaining it right. Look it up. It's like the god is hiding under this blanket of death, but there's life right underneath. Ready to come out. Like spring after winter. Or corn seeds shedding their skins before they sprout.

—You mean snakes. Snakes shed their skins.

—No. I mean corn seeds.

One day, after I entombed everything Davey left at my place in storage bins, Xipe Totec tumbled off a shelf. I pushed it into Brandon's palm without explanation. He didn't ask for any. At the time, I was grateful not to have to speak, but lately it struck me how similar my relationship to Brandon is to Davey's old/new room.

I didn't bother to put the quilt away.

■　■　■

The first Sunday of every month, we eat dinner at Brandon's godson's house. The boy lives with his mother, half sister, aunt, and cousins. We sit on their black wraparound faux leather couch. It's too soft not to sink into, making it impossible to balance plates of food on our knees. There's no room for a dining table. I pretend to like them. I'm supposed to because we're from the same part of the world.

Brandon acts like he's at ease with the two women in his life in the same room. He asks me questions he knows the answer to so she'll take the hint and make small talk. He repeats the ritual with her. He punctuates the conversations with more positivity than a motivational speaker.

He dated his godson's mother in college, over fifteen years ago. He must've been quite the trophy to bring home, a white man. Irish, he always insists, as if that made his reddish-brown hair or blue eyes any darker. Anyway, she and Brandon broke up soon after graduating and she got pregnant from someone else. The baby's father left and she asked Brandon to be the baby's godfather. Then the pregnancy became something to celebrate. It had a patron to sponsor a baby shower, replace outgrown clothes, buy school supplies. She acquired respectability with Brandon's support. He kept the sainthood her family granted him when they were dating. Brandon doesn't attend Mass every Sunday, but being a godfather he considers an unbreakable Catholic duty. He gets to sow his paternal instincts without the pressure to marry.

Sometimes I feel his godson's mother eyeing my natural hair, tracing my tattoos. My cat-eye glasses instead of colored contacts. Wondering what Brandon sees in me. When I feel her looking, I smile back. I study her hair dyed a shade of burgundy not found in nature. Her makeup, I later learn, takes an hour in the bathroom. Her blouse, always a size too small.

I rarely eat rice, never drink soda, never eat anything fried. She makes it a point every single time to say she made a salad just for me, since I don't eat anything. Thank you, that's thoughtful of you, I say. After dinner, Brandon and his godson go outside to play some basketball. If it's too cold or raining, they play video games. *Total War: Shogun 2* or *Crusader Kings II.*

As we're getting ready to leave, she always asks us to wait a minute. She fills a plastic dollar-store container with food for Brandon to take to work for lunch the next day. I make sure to stand right next to him. Brandon always wraps his arm around my waist as we wait.

■   ■   ■

My daughter comes home from Amherst, Massachusetts, in the middle of her sophomore year for spring break. After a few days she's suffocated by the neighborhood, the apartment, and me. She asks why I stay in New York City now that nothing anchors me here. I don't tell her I'm waiting for the lease to end in the summer. I'm crossing my fingers that Brandon suggests moving in with him. I like the Jersey Shore, but Brandon pointed out that my apartment is closer to his job, closer to his godson. He said it's great to share two places instead of one.

My daughter told me she was asexual when she was fourteen. I asked if she meant to come out as a lesbian, but no. She felt attraction toward men but no inclination to act on it. It must be freeing not to need. When she was a teenager, I went on dates every Saturday night. After a breakup, I spent weekends in bed, getting up only to eat baked macaroni and cheese and chocolate ice cream.

She disliked all my boyfriends. She reserved judgment until they showed themselves. Called her stupid in the heat of an argument. Lingered in her doorway when they shouldn't. There was nowhere to go except out the door once she smoked a man out of his sheep's clothing. She became good at it because I failed to see them for what they were, and for that I've always felt guilty. She was a sniper by the time Davey came along, but he was the only one who was what he seemed. A sweet, nervous guy, unprepared for the life of a man.

My daughter says she's never getting married or having children. I wonder if I made her feel that way. Or if watching me lose Davey did.

When Brandon gets busy with work, I won't get a text or phone call for days. I remind myself that I fell for his diligence, how he tends to everything that needs his attention. I busy myself with my daughter to relearn that silence doesn't mean an end.

When he almost fades into a ghost, he reappears with an apologetic text and begs to see me that same night. My anger melts into gratitude when I hug him and feel his arms, solid around me. He changes out of his button-down shirt and slacks, and I sit with him while he eats what I cooked for dinner. He says it's great to come home to me. We are the foundation we rebuilt our lives on.

■ ■ ■

Brandon's cell phone rings. His godson's mother. Brandon measures his replies so that I can't tell what's wrong. He leaves the living room where we're watching a movie but stays within earshot. I try to keep paying attention to the actors on the screen, but my heart pounds.

—Is everything okay?

—She got a dispossess notice on her apartment. She and the kids need a place to stay for a little while.

A war drum beats in my blood. In my head, I scream obscenities and throw things at Brandon.

—I have plenty of room, and they don't have anyone else.

—Of course.

I go to bed early. Brandon tries to rouse me by nuzzling my neck, caressing my thigh. I pretend to be dead asleep.

■ ■ ■

Brandon let Davey keep his old bedroom after buying his parents' house, but Davey took cover at my place whenever he quit or got fired, like he was from that kitchen job. Then he'd call me in the throes of a panic attack on his way to an interview for a new job. The night before his first day of work, he'd snap at me to turn down the TV. I couldn't even turn over in bed, or he'd say I wasn't letting him sleep. He'd come home exuberant about his first week until a bad day struck. The bad days would outnumber the good ones, and he'd quit or get fired again.

He went to work for his uncle's general contracting business. He made it through a whole six months. One night he complained of a headache. I scolded him for overmedicating, taking sleeping pills and pain medication. I woke up in the middle of the night to Davey throwing up in the bathroom. In the morning he said his head felt like it was splitting in two. I told him to take some aspirin. I cooked breakfast. My daughter was already eating, and Davey still hadn't gotten up. When I went to check on him, he'd gone back to sleep. I shook him by the shoulder and told him to get his ass up and go to work. He groaned and rolled over. I told him I left his breakfast in the microwave. I left for work. I texted him during the day to check up on him, but he didn't reply. I figured he was busy at work, but in an eight-hour day everyone stops to eat or take a piss, so I was annoyed. I checked my mailbox. I walked up to my floor. My daughter was home from school. She'd eaten a piece of flan before dinner like I asked her not to. I yelled at her to pick up her laptop and papers, stuff for her SATs, scattered across the kitchen table, forgotten after finishing homework. Davey was taking a bath, but I didn't hear the fizz of water shooting from the showerhead. No splashing. No plastic bottles of shampoo and conditioner knocked down. Only a quiet that made it seem as if beyond that door the world had stopped. I knocked and called his name. Then faster and louder until my hand stung and my throat burned. I kicked the door, and the skinny slide bolt snapped and flew off. Later, my neighbors three floors down told me they could hear me screaming.

—What happened?

My daughter tugged at my elbows. The front of my shirt and pants were drenched. The bathroom tiles were dangerously slippery. I couldn't get words out. Sound, plenty, but not words.

My daughter must've dialed 911.

The pathologist who performed the autopsy found water in Davey's lungs, of course, but also enough Vicodin left over from my last root canal to cast doubt on carelessness. Not enough to declare intention, though. A preexisting heart condition too. The results were inconclusive.

Brandon was the only one who reached out to me. The rest of his family blamed me for not saving Davey from drowning way before that bath. Brandon stopped by every week to check on my daughter and me. He brought us groceries. He threw out the trash. He slept on the couch. He got my daughter out of the house by driving her to the mall under the guise of picking out things for her dorm room. She was so afraid to leave me alone, she would only acquiesce to errands. She wouldn't go to her father's place on the weekends or out with friends. Brandon and I would send long texts back and forth late into the night full of thoughts we could only confess to each other. He was gentle and apologetic with his questions. He drove me to Davey's wake and funeral, against his mother's wishes.

■   ■   ■

Brandon's godson's mother fits into this house like a piece of shrapnel under the skin. The kids take Davey's old room and she takes the other one. Whenever she gets home, she hangs her set of keys up next to Brandon's, opposite from mine. Sometimes I watch Brandon cutting his godson's meat or helping the boy's sister work out a math problem. He looks happy. I'll watch Brandon looking in the cabinets under the sink for a particular pot to cook dinner. Brandon's godson's mother steadies herself with a hand on his shoulder. She tiptoes—poking her ass out—to reach a cabinet over the sink where the pot is.

One night, after sex, during which I am especially vocal for her benefit, Brandon taps his chest. I lay my head where he beckoned. He says it's nice, the house full of people. Reminds him of growing up. Hints at maybe us adding to it.

I won't start all over again with a baby. I tell him how difficult it was to do it alone. How difficult it's been to be alone since Davey. We always end up alone. I'm angry at him for pretending these things aren't true or hoping I've forgotten they are. But something in me also feels victorious.

■ ■ ■

The grass in Brandon's backyard grows lush as spring arrives. I'm helping him plant things. Brandon's godson's mother and the kids have lived here for three months. We overhear her pleading with the storage facility over the phone. We pretend her voice doesn't blast through the air like a car horn. Later, on my way to the bathroom, I overhear her on the phone arguing with her son's father. On a sunny Saturday, we get to Brandon's to find her sniffling and bleary-eyed on the couch. I start dinner. He comes into the kitchen a short while later. She visited a dozen apartments with Realtors, but no one will accept her application. Her credit is bad.

One morning, I hear them in Davey's bedroom. She's crying. Brandon tells her to calm down. He tells her they'll figure it out. That she can always count on him. She says she's too old for this. He says things aren't that bad. That it'll change soon. To be patient.

A sharp pain seizes my chest. I'm breathing too fast like after plunging into cold water. I surface in the room.

—Are you fucking her?

She's startled and jumps away from him. As if he caught on fire. I can't tell if this is an admission of guilt. His shirt is damp where she left her tears.

—What? Are you crazy? No, she's like family.

We're standing in Davey's room. Davey once sat on my couch and said, "I love you." I said it back. I was Davey's girlfriend, and Davey was Brandon's brother. Something even stronger than love binds me to my dead boyfriend's (exboyfriend's?) brother. At first, it was the need to feel alive, yes. Then we were the conduit that kept Davey alive. Now it's the even distribution of the weight of shame between us.

—*I* was like family. I know how good you can be when you're needed.

Brandon blinks. A look of surprise at an injury turns into a look of disbelief at my accusation of betrayal. I cannot take it back.

■　■　■

On Davey's birthday, two months after he died, Brandon drove me to visit his grave. We stood on the plot, staring at the headstone. I felt nothing. If Davey strolled up and clapped Brandon on the shoulder, it would not have shocked me. He existed everywhere except underneath us in the ground.

I grew aware of Brandon's body pulsing with life next to me. His visible breath in the cold. Our arms connected from shoulder to hands. Squeezing each other's hands. Not letting go when we should have. His warm skin underneath layers of wool and denim and cotton. Inhaling. Dropping our gaze to our mouths. His hands never stopped roving over my skin. My skin wasn't numb anymore. On the drive back, we kept the windows rolled up. Our heat, fogging up the windows, created the atmosphere of our world.

On the front porch, Brandon's godson's mother apologizes to me. She says she didn't mean to cause a problem. I bite my lower lip and nod. I hand her the keys to Brandon's car. Her kids dive into the backseat. She's dropping them off at her mother's for the day while she does some overtime at work. Her car sits in the driveway. The two front tires deflated, the car tilting forward. Frozen at the start of a nosedive it will never achieve.

I return to Brandon in Davey's room. We are quiet to match the house. He clutches at me to prove something. I cling to him. We volley ourselves, back and forth, as hard and as fast as we can. He asks if he can come inside of me. Afterward, he lies behind me, the stubble on his chin scratching the crook of my neck. Xipe Totec is in my sightline, draped over the back of an armchair. Brandon says it would make a great blanket for a baby.

IF A BIRD CAN BE A GHOST

Allison Mills

SHELLY'S GRANDMA TEACHES her about ghosts, how to carry them in her hair. If you carry your ghosts in your hair, then you can cut them off when you don't need them anymore. Otherwise, ghosts cling to your skin, dig their fingers in under your ribs, and stay with you long, long after you want them gone.

Shelly's mother doesn't like ghosts. She doesn't like Grandma telling Shelly about them. "You'll scare her," she says. "You'll keep her up at night."

"How is she going to take care of herself if she can't take care of the dead?" Grandma asks, and Shelly's mother never has much of an answer for that. So Grandma teaches Shelly about ghosts, how to keep them, and how to get rid of them too. Not just her own ghosts but other people's.

"My grandma is a Ghostbuster," Shelly tells her friends at school. "I'm going to be one too."

It's true, in a way. People are always coming by the house to see if Grandma will get rid of their ghosts—cats that wind around their ankles and trip them when they walk. Dogs that bark in the middle of the night, startling them out of sleep. Most ghosts Grandma exorcises were someone's pet once.

"People are harder to notice," Grandma says. "Nobody *wants* to see their mother-in-law clinging to their back everywhere they go."

Grandma did a cleansing for a nice white family to get rid of a mother-in-law once. They paid her three hundred dollars and gave her a lasagna for the freezer. Three hundred is a lot for a ghost. Most of Grandma's clients pay in knick-knacks and favors and food. Grandma doesn't charge much, because if people know they have a ghost, they might pay anything—do anything—to get rid of them.

"You've got to be responsible," Grandma tells Shelly. "You can't charge people through the nose to get rid of a ghost. We've got to undercut the frauds so people come to us."

Mom looks over from putting her hair up to go to work, her uniform shirt all nicely pressed. She points a finger at Grandma. "You could charge a little more."

"It's a nice lasagna," Grandma says.

Mom shrugs because Grandma's right. It *is* a nice lasagna.

■　■　■

Grandma doesn't get rid of every ghost she comes across. Sometimes ghosts deserve to do their haunting. Sometimes people deserve to be haunted.

"You don't take ghosts from a graveyard," Grandma says, braiding Shelly's hair so she won't catch any ghosts she doesn't want. "Not unless they want to go; then you can let them out. Most of those ghosts, they'll leave if they really want to. Same with churches and temples, sacred places. They deserve to stay."

The graveyard Grandma takes Shelly to is a twenty-seven-minute bus ride away. It's a nice one—big, with tidy rows of brass plaques and tasteful headstones set in the ground. Shelly keeps to the path so she doesn't walk on anybody's grave.

"This kind of graveyard, you aren't going to find a lot of ghosts," Grandma says, leading Shelly toward the outer limits of the graveyard, the cheaper graves. "Lots of old ladies like me with nothing left to haunt about."

On the outskirts of the graveyard, there are small graves with tiny aluminum stakes and rusted old plaques instead of proper headstones. The graves are closer together, and the undergrowth is creeping toward them. There's a ghost there, a teenage boy, sitting on a grave and playing with a Walkman.

He looks up at Grandma and Shelly with eyes like black holes.

"Hello, Joseph," Grandma says, sticking a hand in her handbag and pulling out a stack of old tapes. She puts them on the grave in front of the boy and he smiles at her.

"Old Lady," he says. His mouth moves, but his voice comes from the headphones around his neck. He pops open his ghostly Walkman and inserts the tapes, one by one, right after each other. They disappear as they slide into place, dissolving into the player. "You want to know who's walking around the yard?"

"I want to introduce you to my granddaughter," Grandma says. "Joseph, this is Shelly."

Joseph turns his disconcerting eyes on Shelly. She does her best not to take a step back. After a moment, she gives Joseph a quick bow because she's not sure what else to do with him staring like that.

Joseph laughs. "I like her," he says. "Old Lady never introduced me to anyone before, Little Shell. You must be special. You ever heard of the Cure?"

Shelly shakes her head.

Joseph opens his Walkman and reaches inside. His hand slips down, down, all the way to his elbow, as he digs around inside, and he pulls out a cassette and holds it out to Shelly. "This is a good one," he says. "Take care of it for me."

Shelly takes the tape—*Disintegration*. It's so icy cold that touching it feels like being burned, but Grandma taught her how to accept gifts from the dead. When they give you something, you must be grateful. You smile and you say thank you and you take good care of it.

"Thank you," Shelly says. "Do you want me to bring it back?"

"Nah," Joseph says. "You keep that one for you."

. . .

The only cassette player Shelly knows about is the one in her mom's car. The next time she goes with her mom to get groceries, she has the tape in her pocket.

"Where did you get a tape?" her mom asks, turning it over in her hands and then sliding it into the deck. "Why *this* tape?"

"Joseph gave it to me. He's one of Grandma's friends."

Shelly's mom fast-forwards through the first song, straight to the second. "A dead friend?"

"His name is Joseph." The music Joseph gave her is all jangly guitar, electric piano, and echoing, sorrowful voices. It sounds like a sad dance party. Shelly likes it.

"Joseph has strong commitment to a theme."

Shelly's mom doesn't approve of ghosts, but she turns the music up and she teaches Shelly the words to the song so they can sing it together.

■　■　■

Despite her mother's fears, Shelly is never afraid of ghosts. Ghosts are nice to little girls who pay them close attention and don't run away screaming. Most ghosts just want to be noticed because they go so long without talking to anyone, and when someone does notice them, they usually just try to get rid of them.

Grandma laughs a lot about people who try to get rid of ghosts on their own.

"We burned sage," one of Grandma's clients—a woman clad in expensive yoga pants with her hair in a high ponytail—says, touring Shelly and Grandma around her haunted apartment. "To cleanse it, you know?"

Grandma smiles, all bland and pointed. "To cleanse it?"

"From the . . . spirits. The demons. You know." The woman gestures vaguely at Grandma, at her brown skin and warm brown eyes. At the little turtle earrings she wears every day. The things that make some people say *Native* and Grandma say *Ililiw*. "It's cleansing. The smoke. We fanned it around the whole house and nothing. The spirits are still here."

Grandma keeps smiling. "I don't use sage to cleanse ghosts."

"Oh. So it's like . . . for other stuff? Bad juju?"

Grandma turns her back on the woman. "This is a tough case. I might have to charge a little more for the work. Do you mind?"

Grandma's right about the money. People will pay more to get rid of a ghost once they're sure it's there.

■　■　■

Sometimes the police come. Not often, and always officers who know Grandma already, with their hats in hand. There are TV shows like that, but when Grandma finally takes Shelly with her, it's not like on TV.

"We can drive you to the river," one of the officers says, looking uncomfortable as Shelly helps Grandma into her raincoat and finds their bus passes.

"In the back of your car?"

"Well, yes."

"No, thank you. We'll meet you at the water," Grandma says, voice so firm the officers have no choice but to leave and drive away as Grandma and Shelly begin their walk to the bus.

"Never get in the back of a car with doors you can't open," Grandma tells Shelly. "You be polite to them, but stay out of that car."

Shelly and Grandma get to the river in less time than it takes to get to the cemetery. The officers have picked up tea for Grandma and hot chocolate for Shelly, which makes the long bus ride worth it.

(At this age, Shelly thinks riding in the back of a police car would be kind of cool. When she grows up, she'll know Grandma was right.)

If Shelly's mother had been home, she wouldn't have let her go to the river. Grandma walks up and down the bank a few times, holding Shelly's hand, the cops trailing after them, and Grandma lets her hair hang loose and long to pull up any ghosts.

She catches the ghost on the third pass. His clothes are plastered to his body and his shivering makes him shift in and out of focus. He doesn't speak, but he keeps glancing over his shoulder toward a little outcrop of rocks on the bank of the water.

"Ah," Grandma says, nodding. She gestures the cops closer and points to the rocks. "He's caught up in there. A nice young man with a red beard."

The cops wait until Shelly and Grandma leave to pull the body from the water. The ghost comes home with them, wet and shivery, even after the bus ride back to the house.

"Do you want me to turn on the heater?" Shelly asks him.

The ghost jumps and looks down at her. "Where did you come from?"

"Leave him alone, Shelly. We'll feed him and send him off," Grandma says. "He doesn't need us confusing him even more."

"I don't understand what happened," the ghost says. "I was just on the bridge. I was just thinking."

Grandma pours the ghost a mug of milk and warms it in the microwave as he drifts around their kitchen, flickering in and out of focus as Shelly watches, fascinated. A new ghost, a ghost who is still deciding if he wants to stick around or not, is new for her.

"What's your name?" Shelly asks, because the cops didn't say.

The ghost gives her a distressed look. "I don't know," he says. "Do you know who I am? Do you know my name?"

Grandma sets the mug of warm milk down on the kitchen table. "Here you go," she says. "This will warm you up, and then we'll make sure you get where you're going.

That sounds nice, doesn't it? Shelly, would you get the scissors from my sewing kit?"

Shelly goes and gets the pair of small silver scissors. The ghost drains the milk on the table. His wet hair drips real water on the floor. He looks like he'll never be fully dry, like if you tried to wring him out, he'd twist and twist and the water would just keep coming. This, Shelly thinks, is probably why Grandma doesn't want to keep him. Having a damp ghost haunting their house would be troublesome.

Grandma wraps a strand of hair around her ring finger and clips it off. By the time the milk is finished, the ghost is nearly gone, just a faint smudge in the air where once there was a man.

"Where do they go?" Shelly asks. "Where do we send them?"

Grandma picks up the mug and refills it with milk. She sticks it in the microwave to heat it up for herself. "We'll find out, won't we? One day, a long time from now."

∙ ∙ ∙

Shelly's mother finds out before Grandma does.

∙ ∙ ∙

Shelly goes looking for her. She lets her hair out and she circles round and round the neighborhood, looking for any sign of her mother's ghost. Not everyone who dies becomes a ghost. Sometimes they just go to whatever's next all on their own. But those people don't know about ghosts. Not like Shelly's mom knew about ghosts. They don't have Shelly waiting for them at home.

Shelly wears her hair loose to the funeral home and has

to comb the ghosts from her hair on the way to the cemetery. She winds her hair into a loose bun when they bury the
coffin, ready to pull loose if she sees her mother. Grandma
wears her hair in braids, wrapped around her head like a
crown. She cries and holds tight to Shelly's hand and doesn't
even tell her off for catching so many ghosts in the funeral
home. Grandma understands grief better than most people.
Grandma makes her living with the dead.

After the funeral, Shelly slips away from all the hugging
and touching and walks to the outskirts of the cemetery.

"Little Shell," Joseph says, looking at her with his black,
blank eyes and his mouth that moves while his headphones
emit the tinny sound of his voice. "Did you bring me a tape?"

Shelly had never stolen anything before, but cassettes
are hard to find. "Do you want to learn French?" she asks,
pulling three tapes from her pockets. "The library had these
language learning tapes."

Joseph looks offended. "No music?"

"My mom died," Shelly says. "I can't find her."

Joseph reaches for the tapes. He feeds them into his
Walkman one by one. "Je suis désolé. That means 'I'm sorry.'
I'm dead. It's not so bad."

"I miss her," Shelly says. "I can't find her. I can't remember
what her voice sounds like. Not exactly. What if I forget how
she smells next?"

Joseph is a ghost, so Joseph doesn't really get how the
impermanence of life affects the living. Shelly can see that
on his face.

Shelly also doesn't know who else to talk to.

"You're a ghost," she says. "You live here. If you see her—"

"I don't live anywhere," Joseph says. He pauses, nods. "If

I see her, I'll tell her Little Shell is looking for her mother. I'll tell her you want to hear her voice again."

Shelly doesn't think to wonder how Joseph will know it's her mother until after she finds Grandma and the rest of the funeral party getting ready to head back home, where there's lots of food and more people waiting to say how sorry they are. Shelly lays her head on Grandma's lap in the back of the car and closes her eyes.

"Do ghosts know things?" she asks.

"They know lots of things," Grandma says. "Most things they knew when they were alive. All the things they've learned since they died. Ghosts have lots of time on their hands."

"About other ghosts," Shelly says. "Would a ghost know who another ghost was before they became a ghost?"

Grandma undoes Shelly's bun and strokes her hair. She cradles Shelly close like she must have once cradled Shelly's mother and whispers that she'll take care of Shelly. She'll make sure Shelly is safe and happy. When the car reaches their home, they don't get out. Shelly falls asleep there, on Grandma's lap.

■ ■ ■

Shelly collects ghosts. She stops cutting her hair and stops combing it most days. She walks around town by herself and snatches up ghosts from the streets she walks down and the buildings she goes into. Old and young, of all different races and genders and everything else. Some so faint they're just smudges and some almost as solid as living people: ghosts you can only tell are dead because they have an uncanny quality that sets them apart—like Joseph and his eyes.

Shelly gathers ghosts and asks them if they've seen her

mother. She asks them if they know anyone like her, if they've run across a woman looking for her daughter.

Grandma is charging more to get rid of ghosts. Sometimes they still get food and trinkets, but only when they're chasing ghosts for one of Grandma's friends. The next time the police come, Grandma tells them she needs to charge a fee for consultation. Shelly isn't allowed to come along because it has to be official. A crime scene is no place for a child, and besides, there won't be any hot chocolate waiting for her at the end of it this time.

Shelly doesn't think she's a child anymore. She's aged since her mother's death. She can't stop getting older and further away from her mom.

■ ■ ■

Shelly sits in an elevator of the oldest hotel downtown and winds a strand of hair around her finger. There's a little boy in the hotel. He likes to ride the elevator up and down, to push all the buttons and watch the living get frustrated with how long it takes to get to their floor. The living are always concerned about time, about running late and running out of it. The little boy has nothing but time now.

"Have you seen my mom?" Shelly asks him, and takes out the photo she carries with her now, of her mom smiling and holding Shelly in her arms.

"I haven't seen any moms," the boy says, running his hands over the bank of buttons so they all light up. "I haven't seen anyone interesting in *forever*. Why aren't there any toys? Why won't anyone play with me?"

"I'll play with you," Shelly says. "Will you look at my photo?"

The boy turns to frown at Shelly. He's a solid ghost, well established in the hotel. They don't want to get rid of him. Tourists come to ride the elevator and stay in the rooms he likes to walk through. They tell people that the ghost is a young woman who got so sad, she jumped from the building's top floor. It was a great tragedy, they say, that someone so pretty and young died. She'd had a young son.

The first time Shelly and Grandma visited the hotel, Grandma told the hotel manager it was the son haunting the hotel and not his mother. The manager said it would be too morbid to tell people it was a little boy haunting them. The death of a young woman was better. It was more romantic that way. Besides, think of all the books that had been published about the haunting. The hotel had a guide to the haunting in their lobby. They couldn't change that.

"I don't want to play with you," the boy says, but he looks at Shelly's photo anyway. "I've never seen her before. Have you seen my mom? Where did she go? She left me here, didn't she? She left me all on my own."

Shelly gets off the elevator at the next floor and takes the stairs down.

■   ■   ■

Shelly does her best to hide the ghosts from Grandma. She buries them in her dresser drawers and tucks them into her hair when she walks into the house so she can carry them down the hall without being stopped. Her room fills up slowly.

Grandma makes them dinner every night and they eat together. Every night Grandma tries to talk to Shelly.

"I have a job tomorrow," Grandma says. "A family keeps

finding things knocked over in their apartment. They say they have a poltergeist, so it's probably a bird."

Sometimes, birds crash into windows of tall buildings and their spirits pass through the glass without their bodies. Birds are always destructive because they flap around trying to get free and throw things about.

"Birds are boring," Shelly says. "They just squawk until you catch them and put them outside. They give me a headache."

"Birds are a good way to make a living," Grandma says. "Birds will always crash into buildings."

Shelly looks down at her dinner. "Do you think there are a lot of chicken ghosts on farms?"

■　■　■

The bird family is nice. They offer Grandma and Shelly lemonade when they arrive.

"I thought it was just Maria throwing her toys around at first," one of the women says as she shows off the cracked glass in picture frames that were knocked off the wall. "Hannah or I would put them away on the shelf and then they'd be scattered everywhere when we got in."

Hannah nods. "When we found the pictures all knocked off the wall we knew Maria wasn't just trying to get out of trouble. She's only four. She can't reach them."

"Besides," says Hannah's wife, "two days ago we were watching TV and something knocked it over."

The bird is sitting on the top of a bookshelf. Its feathers are ruffled up and it looks about as disgruntled as a bird can look. Grandma takes down her hair.

"Don't you worry," she says. "We'll see to your poltergeist problem."

Birds aren't like people. They don't stick to you the same way. Grandma, with her hair down, creeps toward the bookshelf, clucking her tongue at the bird like it's a shy cat. It hops back, away from her, wary, and Grandma stills and coos at it again.

Shelly sometimes wonders what they look like to the women who hire them to free their home of ghosts, and to all the other clients who've seen her and Grandma hop around chasing phantoms. Weird, probably, but they get stuff done. She and Grandma always earn their weirdness.

Shelly moves around the edges of the room and picks up a pillow. She waits until she's sure the bird is entirely focused on Grandma, then whacks it with the pillow, off the shelf and into Grandma's waiting grasp.

■   ■   ■

Shelly kind of wants to keep the bird. All the ghosts she has hidden in her room are human.

"We'll let it out at the park," Grandma says. The bird is still disgruntled but is too wound up in her hair to escape. "Where it can fly around without hurting anything until it gets tired and decides to move on."

"We could take it home and feed it," Shelly says. "We have lots of milk."

"It's just a bird, Shelly," Grandma says. "If it wasn't for people sticking tall buildings everywhere, it wouldn't be here at all. When I was a girl, you never saw as many birds around as you do now. Everything was lower to the ground then. It wasn't nearly as confusing for them."

"Just because it's a bird it doesn't matter?"

"Because it's a bird, we should take it to a park with lots

of trees and other birds and let it go free," Grandma says. "Ghosts like it aren't meant to stay forever. Most of the time it's better to let ghosts fade. You know that."

"Sometimes ghosts deserve to do their haunting. Some things need haunting."

"True." Grandma agrees because she's the one who taught Shelly that. "But those ghosts will let you know. You know that. Those ghosts know where they are. They know what they're about. You know the dead, Shelly. Most ghosts don't realize what's happened to them. They just need a hand getting to where they're going."

Shelly thinks most ghosts are pretty stupid.

Shelly and Grandma walk to the park and Shelly watches Grandma let the bird out of her hair. She watches the bird take off, straight up into the sky, and keeps watching until she loses sight of it in the clouds.

■　■　■

Grandma finds Shelly's ghosts while she's putting laundry away in Shelly's room. She opens a drawer and the dead tumble out. She goes through the dresser and Shelly's closet and finds them both filled with ghosts. Shelly's little bedroom is so full, you could hardly move.

Grandma waits for Shelly when Shelly gets home from school, and she's covered in ghosts.

"Those are *mine*," Shelly says, since she can't pretend they're not.

"These are people," Grandma says. "They belong to themselves. They don't belong here."

Shelly can't tell if Grandma has let some of the ghosts go already or not. Shelly has a lot of ghosts.

"You can't surround yourself with the dead all the time," Grandma says. "You're still alive, Shelly."

Shelly scowls. "You're always with the dead."

"No, Shelly, I'm always with you."

Shelly leaves.

．　．　．

Shelly goes to the cemetery. She storms up to Joseph's grave, where he's sitting and murmuring to himself in French.

"Where is she?" Shelly demands. "Where's my mom?"

Joseph looks up with his black eyes and frowns. "Your mom's not here, Little Shell."

"No," Shelly says. "This is where she's buried."

"Just because you're dead doesn't mean you're a ghost."

"Why not?" Shelly demands. "Why you and not her? If a bird can be a ghost, then why not her? Where did she go?"

Joseph looks terribly, terribly pitying for a dead teenager who talks through a Walkman. "I don't know. I've been here. I've always been here. This place is all I know."

"You have a tape player," Shelly says. "You're not that old."

"This is all I remember," Joseph says. "This place, which is mine, and watching over the graves for the Old Lady and now you, Little Shell. Did you bring me any tapes?"

"Why would I bring you any tapes when you're no good to me?"

Shelly lashes out and kicks her foot through Joseph's im-material body and he topples over from the force of it, com-ing uprooted from his spot on the ground by his grave. Joseph looks startled—at moving, at being suddenly unmoored, sud-denly ghostly in a way he wasn't before. He flickers, like the man that Grandma once dredged up from the river.

"Little Shell, what did you do to me?" Joseph asks, mournful as he twists in place and tries to claw his way back toward his grave, his spot. "Where have you put me?"

Shelly does the only thing she can think to do and catches Joseph up in her hair. She turns and she runs from the cemetery and doesn't take the bus. She runs all the way home, where Grandma is sweeping ghosts out the door and away.

Grandma takes one look at Shelly's frightened face and Joseph in her hair, and sighs. "There's nothing to do, Joseph," she says. "We'll give you some milk and help you get to where you're going."

Shelly carries Joseph into the kitchen and sits with him at the table, quiet and sorry, as Grandma puts a mug full of milk in the microwave and warms it up.

"I didn't mean to," she says when Grandma sets the milk in front of Joseph.

Joseph prods the milk carefully. "I'd rather have music," he says. "Little Shell, you're a kid. You shouldn't be caught up in death all the time anyway. Right, Old Lady?"

"We carry our dead with us everywhere we go," Grandma says, touching Shelly's hair. "The important people don't leave us, even when their ghosts are gone. Even if they never come back."

Grandma combs Shelly's hair, and Joseph gets blurrier and blurrier until he fades away completely and it's just Grandma and Shelly sitting at the table, alone. Shelly blinks tears off her eyelashes and Grandma keeps combing her hair until the tears stop coming.

"Do you feel better?" Grandma asks, handing Shelly Joseph's milk, now just lukewarm.

"No," Shelly says. "Not really." She takes a sip of milk and reaches up to touch her long hair. "I want to cut it."

Grandma hesitates. Cutting your hair has meaning. Cutting your hair is a choice. "Are you sure?"

Once it's out in the air, once Shelly says it out loud, it's obvious it needs to be done. It's time to cut it so it can grow out new and shiny, not tangled up with the dead, not dragging at her shoulders with the weight of the memories it carries. "I need to cut it."

Grandma and Shelly go outside to sit on the steps with Grandma's little silver scissors. The light is fading, but the sky is pink-purple-red as the sun goes down. It's pretty, and Shelly watches the sun setting while Grandma combs her long hair one more time.

Grandma gathers Shelly's hair into little ponytails and cuts them off carefully, her touch gentle, and hands Shelly each lock as she goes, until they're all gone.

Shelly shivers when the evening wind brushes her neck, and shakes out her newly shorn hair, feeling the crisp ends brush against her skin. It feels like sudden weightlessness. All the things she's been carrying with her are still there, but they seem lighter now. Easier.

"We took a lot off," Grandma says, touching Shelly's hair, brushing her fingers through it.

Shelly winds the strands of her hair around and around her hand. There's so much that isn't attached to her the same way anymore, and now she can't fish for ghosts as she walks the street. She can't load her shoulders with the weight of their lives. She can't kidnap anybody from a graveyard.

"What do you think?" Grandma asks. "How do you feel?"

Her hair is gone, and all the feelings from before remain, but it's not bad.

"I like it," she says. "It'll grow back. I'll be ready for it."

■   ■   ■

One day, Shelly will have a baby of her own—a little being to care for like her mother and grandmother cared for her. She will teach her baby about ghosts and how they get caught in your hair and how you can choose to carry them with you or cut them away; about the burden of knowing the past when so many people can forget it so easily. She will teach her baby that not all ghosts need to be exorcised and that some people, some places, need to be haunted.

Shelly will take her baby with her when she exorcises a ghost and will say to the ghost, "See? See this new being that has come into the world? Let the sight of them fill you with hope and good feeling as you go where you're going. Say hello to my mom and Grandma when you get there."

LAST RITES

Dennis Norris II

SOMEONE WILL COME. *Someone will find me.*

Sirens will sound in the distance. Lights will rise from darkness like seraphs, dancing red and blue. Salvation will be brought by men sent from God. These men will come from the east. There is a campus not too far in that direction, a satellite of the state university. The men will move as quickly as possible along the highway, over black ice, close to the barrier that divides east and west.

Tread marks will lead them to an indentation in the guardrail, scratched with white paint. The men, always moving, will jump down from their trucks, rubber boots clomping to the pavement with the strength of hooves. One of them will wonder aloud how that white car got all the way down the hill by the quarry. "You can hardly see it," he'll say, with his hand at attention. His eyes will strain under the swirling clouds that block the moon, that mute the stars. Another, braver, will lead them over the guardrail, hooves romping easily down the hill. They will follow the path cut by the car as it flipped, over and over, and landed on its now caved-in hardtop.

The Reverend remains strapped in his seat, upside down, his nose only inches from the ground, unable to move. His Toyota crashed into a tree with such force that several branches, heaving from the weight of the snow, broke from the trunk, tumbled through the wintry air, and landed on the overturned car. Periodically the tree creaks, warning him. At some point he knows it will give under the excess weight. But by then he will be saved. The men will have come and gone, and in between ripped him free.

They will come shouting into their walkie-talkies, demanding backup, cursing, not caring if their words offend him. The glare from their flashlights will find him, then blind him. Someone will shout for the men at the top of the hill to aim their headlights at the quarry, give them some light. The Toyota's lights will be extinguished by then; the battery will have died. Once there is light, the Reverend will see how the snow has frozen beneath him, how every window has shattered, how the car he gave his sixteen-year-old son eight years ago crumpled around him as though it were nothing more than a toy, a Matchbox model like the ones Davis used to play with.

The youngest, newest trooper will kneel as close to the car as possible. He will extend his arm through the broken window. He will shine his flashlight into the Reverend's face, then up and down his body.

"Are you hurt?" he will ask.

"Davis?" the Reverend will ask the man. "Is it you?"

"Sir, are you hurt? Can you move?" The trooper's voice will ring with easy authority over more sirens sounding in the distance, coming their way; over the slow rumble of traffic that will begin to pile up, though it's after midnight, and the roads are relatively bare. Over the chatter of the Reverend's teeth, for by this time he will be delirious and so cold that his words will be nearly unintelligible.

The Reverend will try to turn his head until he can see the trooper's eyes. He will try, but he will fail. He will know that the trooper's voice is not his son's voice, the trooper's hands—large, pale, and strong—are not his son's hands. He will wonder if these are the hands that will keep him alive, bring him to safety. He will wonder if safety is what Davis sees in That Man, the white one, the one he plans to marry. He will wonder if Davis ever saw these things in him.

"Sir, don't worry. We're going to get you out of here."

"Sunny Boy," he will say.

"Everything is going to be fine."

"I need my son. I need to save my son," he will say.

"Your son isn't here. He's safe. It's only you in this car." The trooper will consider the fact that he, too, would be thinking of his son if it were him trapped in that seat, hanging upside down, waiting for help to come. With his free arm he will slowly reach his hand through the broken window until he can gently press his palm against the driver's shoulder. He will do his best to look the driver in the eye. "Sir, we're going to get you out of here."

■   ■   ■

His intention was to go for a short drive, just a little ride to clear his head. He'd driven past the church, the Popcorn Shoppe, and Shirley's Gourmet Ice Cream Parlor. He'd driven past Montgomery's Country Store, home to the world's chewiest pecan pralines. And though he'd slowed down, that moment as good as any for a drink, eventually he drove right on by the local dive. He'd been done with all that for twenty-five years, minus a few bumps along the way.

He'd turned from Main Street onto Route 34, heading south. He drove past True Value and the Gemini Boutique. Past the post office and Cooke's Violins. It was in the east garret of Cooke's where Davis, at seven years old, first learned how to hold a violin, scratching out two ugly notes before calmly setting the thing down and declaring that he wanted to play an instrument that allowed him to sit. The place finally shut its doors after years spent struggling to stay afloat.

When the Reverend called Davis to tell him the news, Davis had said, "You could have texted me that," and hung up. So the Reverend had texted him, "I'd like to see you, son." But Davis—young, living all the way out there in New York City with That Man, caught up in his life—doesn't make much of an effort. Davis wouldn't know what it is to call your son with news that should be important to him and be dismissed as though you are some kind of nuisance, when at one time, for a long time, you were everything to him.

From home, New York City was an eight-hour drive, a straight shot. The tank was full, the road mostly cleared from the storm that had dumped six feet of snow earlier that week. He paid attention to the signs warning him to watch out for deer crossing and boulders that might stumble to the road from the mountains of Pennsylvania. The Reverend was glad for the late hour and the sparsely populated highway.

■　■　■

The Reverend caught glimpses of the quarry when the car tumbled down the hill. Every so often, because his ears are well-trained to the noise of the creek that travels along his property, he hears the water moving underneath the quarry's icy surface, everything normal, as is, going about its day. He knows he must be perched near water's edge. He listens:

A young boy screams. The sound is faint—distant but present.

He remembers when those horrific screams came from Davis—an aftershock of his mother's death. Davis and Olivia without a mother. A Reverend without a wife. Davis, at five, practically a toddler, a rug rat, his sister already a woman. The first time Davis screamed—just hours after the funeral—Olivia woke, bounding from her bed, and ran to her brother's aid. It was she who stood beside him, momentarily unsure of what to do as she witnessed Davis twisting, turning, shrieking like a thing possessed. Senses gone. Limbs flying every which way. She turned on the bedside lamp, took a seat on the bed, and wrapped her arms around him.

The next morning the Reverend sat at the kitchen table, head aching in his hands, doing his best to listen.

"I stayed with him until his arms stopped moving, until he stopped kicking," Olivia said. She was pouring coffee into a travel mug, her suitcase by the door, her back turned to him. After she set the coffeepot down, she went to the refrigerator, looking for milk.

"You're going to need to watch him. He could hurt himself. He was asleep the whole time." Her voice was low and serious.

"Olivia?"

"What."

She stirred a packet of sugar into the mug and glanced at the Reverend when she tapped the spoon twice against the mug's brim. Her face didn't change—not a smile, nor a glimmer of softness. But she answered his unasked question. "I have to go. Exams."

He remembers the sound of her boots clicking across the hardwood floor as she walked from the kitchen through the living room, pulling her suitcase behind her. How much she looked like her mother—short, darker-skinned, but shapely, as she had been, with a head nearly shaved like hers. She stopped in the foyer and turned around, for a moment looking at him, eyes blinking.

"How could you not have heard him screaming like that?"

He closed the door behind her and slumped against it, his cheek sticking to the glass. Olivia had worn her mother's perfume.

■   ■   ■

First the diagnosis: stage IV lymphoma. Then the symptoms came. Night sweats, weight loss, fatigue so severe that his wife was often unable to pick up her child, to keep up with his endless five-year-old energy. Coughing turned to vomiting blood. They did their best to hide her sickness from Davis and Olivia, but in a matter of weeks she was hospitalized for good.

The Reverend didn't want to bring Davis to the hospital, didn't want him to see Adina like that, nothing more than skin and bones, cheeks sallow and sunken, tubes running in and out of her every which way. A five-year-old was too young to understand. But she repeatedly asked for her boy, and when it became clear that only hours remained, he sent Olivia home for her brother. He worried for them.

The house was nearly an hour-long drive from the hospital, and Olivia was upset, emotional, had walked out of the ICU wiping tears on her sleeve, refusing her father's offer of a handkerchief.

When she returned with Davis, he looked terrified as he slowly entered the room. He held part of his blanket up to his mouth, so long it would've dragged behind him, train-like, on the hospital floor had Olivia not been holding it up.

"Go on," the Reverend said.

Davis didn't move. The boy was going to have to toughen up. The Reverend picked him up and placed him in the bed alongside his mother.

"Sunny Boy," Adina said simply, her voice squeezing out the words. She put her arm around Davis. There was light in her eyes like the Reverend hadn't seen. He watched as Davis—on his knees, his feet curled underneath him, still in his yellow Keds—leaned closer to his mother, his brain trying to make sense of what he saw before him.

"Mommy, what's wrong?"

Adina pulled him as close as he was willing to be pulled, kissing him all over his face, his plump cheeks, his forehead still shiny from the olive oil they used to anoint him every morning, covering him in the Holy Spirit.

Mother and son needed privacy. The Reverend nodded at Olivia. "Let's take a walk."

They walked in silence. Father and daughter, first around the hospital, listening to the machines beeping, the murmuring voices of the doctors and nurses. They'd used those same hushed tones to talk about his wife, and, by extension, his family, their life, their children.

He led Olivia outside, where the warmth of spring was fading into the coolness of night. The wind had picked up, and the Reverend wished for a jacket. This walk was the closest his body had come to his daughter's in years. He wanted to grab her hand, but it was better not to push his luck.

Olivia looked at him as they passed a willow tree. "Are you ready?" she asked.

"No," he said.

"Sometimes you treat him as if you never wanted him."

"Olivia."

She didn't look away. "It's true."

They continued walking until it became too chilly to remain outdoors.

■   ■   ■

Night after night the Reverend and Adina had watched Davis sleep on his back as an infant in his crib, his little brown head dusted with loose dark curls, his chest bobbing up and down ever so slightly—often the only movement he made during slumber. Like a little old man already bored with the world. He was peaceful, quickly learning to sleep through the night.

When the Reverend and Olivia returned to the hospital room, Davis lay stretched in the bed by his mother's side, sleeping once more, his thumb in his mouth, his cheeks streaked with tears. Adina held him, from somewhere mustering the energy to stroke his forehead. She continued to kiss him every so often, even as the Reverend and Olivia walked in. She scrunched her face and brought a finger to her lips so they knew to keep quiet. Olivia settled into a chair and pulled a book out of her bag, but could not tear her eyes from her mother. The Reverend stood by Adina's side and moved to pull his sleeping son from her arms, but she shook her head and gestured for him to come close. He bent down, put his ear by her mouth, the palm of his hand atop hers. She could barely speak.

"Be different, John. He needs you to be different than you were with Olivia."

She kissed them both, first him, then Davis. Olivia rose from her chair and went to the side of the bed opposite her father. She placed one hand on her mother's shoulder and with the other she held Davis, stroking the inside of his palm, which was turned upward to the heavens while he slept, as though he had an offering.

Like that they remained: quiet, clinging to each other, praying that it might be enough.

■ ■ ■

His demons resurfaced.

The Reverend did his best to forget the bottle of bourbon beneath his bed. Three nights in a row he helped Davis move stuffed animals from the rocking chair to the double bed where the boy slept all by himself. He needed company, it seemed. There were giraffes, pigs, monkeys, and a cherished koala bear named Wally, into which his wife had recorded herself singing Davis's favorite song, "The Little Drummer Boy." All Davis had to do was squeeze the bear, hold it close, and his mother's voice rose, seemingly from nowhere. For three nights after the funeral the Reverend sat all night long watching his son sleep soundly, the same as he had always slept: flat on his back, his right cheek against the pillow and his right arm flung above him, bent at the elbow. Olivia had slept the same way until she turned thirteen. The Reverend enjoyed the nightly ritual of getting Davis ready for bed— helping him brush his teeth, setting out his pajamas, and watching him climb into bed and under the covers after plugging in his favorite night-light. It quieted the Reverend, shushed the constant traffic running through his head— visions of Adina, her full thighs, her sharp cheekbones, the three bangles she wore around her wrist. The way she always called him "my love," whispering it in his ear when he woke in the morning, and when she kissed him good night. The way she called Davis "Sunny Boy," because he had slipped out easy, like he was covered in Crisco, on the sunniest day of the year.

Helping that child into bed. Watching him fight to stay awake. Three nights the Reverend observed with care. He paid attention to the ways Davis shifted in his sleep—to the right, the left. If he curled himself into a ball or turned his body around, the tops of his feet searching for the coolest patch of pillow. He slept with his mouth slightly open, his pink lips, always wet like a puppy's nose, parted just enough to release a constant whisper. Nothing more than air passing through those lips, those lungs, that heart.

Everything was normal. Davis's screams from the night after the funeral seemed a fluke, a onetime thing. So for the next two nights the Reverend waited until Davis fell asleep, and then returned to his own bed, where sleep eluded him.

On the sixth night he poured a drink—nothing much, a nightcap. Enough to conjure Adina flitting around the room as she always had, a single lit bulb on her vanity framing her face in a soft yellow bloom as she readied herself for bed.

So many nights he'd watched her—lying on his back, feet crossed at the ankles, arms crossed behind his head, a Bible resting on his chest and his reading glasses slipping down his nose—as he danced in and out of sleep. That night it was a plastic cup that managed to maintain its balance, even as his chest slowly bobbed up and down with each slow, measured breath.

The next morning he woke, not remembering when, or how, he had fallen asleep. And he'd rolled over, the plastic cup crushed underneath him, the remaining drops of bourbon staining the sheets.

On the seventh night he woke, thinking he had heard the wind careening through the valley, skimming the creek, screaming with reckless abandon.

He stared at the emptied plastic cup, this time placed near the edge of the nightstand. It took seconds that felt much longer before he realized the awful sound was coming from the room across the hall where Davis slept.

The Reverend's vision blurred when he stood up. He ran through the room, across the hall, opening Davis's door so hard it smacked into the wall, its knob crashing through the drywall, chunks and dust splattering to the carpet.

There was nothing. No ghost in the closet. No monster under the bed. No intruder. Only Davis sitting upright, his little mouth stretched as wide as it would go, his body whipping around. Teardrops fell from blotchy eyes. The Reverend had never seen a body move like that—disjointed, uncoordinated, as though held together by nothing more than a piece of thread that might split at any moment.

The Reverend was bewildered until he remembered what Olivia had done. He grabbed each of Davis's toothpick legs with one hand and held them down. Then he mounted the bed and rested his left shin across his son's ankles. He needed both hands to trap Davis's arms. Palms open. Palms closed. Twice the boy slapped the Reverend before he caught both arms and brought them down against the bed, where he trapped Davis.

From a window, moonlight poured in across his son's face. Davis's skin was honey-golden in that light. As his body calmed, he opened his eyes. They were the color of amber, filled with panic and confusion—as though the Reverend, this dark-skinned man not far from elderly, was somehow unfamiliar, someone threatening.

The Reverend released him, leaned against the head-board, and motioned to his son, guiding him until the little one sat between his legs. Davis leaned back against his father's bare chest. The Reverend wrapped his arms around his son and began to sing into his ear, "Hush Little Baby." He felt his son relax into his body, heard his breath settle back into its normal rhythm. With one hand he wiped the boy's tears away when he finished the song. Davis turned around and saw the Reverend crying. Davis placed a hand on the Reverend's chest and pulled himself up until he brushed his lips against the Reverend's.

"No." The Reverend jerked away. "That was only for your mother to do."

The Reverend peeled Davis from him and stood away from the bed. "Go back to sleep, boy." He drew the curtain closed. "Under the covers. Now."

Davis slid under his comforter. He scrunched up his face, readying himself for tears once more.

"None of that," the Reverend ordered.

Davis pulled the comforter up to his chin. The Reverend backed out of the room.

"Good night," the Reverend told him, shutting the door.

He walked quietly to the bathroom. Moonlight peered through the window. He stood at the sink, turned on the faucet, and splashed his face with cold water. He studied what he saw before him, trying to see his face through his son's eyes: the thick-skinned wrinkles of his forehead. His wide-set nose and fat nostrils. The mole on his left cheek with the hairs growing out of it.

His wife had loved this face.

He turned the water off. He went back to Davis's room, pushed the door slightly open, and squinted in the dark until he could make out Davis's shape under the covers, clutching a stuffed animal against his scrawny chest, quivering.

Asking, quietly, for his mother.

■　■　■

"Sir, we're going to get you out of here."

The Reverend knows a certain type of man is prone to making promises he can't keep. The trooper will carefully remove his hand from the Reverend's shoulder and pull it back through the damaged car until he can use it freely. The Reverend, unable to move his neck, will hear his boots crunching against the hardened snow as he moves away from the vehicle.

"Don't leave me," he will say. But his voice will barely be audible. He will catch a few of the trooper's words as he speaks with the other men, arriving in quick, successive brushstrokes:

Assistance. Dangerous. Life.

Hurry.

Out of the corner of the Reverend's eye, he will see the trooper return and kneel beside him once more. The image will come, quick as lightning, of Davis on his knees on a white rug in an apartment facing a floor-to-ceiling window, mouth open.

"I have a son, too," the trooper will say while breathing hard. He will bend down, bracing himself against the snow. "How old is yours?"

"Twenty-five." The Reverend will see that Davis's eyes are closed, that his head tilts backward, that his right arm reaches around the front of his neck. Is he praying? Does he know?

"You don't look old enough to have a twenty-five-year-old son, sir." There will be surprise in the trooper's voice. The Reverend will try to smile. The only part of his body he will be able to feel is his face.

Of course. Davis prays not for his father hanging upside down in a white Toyota next to a quarry.

The trooper will continue. "Mine's a baby. Seven months."

The white rug is not a rug but a quilt on a bed. The arm reaching around Davis's neck is not his own but a stronger, paler arm. Their bodies move together, That Man and Davis's, and the Reverend sees how that man presses himself against his son, wraps himself around his son, uses his hands to own his son.

The Reverend will have never been so cold. He'll have things he'll want to tell this man, this young, gentle, kind-faced man who routinely holds a seven-month-old son in his large, pale hands. He'll want to tell him how surprising sons can be, how they never turn out the way you want them to, or the way you think they're going to. He'll want to warn him not to get too used to being a father; it's one of those things that just happens to you, and once it does, it becomes impossible to think of yourself as a person outside of father-hood. He'll want to tell him that moments will come when he will truly hate his child—never long-lasting moments, never yielding dangerous behavior—but they're real, and it's best to accept them, live in them, and let them pass. He'll want to tell him that, in fact, it's the moments when the love floods you, nearly erasing you, that you are most at risk of doing something you shouldn't do.

The Reverend will want to say these things but he will be too cold to move his lips, too cold to feel his tongue. He will close his eyes, hearing the panic in the trooper's voice as he says, "Stay with me, sir! Stay with me," because the other men are just beginning to work. He will try to listen, to tether his wandering mind, as the trooper continues to talk.

In time, voices. Movement. Rubber boots clomping through the snow with the strength of hooves. More men arriving, all of them doing their part. It must be bad. He will no longer be able to open his eyes, but he will know the pres-ence of the flashlights. From an emergency vehicle perched at the top of the quarry, a steady beam will shine upon him. The men will do their job. He will hear them. He will feel them as they tear apart the car, hope rising inside him. They will pull the Reverend free and he will tell himself, *I can survive this.*

I will *survive this.*

. . .

Someone will come.

The words repeat themselves for as long as possible in the Reverend's head, washing over him like a current over stones smoothed, sand densely packed.

Someone will find me.

MOOSEHIDE

Carleigh Baker

IT'S THE MIDDLE of the day—who cares when exactly—
gray on goddamn gray. According to the GPS, we just passed
the Arctic Circle. People get out their iPhones to take pictures of each other—Sean takes mine, since we're paddling
together—and when I smile for the camera I feel a little bit
happy. Or I tell myself I feel happy. Technically, this is an
accomplishment, paddling a million kilometers in the cold
past an arbitrary line on a map that raises eyebrows when
you mention it to your fellow urbanites.

Sean and I both have to reach as far as we can across the
canoe when he passes me the phone to get my approval of
the photo. The skin on his hands is cracked and scratchy;
not the accountant's hands he had two weeks ago. The gaunt
face glowing back at me from the iPhone screen looks pretty
happy. I've lost weight. I guess that will make me happy
when I get back to Vancouver and put on my skinny jeans.
When I only have to wear one layer at a time, and people can
see what I've become. For now, in all these layers, I'm a tiny
face popping out of the Michelin Man. I take Sean's picture

with the phone. He looks handsome. Of course there's no Wi-Fi, so I just save the photos. If you're in the Arctic and you can't Instagram it, does anybody care?

I'm tired.

Early in the trip, the river was all crusty whitewater. I was always paddling a canoe into a bunch of waves that looked like they were beating the shit out of one another. The water roared, and I could hear it all the time. I was excited by the noise at first, but I got used to it. In the evenings, it was a backing track for Sean's banjo serenades. The guides had glanced sideways at each other when he'd added the bulky case to the packing pile, but everyone is happy to listen to him pluck away most nights.

It's all couples on the trip: three couples and the guides, Jan and Eric—also a couple. At night, in addition to the sound of the river, I can hear people rolling around in their tents, groaning like whales. Sean and I tried to get busy the first night, but my back muscles felt like they'd been run through a food processor. Same thing the second night, and the Therm-a-Rest deflated, so I was being pounded onto the rocks. Ugh. Around day six, I pulled Sean into the trees away from everyone and down into a valley dotted with little white flowers. There was this spot with moss so thick that we had to climb up onto it. The whole thing was so badass; we weren't supposed to stray out of sight of the group, and we weren't supposed to go anywhere that might mess up the nature. The tundra is fragile, the guides told us. We were stomping around, ripping out chunks of moss, and when I pulled him down to me, the sanctity of nature was the furthest thing from my mind. But the cold rose up from the ground, deep and penetrating. Sean put his jacket underneath me. We kept as many layers on as we could, his hard dick poking out of wool long johns, my own base layer pulled just low enough to let him in. But we couldn't stop shivering. A hand job under the majestic northern sky just seemed sad, and besides, we'd forgotten to bring wet wipes.

"We'll get it," Sean said. He kissed me on the forehead.

"Yeah."

The other couples are from Toronto, a zillion times more urban than we are. I don't know why they don't seem to have any trouble getting it. From the sound of it, they're getting it constantly.

The river has slowed since we left Aberdeen Canyon; it's big and sluggish and muddy now. For the most part, the only sound comes from the nattering of our fellow travelers, and this happens only when we're rafting, the boats tied together. Sometimes the wings of birds make a *whoop whoop whoop* sound when we startle them into flight. The couples don't mingle much anymore, and I'm not sure if that's because we're comfortable with one another now or because we've given up.

When we pull off the river, the moosehide is just lying there. God. Big, inflated lungs lying next to it, jiggling like jello. Intestines, veiny gray tubes.

"Why is everything inflated?" I ask Sean.

"Botulism," somebody says.

"Don't poke a hole in them," somebody says, "or the worst smell will come out."

How bad, I wonder?

The worst.

Brown-winged birds of prey circle above us.

Everybody loves the hide, prodding and poking it with sticks. Stretching it out so they can see the full length of the inside, mucus membrane and pink blood, a skin cape cut ragged around the edges. I can't look at it. I don't see a dead moose, I see a live moose in the final moments of suffering before its life ends. That kind of empathy is stupid, I know. The moose is dead, and it's feeding someone.

Somebody's going to notice that I'm the only one not looking and ask me why I'm such a wuss. So I make a big show of looking at other things: tiny plants at the river's edge with ice globes surrounding the fruit, broken willow branches, rocks. Scarred rocks that look like patients in a hospital ward; what makes them look like that? I toss a few in the river. Each lands with a fat *plunk*.

Sean's talking to Eric about taking the moosehide with us, and I'm pissed at him for it. Surely bears would smell it and come looking for us, or lynx, or . . . whatever else is out here waiting to kill us. He wants to make something out of it. Whatever. I remember somebody in my Aboriginal Studies class saying that scraping a hide is much harder than it looks, even with expert hands, and we're no experts. We have no tools for this. I may be a mixed-blood—Sean and I are both Cree Métis—but we were also both raised white. All we know are white-people things. But I do know that a perfectly good moosehide shouldn't have been left here. Why did the hunters leave it? Skin it and leave it?

"I think it's female," somebody says, poking around the ass end, playing the expert.

"You're not supposed to kill females," somebody says.

"That's sexist," somebody says.

"The females make more moose, dumbass."

"Not without sperm they don't."

"Maybe she attacked them."

God. It's like reading the comments section on YouTube. I'm hungry.

Somebody passes around a snack, just a big block of cheese cut into a million pieces with a dirty Leatherman. It clogs and sticks in my throat. We got fun size Mars bars, too. Chocolate and cheese. I put the Mars bar in my PFD pocket. My fingers can barely get the zipper down. My fingers, dirty for days despite a river of hand sanitizer. Bloated, with pus around the nails, one finger swollen so big I can barely move it. Rub Polysporin in the cracks before bedtime and hope for the best. I can still paddle just fine. I may have lost weight, but my shoulders are strong now. I can feel the muscle through my merino-wool bottom layer, though I haven't seen much of my actual skin for fifteen days.

"Can you help me with my PFD?" Sean asks. He looks like a little boy when he says it, and for some reason I choke up a little. Get it together, lady.

"Sure," I say. Tug the zipper down hard, even though my fingers might break off.

"Do you want my Mars bar?" he asks.

"Don't drag that moosehide along with us," I say.

"I could make a drum from it."

I turn around so he doesn't see how hard I'm rolling my eyes. A drum. We're *accountants*.

Now it's pictures around the moose remnants, eight of us lined up like so many soldiers. Someone's found an antler, too. Not from the carcass; this one's older. And probably caribou, Eric tells us. People take turns with it, more photo opportunities.

Sean's arm around me, the other holding the antler up to my temple. We'll get back to Vancouver and show this photo to our friends, and they'll be jealous of us. I can't even count how many times people used the word *jealous*, like we were going on an all-expenses-paid five-star Mediterranean yacht cruise or something. You'd have to be a masochist to want to trade places with us right now. There's nothing easy about being out here, and there was nothing easy about getting here. Sean and I trained for months, saved for months. I guess it was good for us to have something to focus on. We barely fought at all. I'm not sure whether we picked the right kind of vacay. I'm not sure whether it's just the tour we chose, because I've never done anything like this before. But I definitely didn't expect things to be this hard. I pictured myself drinking wine and looking out at the river. I'd imagined calm, and a clearing-out of my mind that might make the future easier to see. Anyway. We're doing it now. We're committed.

Time to get back in the boats. It's much warmer when I'm paddling, tied into the spray skirt with my neoprene gloves on. Sean and I always paddle together now. Early in the trip when there was some pretense of friendship among travelers, people switched up paddlemates and made small talk, but not anymore. I don't really care. My friends back home told me this kind of trip forges lifelong connections, so maybe there's something wrong with me.

People take their last pokes at the moose bits. Somebody finally does poke a hole in the lung, and it deflates unceremoniously; no smell. One of the guides persuades Sean that bringing the pelt along is a stupid idea, but I'm still annoyed, so I'm not speaking to him. He points out the same shit we've seen for the last week: stunted trees, exfoliated hills, mud. I just paddle.

When it's finally time to find camp for the night, the atmosphere is thick, the river so still it looks like mercury.

"Taco Bar tomorrow," Eric says.

"Is that some kind of sick joke?" Sean asks. He gets grumpy when I give him the silent treatment.

Eric laughs. "Taco Bar is a checkpoint," he says. "If you need anything flown in or flown out, that's the spot."

"How 'bout some tacos," somebody says. "Hur hur hur."

"They'd be some pretty expensive tacos," Eric says. "Airlift costs about three grand."

"That's our way out," I say to Sean. So much for the silent treatment.

He snorts. "Kiss that ring good-bye, then."

I shrug, knowing it's going to piss him off. He looks at me and laughs. People say traveling together is a true test of a relationship. Those people are correct.

"Smoke," a voice bellows from a canoe behind me. "SMOKE."

I realize I've been looking right at the smoke for a few

minutes, but it hasn't registered. "Smoke," I say to Sean.

"No shit."

"Smoking Hill," Eric says. "Lightning hit a coal seam in the mountain. It's been burning ever since." This generates a lot of delighted conversation. In the absence of Internet access, I guess we're all pretty easily amused. "Let's stop here tonight," Eric says.

We begin the transition back to being land-dwelling mammals: pull the boats up, loosen the spray skirt laces, pull out the gear. Although everyone is tired, this is when we work together best, since the end goal of sleep is finally in sight. The mud is too thick to slog through with a heavy pack, so a line forms, and we pass everything along. Bag after bag: tents, cooking gear, food. Empty boats carried safely above the waterline. Sean and I set up the camp kitchen. I find rocks for a hearth while he collects firewood. Then he builds the fire while I sort through the food barrels for tonight's meal. When everyone else is done with their tasks, they'll all come and circle us like vultures.

"We could leave," Sean says.

"What?"

"We could." He blows into the fire, and sparks fly out. "We could split the three grand and get the fuck out of here."

The water is boiling. I measure out three cups of parboiled rice and dump it in. "Why?"

Sean snorts. "It was your idea."

"We might be waiting a while; I doubt there's a shuttle," I say, watching the rice come to a boil. Fire cooking is not what you'd call precise, but I'm getting better at it.

"I asked Eric," Sean says. "He could call on the satellite phone."

"We could." I think about what our friends would say. It would look like a failure. But they have no idea how hard every day has been. They probably wouldn't *say* much at all, but they would think I'd failed.

"I mean, this is our *vacation*," Sean says. "It's not supposed to be work."

"We could hit that spa in Whitehorse and get four-handed massages."

Sean laughs. "How about six-handed?"

"I like the way you think," I say. We kiss for the first time in a million years.

"Woo, get a room, you two," somebody calls. The vultures are descending.

"A room," Sean says. "We could get one. Think about it."

I do think about it. What heat would feel like. Electric light. Hot water on demand. Mealtime rolls into fire time; people roast marshmallows and laugh among themselves. In the distance, Smoking Hill is glowing a little and still sending a thin white plume up into the night sky. It's a long time before the sky gets dark, and usually by then the northern lights are out. Green streaks across a deep blue twilight. They were so exciting at first; now we just expect them. But tonight, the idea that this could technically be my last night out here has got me looking around again, noticing things.

"Meet you in the tent," Sean says, kissing my cheek.

"I'll be there in a bit," I say.

"Don't be too long; we've got stuff to discuss." He lopes off toward our coffin-sized tent. Handsome.

I leave my comrades at the campfire, but instead of going straight to the tent, I end up down at the edge of the river looking at the burning hill. Big moon. Me in the mud. It's so shitty out here. But still, technically, this is romance. It's hard to remember that, since we're always moving on this stupid river, or too exhausted to think. I stand still for a while. Try to imagine getting picked up by an airplane tomorrow. Removing all future responsibility from ourselves in one simple but expensive maneuver. Crawling into the plane and laughing together like Benjamin and Elaine on the bus at the end of *The Graduate*. Escape! Ha ha ha. Ha ha.

Ha.

Well.

What now?

SURRENDER

Hasanthika Sirisena

AS SUNIL STOOD in his backyard staring at the carcass of
the small unidentifiable animal—a cross between a rat and
a Chihuahua—he realized he was missing something important. Tall concrete walls protected his compound from
the surroundings, but every morning he still found empty
arrack bottles, plastic bags filled with rotten smelling mud,
decaying king coconut husks, and, now, a dead rodent.

Sunil tried to ask the man he'd hired to guard his compound if a storm had dropped these things. Sunil had heard
about such events: objects and animals caught in the eye of
the storm and dumped somewhere far from their origin.
The catcher stared at him, his broad face even more puckered and contorted than usual. Sunil used his best broken
Sinhala to explain again, but the man's eyes grew wider.
Finally, Sunil gave up.

Was it the monsoons that sent that stuff over the compound wall? Sunil demanded of his thirteen-year-old
daughter, Emily.

"Monsoon? Monsoon is months away." Emily replied with that look of scorn, far too common these days.

"Then what's doing that? Leaving those things there."

"Boys from the village. They come at dawn." Of course she was right. He'd seen the boys loitering on the beach, but had thought that they were only beachcombing.

"Why?"

"Because we have a swimming pool and they don't."

Sunil rose very early the next morning and waited near the wall. The first bottle came over, silhouetted against the rising sun. "Stop," Sunil cried out. Nothing happened for a few seconds, then he heard giggling. A boy called out something in Sinhala that Sunil did not understand but knew was a taunt. Sunil peered over the metal gate that separated his yard from the beach just in time to see five boys running across the sand.

■ ■ ■

Sunil was a thirty-five-year-old Sri Lankan–born American engineer. He had returned to the home country a year before to work for an American engineering firm based in the capital. So far, the one thing he loved about Sri Lanka was the house his company had placed him in. After he and Emily had spent eight months in a cramped company apartment in the middle of Colombo, they'd offered him this split-level outside a quiet fishing village a half hour from the capital. Located on a dirt road far from the village and close to the beach, with its air-conditioned office and private swimming pool, the house had felt a haven, the only haven he had in a country that seemed to assault him every day with things the meaning of which he could only barely comprehend. Then the boys started coming.

Sunil decided to ignore them, but they didn't go away. Instead, they became angrier. They stood on the beach each morning, demanding to use the pool. They taunted the catcher, an elderly Tamil man Sunil had hired to clean the grounds and guard the compound gate. The catcher left soon after. The Scotsman who owned the house next to his told Sunil to go to the station house. The chief inspector was a capable man.

Sunil did as the Scotsman suggested. The chief inspector barely acknowledged Sunil as long as he thought Sunil was Sri Lankan, but when Sunil explained he was a supervisor at a foreign engineering firm, the inspector's demeanor changed. Still, nothing was done, and when Sunil returned a week later, the chief inspector frowned. "What to do? This is the way here. They will get bored and go away, sooner or later."

It was a passing conversation that solved the problem. Sunil had complained about what was happening to the cook, Amara, for no other reason than that he had no one else to talk to. Amara had listened carefully and solemnly and had not said a word when Sunil finished. Sunil was sure that once again he had not made himself clear.

Early the next morning, Sunil woke to see Amara standing in his backyard. As the first arrack bottle went sailing through the air, Amara made her way to the back gate and called to the boys. She whispered something to them, and they listened. Whatever Amara said worked. After that, the boys did not come back.

■ ■ ■

Sunil's parents had immigrated to a small town in North Carolina when he was only four. When Sunil was old enough to make such choices, he'd thrown himself into fitting in. For most of his life, he'd referred to himself as a Southerner. He spoke in "y'alls" and qualified every other word with "real": "Y'all have a real good day now." Growing up, he'd listened to Cheap Trick, AC/DC, and Led Zeppelin and hid his parents' baila records. His parents had struggled when they arrived in the States and had put all their energy into keeping the family from poverty; they threw what little they had into giving Sunil the chance to become a good American. They never visited the home country, so he never felt any strong ties.

Two years ago, his parents decided to sell the family business. They packed up their entire life and retired to Boca Raton. The moment they did, Sunil realized he did not have a single connection to the small town in which he'd spent his childhood and young adulthood. He had no friends left there. He had no deep attachment to or interest in Southern history and culture. Maybe it wouldn't have mattered if he wasn't already divorced, if he and Emily hadn't spent their lives moving from one city to the next because of his work. Sunil felt suddenly rootless, bereft. When the position at the engineering firm came along, it seemed a sign: the homeland calling Sunil back, providing an answer to his loss. It would be an adventure for Sunil and his daughter, an opportunity for them both to discover a part of themselves.

But things hadn't quite worked out the way Sunil expected. Since arriving, he'd become isolated in a way he'd never predicted. Sunil's coworkers were mostly Europeans or Sri Lankans. Even if they had shared a culture, Sunil felt as their boss a distance that precluded friendship. The Sri

Lankans he met outside of work thought him odd; maybe if he hadn't looked like them they would have tolerated the difference. Instead, there was a period of discomfited friendship before they'd drop away. He was close only to Sheila, the other American working at his company. He'd started seeing her in part because she reminded him of North Carolina.

Sunil's daughter, on the other hand, woke up one morning, a few months after arriving, able to speak Sinhala fluently. Sunil still tripped over words, so it was Emily who negotiated for him at the kadés and the fishermen's market. Emily explained things to Sunil about the country and its culture. She coached him about the mores and values. He appreciated Emily's intelligence and her willingness to help him, but at times it seemed to him that the country had grossly upended his role in Emily's life. He was supposed to be the one who cared for her, protected her, sheltered her. Now it was the other way around. She was the parent and he was her child.

■　■　■

After six months of dating, Sheila had explained to Sunil over dinner that he was a nice guy but there was something incomplete. Incomplete? Just tell him what, and he'd do whatever she wanted. He'd bring her flowers. He'd take her out for more romantic dinners. Maybe they could take a vacation together? Sheila shook her head slowly. There wasn't something incomplete about their relationship, she elaborated. There was something incomplete about *Sunil himself.*

Sheila's words stung, and Sunil brooded over them for days. Truth was, it wasn't the first time a woman had said something like that to him. Hadn't Emily's mother insinuated something similar just before she left? After the pain of the breakup eased a little, it occurred to Sunil maybe it wasn't completely his fault. Maybe he'd been dating the wrong women. Maybe he should try to date someone more like himself. Maybe, if he was going to return, then he should return as completely as he could.

Sunil had recognized early that Amara, the cook, was special. She was open and charming; there was a genuine sweetness in the way she smiled and laughed. She was also smoking hot. In the mornings, Sunil would watch from the upstairs window as she walked down the dirt road leading to the house. The men, the women, even the cows ambling among the piles of roadside garbage, stepped into the drainage ditch to let her pass. Sunil observed on more than one occasion the Scotsman next door watching Amara over the compound wall. One time, Sunil stepped into the yard to see his neighbor seated on the balcony, binoculars in hand, watching Amara as she hung the laundry to dry. When the Scotsman realized Sunil had seen him, he trained his binoculars at some distant seabirds.

Recently, Amara had started taking classes to improve her English. She'd asked Sunil if she could practice by talking to him. She began by telling him she had two sons, a six-year-old and a twelve-year-old. The reason she was learning English was so that she could get a job in Jordan. Her husband was already living there—had left five years ago—and was working as a driver for a wealthy family. Her husband had learned English in school, but she needed to make her English better if she wanted to work outside the country. Sunil was grateful for the conversations. And why not? Amara needed someone to help her with her English. He needed someone to teach him about the country so he wouldn't have to rely so much on Emily.

Amara became more flirtatious. She giggled when Sunil spoke to her, and she stood closer to him. One day he reached out and touched her gently on the arm. She shivered.

A few days later, Amara told him that her cousin had given her an old tape recorder. He'd told her to listen to music—American and British music. "Learn from book not good." She tapped her ear. "Music fun and give how real people talk." Her cousin had given her old tapes he'd kept since he was a teenager. She listened to the tapes in the evening after she returned home from Sunil's. Her eldest son helped her with the lyrics. He was learning English at school.

One day Sunil asked her what American music she liked.

"Eagles. Chick-a-go. Michael Jackson. Cheap Trick."

Sunil perked up. "Cheap Trick? I listened to Cheap Trick growing up."

"You learn good English from Cheap Trick, no?"

"No, not really. I mean, I knew English before I started listening." He drew closer to her. "But I love Cheap Trick. What's your favorite album?"

"Album?" Amara enunciated carefully.

"Song? What's your favorite song?" Sunil waved his hands about but wasn't sure how to mime "Cheap Trick." "Fav-o-rite song by Cheap Trick."

Amara nodded that she understood. "I want you to want me." She said the words clearly and precisely, looking straight at Sunil. Amara smiled coyly. "I beg you to beg me," she continued.

He coughed, hoping to hide that he'd forgotten to breathe. "Yeah, good song."

"What is your favorite song?"

Sunil knew he should stop, but the answer came to him naturally, without much thought. "Surrender."

Amara stared at him blankly, so Sunil began to sing. "*Mommy's all right / Daddy's all right / They just seem a little weird / Surrender—*"

She giggled. "*Surrender*," she sang.

"*But don't give yourself away.*" They sang in chorus. Or at least Amara sang something that sounded like that. Sunil couldn't really be sure.

■ ■ ■

Sunil's encounter with Amara was easy to arrange. Sunil told Emily that he needed the afternoon to catch up on some reading. He found Amara in the kitchen filling pastry dough with ground meat. She didn't seem surprised to see Sunil, and she didn't seem at all curious when he stood in the doorway of the kitchen watching her. He finally worked up the nerve to ask her to make a pot of tea and went to sit on the patio.

Amara brought out the tea on a serving tray and placed it on the table in front of him. When she leaned forward to nudge the sugar bowl closer, her hand grazed his knee.

He didn't know how exactly they made it to his bedroom. Amara led and he followed mutely behind. Later, when he replayed the moment, he could not remember moving, placing one foot in front of the other. Upstairs, she sat on the edge of the bed and looked up at him.

"What about your husband?" he whispered. As soon as it came out of his mouth, he wanted to kick himself.

But Amara remained unruffled. "In Kandy, in the time before—"

"Old days," Sunil offered helpfully.

"Yes, in the old days. The woman run house. She can choose and have many husbands."

"A woman could choose to marry multiple men?"

Amara nodded. "She could choose one brother. Then choose the other. When she with one brother, she hang shirt belong to him in door."

Sunil laughed. "Like this?" He took off his shirt and walked out onto the sun deck. He tied it to the railing. The fabric billowed and fluttered in the breeze. When he turned to go back in, he noticed the Scotsman on the balcony, watching a pair of terns flying in the distance. He suppressed the urge to call and wave.

Amara was still giggling when Sunil returned. She unfastened the hooks and eyes that held the front of her blouse together. When she reached the bottom one, she stopped. "Mahattaya . . ." she began.

"Sunil, please call me Sunil."

"I bring my sons to pool?" She pointed outside.

Sunil's stomach dropped. Good God, why hadn't he thought of that sooner. Something so simple like letting her sons use the pool. "Sure," he stammered. "That won't be a problem."

She undid the last fastener and removed her blouse. She pulled off the skirt and then her bra. She lay back on Sunil's bed. She'd let down her hair for the first time since he'd known her; the tendrils formed black curlicues along the surface of Sunil's pillow. He lay down next to her and traced the silky outline of one.

Later, he told Amara, though he was not sure how much she understood, something he had not told anyone—not Sheila, not Emily. He had family to the east, near Trincomalee. He'd been to visit only once. Up until he reached the border of the war zone, he was surrounded by the lush, tropical landscape he'd grown to expect. Then suddenly nothing. No animals. No houses. Just bleached and barren land. They passed men on bikes with AK-47s slung over their shoulders, and army convoys. When he came to the shack where his aunt lived, an old woman ran out and pulled him into the house. According to Sunil's mother, her sister was in her late forties but this woman looked, with her gray hair and worn skin, nearly eighty. It took him several minutes to realize this was his aunt, his mother's younger sister. The house she lived in had no doors, no glass in the windows. There was only an ancient electric range in the back and a small radio/television balanced on a crate. The pair muddled through a brief conversation. Finally, Sunil promised to return, and bring Emily with him. He hadn't yet. He sent his aunt money every week, but every time he considered a second visit, he told himself it was too dangerous because of the war. The truth was he could not face his aunt again: her poverty, the enormity of her loss.

As Sunil finished his story, he realized Amara had fallen asleep. Gravity had flattened her breasts to reveal the skin along her breastbone, not brown like the rest of her but a creamy yellow. The base of her stomach sloped into a nest of coarse thatched hair that extended down the insides of her thighs. Sunil nudged Amara awake and explained that Emily would be home soon. Amara dressed quickly without any mention of what had just happened between them. Their day ended as it always did with an exchange of wages, a list of items that needed to be bought at the market, and a polite good-bye.

■ ■ ■

"Dad, why is your shirt tied to the deck rail?"

Emily was standing, hands on hips, at the edge of the swimming pool. She was peering up at his bedroom.

Sunil nearly dropped his beer bottle. "I was drying it," he stammered.

"Why didn't you hang it on the clothesline?"

"I was in a hurry." Sunil took a swig of his beer.

Emily considered this response for a moment and then tucked her long brown hair under her swimming cap. She dove into the pool.

Sunil crouched at the edge. He watched as his daughter did backflips underwater. It still took his breath away to watch this glorious creature that he had somehow created. He was only a baby when she was born—though he had thought at the time he was mature beyond his years and perfectly capable of raising a child. Now he wanted to apologize again and again for all the mistakes he'd made. Emily made his life more real. At twenty-two, twenty-eight, thirty, his friends were going to bars, picking up women, and then complaining to Sunil that their lives were shallow. Not Sunil. He had to take Emily to school, help her with her homework, make sure she was clothed, fed, bathed. He'd nursed her when she was sick. They'd grown up together.

But she was also, especially in the past few years, an alien. He'd expected his child to be an extension of him—the better part. She would be the blank slate on which he'd write the things he'd learned about life, a means for correcting all the mistakes. Instead, she seemed to contain a whole other world, replete with foreign signs and cues, and someone had forgotten to provide Sunil with the guidebook.

Emily swam over and propped her arms on the side of the pool. "What?" she demanded.

The water gave her skin a fine sheen. Even though she still had the unformed features and ungainliness of a thirteen-year-old, he knew she was going to be a stunning woman: one more thing that would pull her away from him.

"I'm thinking of letting Amara's sons use the pool. Once. Maybe twice."

Emily scrunched her eyebrows together and puckered her lips. "You can't let her use the pool. It's just not done."

"What does that mean?"

"Servants have their place. And we have ours. If you're not careful, the servants will manipulate you."

Sunil clenched his jaw. Why was it so hard to get her to listen to him? "She's not a servant," Sunil insisted. "And this is my house. If I want Amara to use the pool, then she can. Because I'm the adult and I say so."

Emily smiled slyly. "I don't know, Dad. This may be your house, and you may be an adult, but this isn't *your* country. There are ways that things are done here and the truth is you don't always know what they are." He blinked at her. "You should listen to me," she added, "like you usually do."

She kicked off from the side of the pool and backstroked away. Sunil stood up. Just as he reached the house, she called. "I think your shirt's dry."

Sunil flinched but kept moving.

■ ■ ■

When Sunil went to sleep that night, he could still smell Amara on his sheets. He reveled in the scent and imagined her body. Even without language, they'd connected. He couldn't explain how or why, but she was not a stranger. He imagined continuing the affair—quietly, of course. Still, the next day when he saw her approaching the house, Sunil fought the urge to sneak away. Amara smiled shyly when she saw him. "Sir, I bring sons to pool tomorrow."

Sunil thought of Emily. Just to make things easier, he should probably arrange this on a day his daughter wouldn't be around. "How about we make it another day?"

Amara looked dismayed.

"The day after tomorrow." Sunil offered quickly.

"But that is—"

"A school day, I know. But Emily stays for tutoring. I'll come back from work early."

Amara hesitated. When she spoke, her voice was surprisingly firm. "Sir, you not be here."

"Why not?"

"Four months we no come to pool. Now you tell come. Older boy see you and understand too much. I tell him you and Emily go away. You leave gate open. We sneak in."

Sunil wanted to protest, but he couldn't deny a sense of relief at not having to face her sons.

At work, away from the house and Emily, Sunil dwelled on Amara. With his staff popping in and out of the office, with Sheila e-mailing details about a new obstacle to the project, his time with Amara felt an idyll. He called his secretary into his office.

"I need to find a tape."

She looked confused. "There is sticking tape in your desk drawer."

"No, a music tape. An album. You know, songs."

The secretary scowled. "A music tape? We are a third-world country, but we are not that backward. CDs and DVDs now, sir."

"I need a tape of an album. *Cheap Trick at Budokan*. It's a concert album."

The secretary began to protest.

"eBay it," demanded Sunil. "Buy the CD and tape it. Just get me the tape."

Sunil's secretary closed the door behind her.

That evening at home, Emily was going on about some trip she wanted to take the day after next, but Sunil was lost in his dream of presenting Amara with one of the best concert albums ever made. Of course, she wouldn't really be able to appreciate it, but she could listen to it and think of him. It was innocuous. Something she needn't be embarrassed to play around her kids. Emily prodded him, asking his approval to do something. Sunil just nodded.

The next day Sheila sent several e-mails with the heading "Reminder." He opened none of them. When Sheila was feeling unsure about her effectiveness, she tended to send a rush of urgent e-mails. All of them could be ignored.

The day Amara was supposed to bring her boys, Sunil made sure to see his daughter off. Emily gave him a quick peck on the cheek and got into her friend Harishini's car. For a moment he wondered when Harishini's driver had started picking Emily up for school. But he didn't think any more about it. Work was especially quiet. It wasn't until late after lunch that Sunil realized he hadn't seen any of his Sri Lankan employees: not Ranil, or Harry, or Sujeeva, or Bavan. When Sheila came into his office, he asked where everybody was.

"Didn't you get any of my e-mails?" Sheila demanded. "Today is the new moon."

He stared at her blankly.

"It's poya. A government holiday. Can you really be so out of it?" She shook her head. "This happens every month, Sunil. And you're a Buddhist. How can you not know about your own religious holidays?"

Sunil sat up in his seat. "School's out today, isn't it?" But he already knew the answer. Sunil made some excuse about having to go home for some papers. He picked up his briefcase and ran out the door.

During the ride home, Sunil replayed his conversation with Emily the night before last. Hadn't she said she was going on a trip? She'd be gone all day, no doubt. There was nothing to be worried about.

When he reached his house, two boys, soggy swim trunks clinging to their bony legs, were standing in the doorway. Sunil tried to smile at them, but the oldest one glowered and shielded the younger brother with his body.

Emily was seated inside. Amara stood in the shadows.

"Guess what I caught them doing?" Emily demanded.

Sunil glanced at Amara. He said her name softly.

"They were in the swimming pool, Dad!"

He took a deep breath. "I let them, honey. I told Amara she could."

Emily's face contorted with anger. "Why?" she cried. "I told you not to." She stamped her foot. Amara's son was peering through the gap in the door, following everything that was being said. Emily turned and spoke in Sinhala to Amara. Sunil did not understand but somehow he knew she was firing her. Amara blanched.

"Give us a few days, Amara," Sunil said softly. "Think of it as a temporary suspension. Come back in a week, when everything has calmed down."

Emily sat in her chair, her body contracted with rage. Amara shooed her boys out the compound gate. After Amara was gone, Emily sat fuming. "How could you, Dad? How could you humiliate me like that?"

"Humiliate you? How did I humiliate you?"

"You went against me. You let them use the pool! I told you not to."

"And I told you this is my house."

Emily stamped her foot. "But you wouldn't even know what to do with it if it wasn't for me." She hiccupped loudly and then burst into tears. "You told her to come back," she wailed. "Why?"

When Sunil didn't respond, Emily covered her face with her hands and ran into her room.

■ ■ ■

For the next week, Sunil and Emily avoided each other. Avoided speaking. Avoided contact. Sunil had brooded, hurt and angered by Emily's callousness. Then he received a call from the village police. The constable informed him that his daughter was with the chief inspector at the station house and that he should come. The line went dead before Sunil could ask any questions. He ran into Sheila as he was leaving work. She insisted on accompanying him.

At the station house, the constable, a woman, led Sunil

through the station house to the chief inspector's office. As they walked, the constable informed Sunil that his house had been attacked when Emily was inside. Some boys from the village had scaled the compound wall. Emily had hidden under a computer table in the home office while they'd ransacked the rooms. Eventually she'd come out and confronted them. When they saw her, the boys had run off. She'd gone to the neighbor's house for help.

Sunil barely listened to the story. He only wanted to know if Emily had been hurt in any way. No, Emily was not hurt, the constable reported, but she was in shock. She had identified one of the vandals, the leader, as the son of Sunil's cook. Sunil stopped in mid-stride. The constable turned her dark, slanted eyes on him. "Sir, do not be upset. The chief inspector has arrested him. The cook is with the inspector now."

Amara and Emily sat on either side of the inspector's office. The chief inspector presided over the scene from behind an ancient teakwood desk. Emily was huddled, despite the heat, her face stained with grime and tears. Sheila ran to her and took her into her arms. Amara sat quietly. She did not acknowledge Sunil.

"You have Amara's son in custody?" asked Sunil. The chief inspector nodded. Sunil turned to Emily. "You're okay, baby? You weren't hurt?"

His daughter smiled bravely as Sheila rubbed her shoulders. "I'm okay, Dad. But they messed up the house."

The room was badly lit; a cloud of clay dust hung heavy in the air. Sunil had to squint to see. "What will happen?" he asked.

"Her son"—the inspector gestured in Amara's direction—"will go before the magistrate. In his favor, he didn't know your daughter was there. He seems sorry. Still, there must be punishment." Amara tried to speak, but the inspector put up a hand to stop her.

"The boy's only twelve," Sunil began. "That's pretty young. And if he's sorry?" Amara and Emily were there only because of him. He had to do something. "We don't want more people to get hurt. We could"—he hesitated—"we could drop the charges. Couldn't we? I'm sure Amara—I mean, our cook—will punish her son."

Sheila frowned. Emily's body tensed. The inspector smiled grimly. "This is not some American police show, sir. This is not the *NYPD Blues*. We cannot just drop charges against boys, even twelve-year-old boys, who attack foreigners. Imagine what your firm will say. Imagine what your Scottish neighbor will say if we let this boy loose without punishment. The uproar will come down on my head."

"But you don't get it," Sunil sputtered.

The inspector thrust his face toward Sunil. "What, sir, do I not get?"

It came then: the words of Sunil's nearly full confession. He explained how, because he liked Amara—even cared deeply for her—he'd promised her and her kids they could use the pool. He had also, in a way, reneged. It was obvious how anyone, especially a little boy, would be angry about that. Sunil was new to the country and didn't know the way things worked. He'd made some mistakes that he didn't want to go into. Anyone could easily see everything was his fault. He was the only one to blame.

As he spoke, Sunil knew his admission was not having the intended effect. Before Amara and the boys, maybe even before he came to Sri Lanka, there had existed a point when his words had carried import, had had weight and significance, but Sunil couldn't remember now when or where that point was. How, he wondered, had he become so lost?

The chief inspector listened with the tips of his fingers pressed together as if in prayer. After Sunil had finished, the inspector was quiet for a beat. When he spoke, he pronounced each word carefully, as if he were addressing a small, especially dim child. "There is only so long," the inspector intoned, "that a man can pretend to be a fool before he really becomes one. No?"

Sheila had left Emily's side and stood now beside Sunil. She considered Amara and then Sunil, a woman doing a complicated calculation. She placed a hand on Sunil's shoulder and whispered, "Take your daughter home." When he did nothing, she said firmly. "For God's sake, let it go."

■ ■ ■

As he entered his office the next day, Sunil's secretary handed him a package. "What's this?" he asked.

"That tape you wanted, sir. *Cheap Trick at Budokan*. I found it on eBay like you asked. I am very sorry, sir, it took so many days to come."

Sunil unwrapped the package and took out the tape. The cover was tattered; the label had long ago worn away. He wondered if it was even listenable. He held it in his hands, wound and unwound the strip of shiny brown plastic. Sunil considered keeping it, stashing the tape in his desk. But what was the point? He ran his finger one more time across the cassette before chucking it, brown paper wrapping and all, into the trash.

Reading List of Contemporary Works by Women, Nonbinary, and Transgender Writers of Color/Indigenous Writers

This list is in no way comprehensive. The hope is that it serves as a helpful guide to seeking out various books by writers of color. There are many more works to look forward to (and invest in) that are not included here or are yet to be published. Thank you to those who offered additional title suggestions, as well as to those who continue with the work of collating lists of books by Black, Indigenous, and PoC (BIPOC) artists. These resources helped to make this section as reflective as possible. Additionally, many thanks to my friend Maya Davis, who suggested this list.

Novels and Graphic Novels

Leila Abdelrazaq, *Baddawi*

Susan Abulhawa, *Mornings in Jenin*

Chimamanda Ngozi Adichie, *Half of a Yellow Sun*

Dylan Allen, *Rise*

Stephanie Allen, *Tonic and Balm*

Isabel Allende, *The House of the Spirits*

Julia Alvarez, *In the Time of the Butterflies*

Hala Alyan, *Salt Houses*

Ryka Aoki, *He Mele a Hilo*

Gina Apostol, *Gun Dealers' Daughter*

Nathacha Appanah, *The Last Brother*

Hannah Lillith Assadi, *Sonora*

Sandra Rodriguez Barron, *Stay with Me*

Brit Bennett, *The Mothers*

Champa Bilwakesh, *Desire of the Moth*

Nicole Blades, *The Thunder Beneath Us*

Paulette Boudreaux, *Mulberry*

Oyinkan Braithwaite, *My Sister, the Serial Killer*

Nana Ekua Brew-Hammond, *Powder Necklace*

Octavia E. Butler, *Lilith's Brood*

Zoey Castile, *Stripped*

Nidhi Chanani, *Pashmina*

Jade Chang, *The Wangs vs. the World*

Janie Chang, *Dragon Springs Road*

Lan Samantha Chang, *Inheritance*

Ching-In Chen, *recombinant*

Kirstin Chen, *Bury What We Cannot Take*

Wai Chim, *Freedom Swimmer*

Zen Cho, *Sorcerer to the Crown*

Andie J. Christopher, *Stroke of Midnight*

Pearl Cleage, *Seen It All and Done the Rest*

Zinzi Clemmons, *What We Lose*

Michelle Cliff, *Abeng*

Camille Collins, *The Exene Chronicles*

Maryse Condé, *I, Tituba, Black Witch of Salem*

Ingrid Rojas Contreras, *Fruit of the Drunken Tree*

Kia Corthron, *The Castle Cross the Magnet Carter*

Naima Coster, *Halsey Street*

Patty Yumi Cottrell, *Sorry to Disrupt the Peace*

Leesa Cross-Smith, *Whiskey & Ribbons*

Jennine Capó Crucet, *Make Your Home among Strangers*

Angie Cruz, *Soledad*

Tsitsi Dangarembga, *This Mournable Body*

Edwidge Danticat, *Claire of the Sea Light*

Alexis Daria, *Take the Lead*

Jasmin Darznik, *Song of a Captive Bird*

Bridgett M. Davis, *Into the Go-Slow*

Aliette de Bodard, *The House of Shattered Wings*

Rios de la Luz, *Itzá*

Aya de León, *The Boss*

Ella Cara Deloria, *Waterlily*

Nicole Dennis-Benn, *Here Comes the Sun*

Carolina De Robertis, *Perla*

Margaret Dilloway, *How to Be an American Housewife*

Négar Djavadi, *Disoriental*

Farzana Doctor, *All Inclusive*

Tananarive Due, *My Soul to Keep*

Jenny Kay Dupuis, Kathy Kacer, and Gillian Newland,
   I Am Not a Number

Heidi W. Durrow, *The Girl Who Fell from the Sky*

Anjali Mitter Duva, *Faint Promise of Rain*

Akwaeke Emezi, *Freshwater*

Patricia Engel, *The Veins of the Ocean*

Louise Erdrich, *The Round House*

Ro Esterhazy, *Queen of Corona*

Angela Flournoy, *The Turner House*

Aminatta Forna, *Happiness*

Lauren Francis-Sharma, *'Til the Well Runs Dry*

Tee Franklin, Jenn St-Onge, and Joy San, *Bingo Love*

Savannah J. Frierson, *Being Plumville*

Kim Fu, *The Lost Girls of Camp Forevermore*

Diana Gabaldon, the Outlander series

Aja Gabel, *The Ensemble*

M. Evelina Galang, *Angel de la Luna and the 5th Glorious
   Mystery*

V. V. Ganeshananthan, *Love Marriage*

Cristina García, *Dreaming in Cuban*

Vanessa Garcia, *White Light*

Hiromi Goto, *Chorus of Mushrooms*

Kaitlyn Greenidge, *We Love You, Charlie Freeman*

Jasmine Guillory, *The Wedding Date*

Yaa Gyasi, *Homegoing*

Jessica Hagedorn, *Dogeaters*

Nafisa Haji, *The Sweetness of Tears*

Janet Campbell Hale, *The Jailing of Cecelia Capture*

Gail Vida Hamburg, *Liberty Landing*

Jimin Han, *A Small Revolution*

Anita Heiss, *Tiddas*

Cristina Henríquez, *The Book of Unknown Americans*

Linda Hogan, *People of the Whale*

Jasmine Hong, *The Witch Stone*

Nalo Hopkinson, *Sister Mine*

Vanessa Hua, *A River of Stars*

Tanwi Nandini Islam, *Bright Lines*

Naomi Jackson, *The Star Side of Bird Hill*

Mira Jacob, *The Sleepwalker's Guide to Dancing*

S. Jae-Jones, *Wintersong*

Randa Jarrar, *A Map of Home*

N. K. Jemisin, the Broken Earth series

Gish Jen, *Typical American*

Stephanie Jimenez, *They Could Have Named Her Anything*

Tayari Jones, *Leaving Atlanta*

Soniah Kamal, *An Isolated Incident*

Han Kang, *The Vegetarian*

Kirsten Imani Kasai, *The House of Erzulie*

Rosalie Morales Kearns, *Kingdom of Women*

Porochista Khakpour, *Sons and Other Flammable Objects*

Crystal Hana Kim, *If You Leave Me*

Lisa Ko, *The Leavers*

Joy Kogawa, *The Rain Ascends*

R. O. Kwon, *The Incendiaries*

Bunmi Laditan, *Confessions of a Domestic Failure*

Larissa Lai, *Salt Fish Girl*

Yi Shun Lai, *Not a Self-Help Book: The Misadventures of Marty Wu*

Ana-Maurine Lara, *Erzulie's Skirt*

J. S. Lee, *Keurium*

Marie Myung-Ok Lee, *Somebody's Daughter*

Min Jin Lee, *Pachinko*

Mira T. Lee, *Everything Here Is Beautiful*

Carrianne Leung, *That Time I Loved You*

Lillian Li, *Number One Chinese Restaurant*

Dahlma Llanos-Figueroa, *Daughters of the Stone*

Inverna Lockpez, Dean Haspiel, and José Villarrubia, *Cuba: My Revolution*

Nilah Magruder, *M. F. K.*

Sujata Massey, *The Widows of Malabar Hill*

Bernice L. McFadden, *The Book of Harlan*

Terry McMillan, *How Stella Got Her Groove Back*

Harper Miller, *The Sweetest Taboo: An Unconventional Romance*

Mitzi Miller and Denene Millner, *Hotlanta*

Toni Morrison, *God Help the Child*

Bethany C. Morrow, *MEM*

Nayomi Munaweera, *What Lies Between Us*

Sayaka Murata, *Convenience Store Woman*

Celeste Ng, *Everything I Never Told You*

Fae Myenne Ng, *Bone*

Bich Minh Nguyen, *Pioneer Girl*

Sigrid Nunez, *The Last of Her Kind*

Brooke C. Obie, *Book of Addis: Cradled Embers*

Trifonia Melibea Obono, *La Bastarda*

Nnedi Okorafor, *Akata Witch*

Chinelo Okparanta, *Under the Udala Trees*

Priscilla Oliveras, *His Perfect Partner*

Azareen Van der Vliet Oloomi, *Call Me Zebra*

Tracy O'Neill, *The Hopeful*

Ruth Ozeki, *A Tale for the Time Being*

Melinda Palacio, *Ocotillo Dreams*

Madhuri Pavamani, the Keeper series

L. Penelope, *Song of Blood & Stone*

Hoa Pham, *Wave*

Caridad Pineiro, *What Happens in Summer*

Emily Raboteau, *The Professor's Daughter*

Marcie R. Rendon, *Murder on the Red River*

Laura Restrepo, *Delirium*

Melissa Rivero, *The Affairs of the Falcons*

Rebecca Roanhorse, *Trail of Lightning*

Eden Robinson, *Son of a Trickster*

Nelly Rosario, *Song of the Water Saints*

Lydia San Andres, *The Infamous Miss Rodriguez*

Cristina Sánchez-Andrade, *The Winterlings*

Chaitali Sen, *The Pathless Sky*

Danzy Senna, *New People*

Kamila Shamsie, *Home Fire*

Jade Sharma, *Problems*

Nisi Shawl, *Everfair*

Jude Sierra, *A Tiny Piece of Something Greater*

Leslie Marmon Silko, *Ceremony*

S. J. Sindu, *Marriage of a Thousand Lies*

Monique Gray Smith, *Tilly: A Story of Hope and Resilience*

Zadie Smith, *On Beauty*

Marivi Soliven, *The Mango Bride*

Rivers Solomon, *An Unkindness of Ghosts*

Mia Sosa, *Acting on Impulse*

Martha Southgate, *The Taste of Salt*

Arigon Starr, *Tales of the Mighty Code Talkers*

Jen Storm, Scott B. Henderson, and Donovan Yaciuk, *Fire Starters*

Natalia Sylvester, *Everyone Knows You Go Home*

Nafkote Tamirat, *The Parking Lot Attendant*

Amy Tan, *The Joy Luck Club*

Cheryl Lu-Lien Tan, *Sarong Party Girls*

Lucy Tan, *What We Were Promised*

Whit Taylor, *Ghost Stories*

Madeleine Thien, *Do Not Say We Have Nothing*

Monique Truong, *Bitter in the Mouth*

Addie Tsai, *Dear Twin*

Jennifer Tseng, *Mayumi and the Sea of Happiness*

Thrity Umrigar, *The Secrets Between Us*

Ellen van Neerven, *Heat and Light*

Piper Vaughn, *Bookmarked*

Sabrina Vourvoulias, *Ink*

Alice Walker, *Possessing the Secret of Joy*

Esmé Weijun Wang, *The Border of Paradise*

Weike Wang, *Chemistry*

Jesmyn Ward, *Salvage the Bones*

Stephanie Powell Watts, *No One Is Coming to Save Us*

Jacqueline Woodson, *Another Brooklyn*

Karen Tei Yamashita, *I Hotel*

Désirée Zamorano, *The Amado Women*

Story Collections

Camille Acker, *Training School for Negro Girls*

Sharbari Z. Ahmed, *The Ocean of Mrs. Nagai*

Mia Alvar, *In the Country*

Lesley Nneka Arimah, *What It Means When a Man Falls from the Sky*

Alexia Arthurs, *How to Love a Jamaican*

Carleigh Baker, *Bad Endings*

Chaya Bhuvaneswar, *White Dancing Elephants*

Octavia E. Butler, *Bloodchild and Other Stories*

May-lee Chai, *Useful Phrases for Immigrants*

Y. Z. Chin, *Though I Get Home*

Tom Cho, *Look Who's Morphing*

Sandra Cisneros, *Woman Hollering Creek and Other Stories*

Tyrese L. Coleman, *How to Sit*

Hilma Contreras, *Entre Dos Silencios*

Jennani Durai, *Regrettable Things That Happened Yesterday*

Danielle Evans, *Before You Suffocate Your Own Fool Self*

Anita Felicelli, *Love Songs for a Lost Continent*

Roxane Gay, *Ayiti*

Stephanie Han, *Swimming in Hong Kong*

Yang Huang, *My Old Faithful*

Toni Jensen, *From the Hilltop*

Kristiana Kahakauwila, *This Is Paradise*

Barbara F. Kawakami, *Picture Bride*

Julie Koh, *Portable Curiosities*

Jhumpa Lahiri, *Unaccustomed Earth*

Krys Lee, *Drifting House*

Yiyun Li, *Gold Boy, Emerald Girl*

Jocelyn Lieu, *Potential Weapons*

Lorraine M. López, *Homicide Survivors Picnic and Other Stories*

Carmen Maria Machado, *Her Body and Other Parties*

Sharanya Manivannan, *The High Priestess Never Marries*

Annam Manthiram, *Dysfunction*

Donna Miscolta, *Hola and Goodbye: Una Familia in Stories*

Mary Anne Mohanraj, *Bodies in Motion*

Meera Nair, *Video*

Helen Oyeyemi, *What Is Not Yours Is Not Yours*

Z. Z. Packer, *Drinking Coffee Elsewhere*

Wang Ping, *The Last Communist Virgin*

Toni Margarita Plummer, *The Bolero of Andi Rowe*

Shona Ramaya, *Operation Monsoon*

Ivelisse Rodriguez, *Love War Stories*

Anjali Sachdeva, *All the Names They Used for God*

Sofia Samatar, *Tender*

Renee Simms, *Meet Behind Mars*

Hasanthika Sirisena, *The Other One*

Krystal A. Smith, *Two Moons*

Mecca Jamilah Sullivan, *Blue Talk & Love*

Nafissa Thompson-Spires, *Heads of the Colored People*

Novuyo Rosa Tshuma, *Shadows*

Ruvanee Pietersz Vilhauer, *The Water Diviner and Other Stories*

Stephanie Powell Watts, *We Are Taking Only What We Need*

Jia Qing Wilson-Yang, *Small Beauty*

Tara June Winch, *After the Carnage*

Erika T. Wurth, *Buckskin Cocaine*

Tiphanie Yanique, *How to Escape from a Leper Colony*

Jenny Zhang, *Sour Heart*

Nonfiction

Stacy Parker Aab, *Government Girl: Young and Female in the White House*

Faith Adiele, *Meeting Faith: An Inward Odyssey*

Nancy Agabian, *Me as Her Again: True Stories of an Armenian Daughter*

Luvvie Ajayi, *I'm Judging You: The Do-Better Manual*

Amani Al-Khatahtbeh, *Muslim Girl: A Coming of Age*

Huda Al-Marashi, *First Comes Marriage: My Not-So-American Love Story*

Kathleen Alcalá, *The Deepest Roots: Finding Food and Community on a Pacific Northwest Island*

Paula Gunn Allen, *Grandmothers of the Light: A Medicine Woman's Sourcebook*

Elizabeth Alexander, *The Light of the World: A Memoir*

Michelle Alexander, *The New Jim Crow: Mass Incarceration in the Age of Colorblindness*

Carol Anderson, *White Rage: The Unspoken Truth of Our Racial Divide*

Maya Angelou, *I Know Why the Caged Bird Sings*

Gloria Anzaldúa, *Borderlands*/La Frontera: *The New Mestiza*

Ifeanyi Awachie, *Summer in Igboland*

Cinelle Barnes, *Monsoon Mansion: A Memoir*

adrienne maree brown, *Emergent Strategy: Shaping Change, Changing Worlds*

Austin Channing Brown, *I'm Still Here: Black Dignity in a World Made for Whiteness*

Keah Brown, *The Pretty One*

Thi Bui, *The Best We Could Do*

Shuly Xóchitl Cawood, *The Going and Goodbye: A Memoir*

Raquel Cepeda, *Bird of Paradise: How I Became Latina*

Ying-Ying Chang, *The Woman Who Could Not Forget: Iris Chang Before and Beyond* The Rape of Nanking

Ava Chin, *Eating Wildly: Foraging for Life, Love and the Perfect Meal*

Nicole Chung, *All You Can Ever Know: A Memoir*

Maxine Beneba Clarke, *The Hate Race: A Memoir*

Allison Adelle Hedge Coke, *Rock, Ghost, Willow, Deer: A Story of Survival*

Brittney C. Cooper, Susana M. Morris, and Robin M. Boylorn, *The Crunk Feminist Collection*

Marguerite Dabaie, *The Hookah Girl and Other True Stories*

M. B. Dallocchio, *The Desert Warrior*

Kavita Das, *Poignant Song: The Life and Music of Lakshmi Shankar*

Sayantani Dasgupta, *Fire Girl: Essays on India, America & the In-Between*

Bridgett M. Davis, *The World According to Fannie Davis: My Mother's Life in the Detroit Numbers*

Sarah Deer, *The Beginning and End of Rape: Confronting Sexual Violence in Native America*

Jaquira Díaz, *Ordinary Girls*

Mary Crow Dog, *Lakota Woman*

Erica Armstrong Dunbar, *Never Caught: The Washingtons' Relentless Pursuit of Their Runaway Slave, Ona Judge*

Roxanne Dunbar-Ortiz and Dino Gilio-Whitaker, *"All the Real Indians Died Off": And 20 Other Myths about Native Americans*

Camille T. Dungy, *Guidebook to Relative Strangers: Journeys into Race, Motherhood, and History*

Nawal El-Saadawi, *A Daughter of ISIS*

Melissa Febos, *Abandon Me: Memoirs*

Linda Furiya, *Bento Box in the Heartland: My Japanese Girlhood in Whitebread America*

M. Evelina Galang, *Lolas' House: Filipino Women Living with War*

Erica Garza, *Getting Off: One Woman's Journey through Sex and Porn Addiction*

Lorna Goodison, *From Harvey River: A Memoir of My Mother and Her Island*

Patrice Gopo, *All the Colors We Will See: Reflections on Barriers, Brokenness, and Finding Our Way*

Natasha Gordon-Chipembere, *Representation and Black Womanhood: The Legacy of Sarah Baartman*

Annette Gordon-Reed, *The Hemingses of Monticello: An American Family*

Alexis Pauline Gumbs, *Spill: Scenes of Black Feminist Fugitivity*

Myriam Gurba, *Mean*

Minal Hajratwala, *Leaving India: My Family's Journey from Five Villages to Five Continents*

Joy Harjo, *Crazy Brave: A Memoir*

Ernestine Hayes, *The Tao of Raven: An Alaska Native Memoir*

Claudia D. Hernández, *Knitting the Fog*

Daisy Hernández, *A Cup of Water Under My Bed: A Memoir*

Sheena C. Howard, *Encyclopedia of Black Comics*

LeAnne Howe, *Choctalking on Other Realities*

Madeline Y. Hsu, *The Good Immigrants: How the Yellow Peril Became the Model Minority*

Jade Ngoc Quang Huynh, *South Wind Changing*

Karen M. Inouye, *The Long Afterlife of Nikkei Wartime Incarceration*

Samantha Irby, *We Are Never Meeting in Real Life*

Morgan Jerkins, *This Will Be My Undoing: Living at the Intersection of Black, Female, and Feminist in (White) America*

Ji-li Jiang, *Red Scarf Girl: A Memoir of the Cultural Revolution*

Kapka Kassabova, *Border: A Journey to the Edge of Europe*

Porochista Khakpour, *Sick: A Memoir*

Patrisse Khan-Cullors & asha bandele, *When They Call You a Terrorist: A Black Lives Matter Memoir*

Maxine Hong Kingston, *The Woman Warrior: Memoirs of a Girlhood among Ghosts*

Alison Kinney, *Hood*

Srilata Krishnan, *Table for Four*

Winona LaDuke, *Recovering the Sacred: The Power of Naming and Claiming*

Christine Hyung-Oak Lee, *Tell Me Everything You Don't Remember: The Stroke That Changed My Life*

Deborah Jian Lee, *Rescuing Jesus: How People of Color, Women, & Queer Christians Are Reclaiming Evangelicalism*

Erika Lee, *The Making of Asian America: A History*

Katherine Reynolds Lewis, *The Good News about Bad Behavior: Why Kids Are Less Disciplined Than Ever—and What to Do about It*

Haiming Liu, *From Canton Restaurant to Panda Express: A History of Chinese Food in the United States*

Audre Lorde, *A Burst of Light and Other Essays*

Valeria Luiselli, *Tell Me How It Ends: An Essay in Forty Questions*

T. Kira Madden, *Long Live the Tribe of Fatherless Girls: A Memoir*

Terese Marie Mailhot, *Heart Berries: A Memoir*

Jasminne Méndez, *Night-Blooming Jasmin(n)e: Personal Essays and Poetry*

Dunya Mikhail, *The Beekeeper: Rescuing the Stolen Women of Iraq*

Caille Millner, *The Golden Road: Notes on My Gentrification*

Deborah A. Miranda, *Bad Indians: A Tribal Memoir*

Janet Mock, *Redefining Realness: My Path to Womanhood, Identity, Love & So Much More*

Angela Morales, *The Girls in My Town*

Sally Morgan, *My Place*

Mari Naomi, *Dragon's Breath and Other True Stories*

Olivia Olivia, *No One Remembered Your Name but I Wrote It Down*

Ijeoma Oluo, *So You Want to Talk about Race*

Wendy C. Ortiz, *Bruja*

Ruth Ozeki, *The Face: A Time Code*

Nell Painter, *Old in Art School: A Memoir of Starting Over*

Ellen Pao, *Reset: My Fight for Inclusion and Lasting Change*

Stacey Patton, *That Mean Old Yesterday*

Leah Lakshmi Piepzna-Samarasinha, *Care Work: Dreaming Disability Justice*

Dianca London Potts, *Planning for the Apocalypse*

Franchesca Ramsey, *Well, That Escalated Quickly: Memoirs and Mistakes of an Accidental Activist*

Sharifa Rhodes-Pitts, *Harlem Is Nowhere: A Journey to the Mecca of Black America*

Andrea J. Ritchie, *Invisible No More: Police Violence against Black Women and Women of Color*

Lori S. Robinson, *I Will Survive: The African-American Guide to Healing from Sexual Assault and Abuse*

Phoebe Robinson, *You Can't Touch My Hair and Other Things I Still Have to Explain*

Rokudenashiko, *What Is Obscenity? The Story of a Good for Nothing Artist and Her Pussy*

Joshunda Sanders, *The Beautiful Darkness: A Handbook for Orphans*

Esmeralda Santiago, *When I Was Puerto Rican*

Margot Lee Shetterly, *Hidden Figures: The American Dream and the Untold Story of the Black Women Mathematicians Who Helped Win the Space Race*

Vivek Shraya, *I'm Afraid of Men.*

Leslie Marmon Silko, *The Turquoise Ledge*

Anneliese Singh, *The Queer & Transgender Resilience Workbook: Skills for Navigating Sexual Orientation & Gender Expression*

Krystal A. Sital, *Secrets We Kept: Three Women of Trinidad*

Tracy K. Smith, *Ordinary Light: A Memoir*

C. Riley Snorton, *Black on Both Sides: A Racial History of Trans Identity*

Janet Stickmon, *Crushing Soft Rubies: A Memoir*

Sonya Renee Taylor, *The Body Is Not an Apology: The Power of Radical Self-Love*

Laura Tohe, *Code Talker Stories*

Jane Jeong Trenka, *Fugitive Visions: An Adoptee's Return to Korea*

Eleanor Ty, *Asianfail: Narratives of Disenchantment and the Model Minority*

Neela Vaswani, *You Have Given Me a Country*

Chelsea Vowel, *Indigenous Writes: A Guide to First Nations, Métis & Inuit Issues in Canada*

Elissa Washuta, *My Body Is a Book of Rules*

Isabel Wilkerson, *The Warmth of Other Suns: The Epic Story of America's Great Migration*

Mai'a Williams, *This Is How We Survive: Revolutionary Mothering, War, and Exile in the 21st Century*

Jenna Wortham and Kimberly Drew, *The Black Futures Project*

Alexis Wright, *Tracker*

Kao Kalia Yang, *The Latehomecomer: A Hmong Family Memoir*

Malala Yousafzai, *I Am Malala: The Girl Who Stood Up for Education and Was Shot by the Taliban*

Zane, *Infinite Words: A Comprehensive Guide to Writing and Publishing*

Anthologies

Hadeel al-Massari and Nyala Ali, *Habibi: A Muslim Love Story Anthology*

S. Andrea Allen and Lauren Cherelle, *Lez Talk: A Collection of Black Lesbian Short Fiction*

Piyali Bhattacharya, *Good Girls Marry Doctors: South Asian American Daughters on Obedience and Rebellion*

adrienne maree brown and Walidah Imarisha, *Octavia's Brood: Science Fiction Stories from Social Justice Movements*

Mahogany L. Browne, Idrissa Simmonds, and Jamila Woods, *The BreakBeat Poets, Volume 2: Black Girl Magic*

Rowan Hisayo Buchanan, *Go Home!*

Jocelyn Burrel, *Word. On Being a [Woman] Writer*

Lori Marie Carlson, *Moccasin Thunder: American Indian Stories for Today*

Lisa Charleyboy and Mary Beth Leatherdale, *#NotYour Princess: Voices of Native American Women*

Edwidge Danticat, *Haiti Noir*

jayy dodd, *A Portrait in Blues: An Anthology of Identity, Gender & Bodies*

Qwo-Li Driskill, Daniel Heath Justice, Deborah Miranda, and Lisa Tatonetti, *Sovereign Erotics: A Collection of Two-Spirit Literature*

Camille T. Dungy, *Black Nature: Four Centuries of African American Nature Poetry*

Glory Edim, *Well-Read Black Girl: Finding Our Stories, Discovering Ourselves*

Lisa Factora-Borchers, *Dear Sister: Letters from Survivors of Sexual Violence*

Roberta Fernández, *In Other Words: Literature by Latinas of the United States*

Cristina García, *¡Cubanísmo! The Vintage Book of Contemporary Cuban Literature*

Roxane Gay, *Not That Bad: Dispatches from Rape Culture*

Farah Ghuznavi, *Lifelines: New Writing from Bangladesh*

Diane Glancy & Linda Rodriguez, *The World Is One Place: Native American Poets Visit the Middle East*

Alexis Pauline Gumbs, China Martens, and Mai'a Williams: *Revolutionary Mothering: Love on the Front Lines*

Joy Harjo and Gloria Bird, *Reinventing the Enemy's Language: Contemporary Native Women's Writings of North America*

Daisy Hernández and Bushra Rehman, *Colonize This! Young Women of Color on Today's Feminism*

Tobi Hill-Meyer, *Nerve Endings: The New Trans Erotic*

Tayari Jones, *Atlanta Noir*

Mikki Kendall & Chesya Burke, *Hidden Youth: Speculative Fiction from the Margins of History*

Nia King, Jessica Glennon-Zukoff, and Terra Mikalson, *Queer & Trans Artists of Color: Stories of Some of Our Lives*

Wilma Mankiller, *Every Day Is a Good Day: Reflections by Contemporary Indigenous Women*

Erika M. Martínez, *Daring to Write: Contemporary Narratives by Dominican Women*

Ayesha Mattu & Nura Maznavi, *Love, InshAllah: The Secret Love Lives of American Muslim Women*

Cherríe Moraga & Gloria Anzaldúa, *This Bridge Called My Back: Writings by Radical Women of Color*

Rosalie Morales Kearns, *The Female Complaint: Tales of Unruly Women*

Native Realities, *Deer Woman: An Anthology*

Hope Nicholson, *Love Beyond Body, Space & Time: An Indigenous LGBT Sci-Fi Anthology*

Nadxieli Nieto & Lincoln Michel, *Tiny Crimes: Very Short Tales of Mystery and Murder*

Achy Obejas and Megan Bayles, *Immigrant Voices: 21st Century Stories*

Ellen Oh and Elsie Chapman, *A Thousand Beginnings and Endings: 15 Retellings of Asian Myths and Legends*

Stephanie Stokes Oliver, *Black Ink: Literary Legends on the Peril, Power, and Pleasure of Reading and Writing*

Jina Ortiz and Rochelle Spencer, *All About Skin: Short Fiction by Women of Color*

Nausheen Pasha-Zaidi and Shaheen Pasha, *Mirror on the Veil: A Collection of Personal Essays on Hijab and Veiling*

Retha Powers, *Black Silk: A Collection of African American Erotica*

Rochelle Riley, *The Burden: African Americans and the Enduring Impact of Slavery*

Sonia Shah, *Dragon Ladies: Asian American Feminists Breathe Fire*

Sheree R. Thomas, *Dark Matter: Reading the Bones— Speculative Fiction from the African Diaspora*

Jael Uribe, *Grito de Mujer: Antología Internacional de Mujeres Poetas*

Jesmyn Ward, *The Fire This Time: A New Generation Speaks about Race*

Ibi Zoboi, *Black Enough: Stories of Being Young & Black in America*

Poetry

Elizabeth Acevedo, *Beastgirl & Other Origin Myths*

Hala Alyan, *Hijra*

Maya Angelou, *A Brave and Startling Truth*

Fatimah Asghar, *If They Come for Us*

Shauna Barbosa, *Cape Verdean Blues*

Mildred Kiconco Barya, *Give Me Room to Move My Feet*

Lisa Bellear, *Dreaming in Urban Areas*

Gwen Benaway, *Passage*

Xochitl-Julisa Bermejo, *Posada: Offerings of Witness and Refuge*

Tamiko Beyer, *We Come Elemental*

Kimberly Blaeser, *Apprenticed to Justice*

Mahogany L. Browne, *Kissing Caskets*

Maya Chinchilla, *The Cha Cha Files: A Chapina Poética*

Sandra Cisneros, *Loose Woman*

Laura Da', *Tributaries*

Yrsa Daley-Ward, *bone*

Natalie Diaz, *When My Brother Was an Aztec*

Demian DinéYazhi', *Ancestral Memory*

jayy dodd, *Mannish Tongues*

Rita Dove, *Mother Love*

r. erica doyle, *proxy*

Carlina Duan, *I Wore My Blackest Hair*

Heid E. Erdrich, *Curator of Ephemera at the New Museum for Archaic Media*

Rhina P. Espaillat, *Where Horizons Go*

Eve L. Ewing, *Electric Arches*

Nikky Finney, *Head Off & Split*

t'ai freedom ford, *how to get over*

Tonya M. Foster, *A Swarm of Bees in High Court*

Nikita Gill, *Wild Embers: Poems of Rebellion, Fire, and Beauty*

Nikki Giovanni, *Cotton Candy on a Rainy Day*

Rain C. Goméz, *Smoked Mullet Cornbread Crawdad Memory*

liz gonzález, *Dancing in the Santa Ana Winds: Poems y Cuentos New and Selected*

Rachel Eliza Griffiths, *Lighting the Shadow*

Suheir Hammad, *Born Palestinian, Born Black: & the Gaza Suite*

Joy Harjo, *Conflict Resolution for Holy Beings*

J. P. Howard, *Say/Mirror*

Honorée Fanonne Jeffers, *The Glory Gets*

Allyson Jeffredo, *Songs after Memory Fractures*

Maisha Z. Johnson, *No Parachutes to Carry Me Home*

June Jordan, *Directed by Desire: The Collected Poems of June Jordan*

Janine Joseph, *Driving Without a License*

Joan Naviyuk Kane, *Hyperboreal*

Donika Kelly, *Bestiary*

Mari L'Esperance, *The Darkened Temple*

Makeda Lewis, *Avie's Dreams: An Afro-Feminist Coloring Book*

Robin Coste Lewis, *Voyage of the Sable Venus*

Ada Limón, *Bright Dead Things*

Michelle Lin, *A House Made of Water*

Casandra Lopez, *Where Bullet Breaks*

Do Nguyen Mai, *Ghosts Still Walking*

Cynthia Manick, *Blue Hallelujahs*

Janet McAdams, *Feral*

Tiffany Midge, *Outlaws, Renegades, and Saints: Diary of a Mixed-Up Halfbreed*

Aja Monet, *My Mother Was a Freedom Fighter*

Kamilah Aisha Moon, *Starshine & Clay*

Pat Mora, *Agua Santa: Holy Water*

Aimee Nezhukumatathil, *Oceanic*

Naomi Shihab Nye, *Fuel*

Venetta Octavia, *Prelude to Light*

Cynthia Dewi Oka, *Salvage*

Ife-Chudeni A. Oputa, *Rummage*

Morgan Parker, *There Are More Beautiful Things Than Beyoncé*

Cina Pelayo, *Poems of My Night*

Kiki Petrosino, *Hymn for the Black Terrific*

Leah Lakshmi Piepzna-Samarasinha, *Love Cake*

Khadijah Queen, *I'm So Fine: A List of Famous Men & What I Had On*

Shivanee Ramlochan, *Everyone Knows I Am a Haunting*

Camille Rankine, *Incorrect Merciful Impulses*

Claudia Rankine, *Citizen*

Barbara Jane Reyes, *Poeta en San Francisco*

Margaret Rhee, *Love, Robot*

Linda Rodriguez, *Dark Sister*

Jenny Sadre-Orafai, *Malak*

Trish Salah, *Lyric Sexology, Vol. 1*

Erika L. Sánchez, *Lessons on Expulsion*

Leslie Contreras Schwartz, *Nightbloom & Cenote*

Nicole Sealey, *Ordinary Beast*

Ntozake Shange, *For Colored Girls Who Have Considered Suicide When the Rainbow Is Enuf*

Solmaz Sharif, *Look*

Warsan Shire, *Teaching My Mother How to Give Birth*

Vivek Shraya, *even this page is white*

Safiya Sinclair, *Cannibal*

Danez Smith, *Don't Call Us Dead*

Patricia Smith, *Blood Dazzler*

Tracy K. Smith, *Wade in the Water*

Layli Long Soldier, *Whereas*

Krishnan Srilata, *Bookmarking the Oasis*

Aimee Suzara, *Souvenir*

Sokunthary Svay, *Apsara in New York*

Lehua M. Taitano, *A Bell Made of Stones*

Kai Cheng Thom, *A Place Called No Homeland*

Natasha Trethewey, *Native Guard*

Jennifer Tseng, *Red Flower, White Flower*

Alok Vaid-Menon, *Femme in Public*

Patricia Jabbeh Wesley, *Becoming Ebony*

Sherley Anne Williams, *The Peacock Poems*

Tanaya Winder, *Why Storms Are Named after People and Bullets Remain Nameless*

Joyce E. Young, *How It Happens*

Young People's Literature

Elizabeth Acevedo, *The Poet X*

Tomi Adeyemi, *Children of Blood and Bone*

Marjorie Agosín, *I Lived on Butterfly Hill*

Samira Ahmed, *Love, Hate & Other Filters*

Kwame Alexander and Ekua Holmes, *Out of Wonder: Poems Celebrating Poets*

S. K. Ali, *Saints and Misfits*

Julia Alvarez, *Return to Sender*

Swati Avasthi and Craig Phillips, *Chasing Shadows*

Jane Bahk and Felicia Hoshino, *Juna's Jar*

Nandini Bajpai, *A Match Made in Mehendi*

Tracey Baptiste, *The Jumbies*

Ysaye M. Barnwell, *No Mirrors in My Nana's House*

Ruth Behar, *Lucky Broken Girl*

Rhoda Belleza, *Empress of a Thousand Skies*

Estela Bernal, *Can You See Me Now?*

Carmen T. Bernier-Grand, *Frida: ¡Viva la vida! Long Live Life!*

Rudine Simms Bishop and Lois Mailou Jones, *Wonders: The Best Children's Poems of Effie Lee Newsome*

Kendare Blake, *Three Dark Crowns*

Tonya Bolden, *Crossing Ebenezer Creek*

Victoria Bond and T. R. Simon, *Zora and Me*

Monica Brown and Sara Palacios, *Marisol McDonald Doesn't Match/Marisol McDonald no combina*

JaNay Brown-Wood and Hazel Mitchell, *Imani's Moon*

Mahogany L. Browne and Jess X. Snow, *Black Girl Magic*

Ashley Bryan, *Freedom over Me: Eleven Slaves, Their Lives and Dreams Brought to Life*

Ahlam Bsharat, *Code Name: Butterfly*

Marina Budhos, *Watched*

Hilda Eunice Burgos, *Ana Maria Reyes Does Not Live in a Castle*

Kheryn Callender, *Hurricane Child*

Nicola I. Campbell and Julie Flett, *A Day with Yayah*

Viola Canales, *The Tequila Worm*

Meg Cannistra, *The Trouble with Shooting Stars*

Angela Cervantes, *Gaby, Lost and Found*

May-lee Chai, *Tiger Girl*

Ruth Chan, *Where's the Party?*

Elsie Chapman, *Along the Indigo*

Sona Charaipotra & Dhonielle Clayton, *Shiny Broken Pieces*

Sheela Chari, *Vanished*

Roshani Chokshi, *The Star-Touched Queen*

Lesa Cline-Ransome and James E. Ransome, *Young Pelé: Soccer's First Star*

Brandy Colbert, *Little & Lion*

Ying Chang Compestine, *Revolution Is Not a Dinner Party*

Zoraida Córdova, *The Savage Blue*

Pat Cummings, *Harvey Moon, Museum Boy*

Julie C. Dao, *Forest of a Thousand Lanterns*

Sayantani DasGupta, *The Serpent's Secret*

Tanita S. Davis, *Mare's War*

Monalisa DeGross and Cheryl Hanna, *Donovan's Word Jar*

Alexandra Diaz, *The Only Road*

Cherie Dimaline, *The Marrow Thieves*

Angela Dominguez, *Maria Had a Little Llama/María tenía una llamita*

Sharon M. Draper, *Stella by Starlight*

Firoozeh Dumas, *It Ain't So Awful, Falafel*

Zetta Elliott and Shadra Strickland, *Bird*

Susan Middleton Elya and Susan Guevara, *Little Roja Riding Hood*

Margarita Engle, *Enchanted Air: Two Cultures, Two Wings: A Memoir*

Sara Farizan, *If You Could Be Mine*

Reem Faruqi and Lea Lyon, *Lailah's Lunchbox*

Sharon G. Flake, *The Skin I'm In*

Jessika Fleck, *The Castaways*

Julie Flett, *Wild Berries*

Debbi Michiko Florence, *Jasmine Toguchi, Mochi Queen*

Sundee T. Frazier, *Cleo Edison Oliver in Persuasion Power*

Shannon Gibney, *See No Color*

Lucía González and Lulu Delacre, *The Storyteller's Candle/ La velita de los cuentos*

Xelena González and Adriana M. Garcia, *All Around Us*

Maurene Goo, *I Believe in a Thing Called Love*

Eloise Greenfield and Jan Spivey Gilchrist, *The Great Migration: Journey to the North*

I. W. Gregorio, *None of the Above*

Nikki Grimes, *One Last Word: Wisdom from the Harlem Renaissance*

Glynis Guevara, *Black Beach*

Guojing, *The Only Child*

Virginia Hamilton, *Second Cousins*

Jenny Han, *P.S. I Still Love You*

Vashti Harrison, *Little Leaders: Bold Women in Black History*

Barbara Hathaway, *Missy Violet & Me*

Leah Henderson, *One Shadow on the Wall*

Tanuja Desai Hidier, *Bombay Blues*

Naomi Hirahara, *1001 Cranes*

Nadia L. Hohn and Irene Luxbacher, *Malaika's Costume*

Elizabeth Fitzgerald Howard and James Ransome, *Aunt Flossie's Hats (and Crab Cakes Later)*

Cheryl Willis Hudson and Cathy Johnson, *Glo Goes Shopping*

Justina Ireland, *Promise of Shadows*

Malathi Michelle Iyengar and Jamel Akib, *Tan to Tamarind: Poems about the Color Brown*

Tiffany D. Jackson, *Monday's Not Coming*

Angela Johnson, *The First Part Last*

Jen Cullerton Johnson and Sonia Lynn Sadler, *Seeds of Change*

Traci L. Jones, *Finding My Place*

Imani Josey, *The Blazing Star*

N. Joy and Nancy Devard, *The Secret Olivia Told Me*

Cynthia Kadohata, *The Thing about Luck*

Suzanne Kamata, *Gadget Girl: The Art of Being Invisible*

Hildi Kang, *Chengli and the Silk Road Caravan*

Claire Kann, *Let's Talk about Love*

Keshni Kashyap and Mari Araki, *Tina's Mouth: An Existential Comic Diary*

Erin Entrada Kelly, *Blackbird Fly*

Christine Kendall, *Riding Chance*

Hena Khan, *Amina's Voice*

Rukhsana Khan and Nasrin Khosravi, *A New Life*

Intisar Khanani, *Sunbolt*

Aditi Khorana, *Mirror in the Sky*

Uma Krishnaswami, *Step Up to the Plate, Maria Singh*

R. F. Kuang, *The Poppy War*

Stephanie Kuehn, *Charm & Strange*

Sarah Kuhn, *Heroine Complex*

Ambelin Kwaymullina, *The Interrogation of Ashala Wolf*

Thanhhà Lai, *Listen, Slowly*

C. B. Lee, *Not Your Sidekick*

Fonda Lee, *Jade City*

Stacey Lee, *Under a Painted Sky*

Julie Leung, *The Mice of the Round Table: A Tail of Camelot*

Grace Lin, *Where the Mountain Meets the Moon*

Malinda Lo, *Ash*

Marie Lu, *Warcross*

Many Ly, *Home Is East*

Kelly Starling Lyons, the Jada Jones series

Samantha Mabry, *All the Wind in the World*

Valynne E. Maetani, *Ink and Ashes*

Kekla Magoon, *Camo Girl*

Nilah Magruder, *How to Find a Fox*

Sonia Manzano, *The Revolution of Evelyn Serrano*

Claudia Guadalupe Martinez, *The Smell of Old Lady Perfume*

Guadalupe Garcia McCall, *Under the Mesquite*

Janet McDonald, *Harlem Hustle*

Patricia C. McKissack and Jerry Pinkney, *Goin' Someplace Special*

Anna-Marie McLemore, *The Weight of Feathers*

Juana Medina, *Juana & Lucas*

Meg Medina, *Yaqui Delgado Wants to Kick Your Ass*

Rati Mehrotra, *Markswoman*

Sandhya Menon, *When Dimple Met Rishi*

Anna Meriano, *Love Sugar Magic: A Dash of Trouble*

Ki-Wing Merlin, *Weaving a Net Is Better Than Praying for Fish*

Sharee Miller, *Don't Touch My Hair!*

Marisa Montes and Yuyi Morales, *Los Gatos Black on Halloween*

Pat Mora and Cecily Lang, *A Birthday Basket for Tía*

Yuyi Morales, *Viva Frida*

Shelia P. Moses, *The Legend of Buddy Bush*

An Na, *A Step from Heaven*

Marilyn Nelson and Hadley Hooper, *How I Discovered Poetry*

Vaunda Micheaux Nelson and Elizabeth Zunon, *Don't Call Me Grandma*

Christina Newhard and Robbie Bautista, *Amina and the City of Flowers*

Eucabeth Odhiambo, *Auma's Long Run*

Ellen Oh, *Spirit Hunters*

Nancy Osa, *Cuba 15*

Emily X. R. Pan, *The Astonishing Color of After*

Linda Sue Park, *A Single Shard*

Amada Irma Pérez and Maya Christina Gonzalez, *My Very Own Room/Mi propio cuartito*

Celia C. Pérez, *The First Rule of Punk*

Bao Phi and Thi Bui, *A Different Pond*

Dow Phumiruk and Ziyue Chen, *Mela and the Elephant*

Andrea Davis Pinkney and Shane W. Evans, *The Red Pencil*

Anita Poleahla and Emmett Navakuku, *Celebrate My Hopi Toys*

Cindy Pon, *Want*

Connie Porter, *Imani All Mine*

Dawn Quigley, *Apple in the Middle*

Isabel Quintero, *Gabi, a Girl in Pieces*

Sofia Quintero, *Show and Prove*

Jewell Parker Rhodes, *Bayou Magic*

Olugbemisola Rhuday-Perkovich, *8th Grade Superzero*

Karuna Riazi, *The Gauntlet*

Caroline Tung Richmond, *The Only Thing to Fear*

Faith Ringgold, *Tar Beach*

Gabby Rivera, *Juliet Takes a Breath*

Lilliam Rivera, *The Education of Margot Sanchez*

Cindy L. Rodriguez, *When Reason Breaks*

Katheryn Russell-Brown and Frank Morrison, *Little Melba and Her Big Trombone*

Pam Muñoz Ryan and Peter Sís, *The Dreamer*

Aisha Saeed, *Amal Unbound*

Erika L. Sánchez, *I Am Not Your Perfect Mexican Daughter*

N. H. Senzai, *Shooting Kabul*

Wendy Wan-Long Shang, *The Great Wall of Lucy Wu*

Kashmira Sheth, *Blue Jasmine*

Sheetal Sheth and Jessica Blank, *Always Anjali*

Irene Smalls and Colin Bootman, *Don't Say Ain't*

Cynthia Leitich Smith, *Hearts Unbroken*

Hope Anita Smith and E. B. Lewis, *Keeping the Night Watch*

Nic Stone, *Odd One Out*

Misa Sugiura, *It's Not Like It's a Secret*

Carmen Tafolla and Amy Córdova, *Fiesta Babies*

Sabaa Tahir, *An Ember in the Ashes*

Jillian Tamaki, *They Say Blue*

Liara Tamani, *Calling My Name*

Susan Tan and Dana Wulfekotte, *Cilla Lee-Jenkins: Future Author Extraordinaire*

Natasha Anastasia Tarpley and Adjoa J. Burrowes, *Destiny's Gift*

Mildred D. Taylor, *The Land*

Kai Cheng Thom, *Fierce Femmes and Notorious Liars: A Dangerous Trans Girl's Confabulous Memoir*

Angie Thomas, *On the Come Up*

Joyce Carol Thomas and Floyd Cooper, *The Blacker the Berry*

Jamilah Thompkins-Bigelow and Ebony Glenn, *Mommy's Khimar*

Chieri Uegaki and Qin Leng, *Hana Hashimoto, Sixth Violin*

Samantha R. Vamos and Rafael López, *The Cazuela that the Farm Maiden Stirred*

Padma Venkatraman, *A Time to Dance*

Booki Vivat, *Frazzled: Everyday Disasters and Impending Doom*

Quvenzhané Wallis and Vanessa Brantley-Newton, *A Night Out with Mama*

Andrea Wang and Alina Chau, *The Nian Monster*

Renée Watson, *Piecing Me Together*

Carole Boston Weatherford and Ekua Holmes, *Voice of Freedom: Fannie Lou Hamer: Spirit of the Civil Rights Movement*

Carole Boston Weatherford and Eric Velasquez, *Schomburg: The Man Who Built a Library*

Ebony Joy Wilkins, *Sellout*

Rita Williams-Garcia, *Jumped*

Jamia Wilson and Andrea Pippins, *Young, Gifted and Black: Meet 52 Black Heroes from Past and Present*

Brenda Woods, *A Star on the Hollywood Walk of Fame*

Jacqueline Woodson, *Feathers*

Kat Yeh, *The Way to Bea*

Paula Yoo, *Good Enough*

Nicola Yoon, *The Sun Is Also a Star*

Hyewon Yum, *Puddle*

F. Zia and Ken Min, *Hot, Hot Roti for Dada-ji*

Ibi Zoboi, *Pride*

ABOUT THE AUTHORS

JENNIFER BAKER is a contributing editor to *Electric Literature* and creator/host of the *Minorities in Publishing* podcast. In 2017, she was awarded a NYSCA/NYFA Artist Fellowship and a Queens Council on the Arts New Work Grant (as well as their award for Artistic Excellence) for Nonfiction Literature. Her writing has appeared in *Newtown Literary* (for which her short story "The Pursuit of Happiness" was nominated for a 2017 Pushcart Prize), *Boston Literary Magazine, Eclectic Flash, The Offing, Poets & Writers,* the *Other Stories* podcast, *Kweli Journal,* and *The Female Complaint* anthology from Shade Mountain Press. She has also contributed to Forbes.com, Literary Hub, *The Billfold, School Library Journal,* and *Bustle,* among other online publications. Her website is jennifernbaker.com.

MIA ALVAR's collection of short stories, *In the Country,* won the PEN/Robert W. Bingham Prize for Debut Fiction, the University of Rochester's Janet Heidinger Kafka Prize, and the Barnes & Noble Discover Great New Writers Award.

CARLEIGH BAKER is a Canadian writer whose debut short story collection, *Bad Endings*, was a shortlisted finalist for the 2017 Rogers Writers' Trust Fiction Prize and won the City of Vancouver Book Award. Her work has also appeared in *subTerrain*, *PRISM International*, *Joyland*, and *This Magazine*.

NANA EKUA BREW-HAMMOND is the author of *Powder Necklace* (Washington Square Press, 2010), which *Publishers Weekly* called "a winning debut." Named among thirty-nine of the most promising African writers under thirty-nine, her short fiction was included in the anthology *Africa39: New Writing from Africa South of Sahara* (Bloomsbury, 2014). She was shortlisted for a Miles Morland Writing Scholarship in 2014 and 2015, and has contributed fiction to *African Writing*, the *Los Angeles Review of Books*, *Sunday Salon*, and the short story collection *Woman's Work*. Her think pieces have appeared at online destinations including Ebony.com and TheGrio.com; and she has contributed commentary on everything from Michelle Obama's role in the US presidential campaign to Nelson Mandela's legacy on MSNBC, NY1, SaharaTV, and Arise TV. In April 2015, she was the opening speaker at TEDxAccra. Brew-Hammond coleads a monthly writing fellowship at the Center for Faith & Work. Also noted for her personal style, Brew-Hammond's fashion looks have appeared in the street style slideshows and print editions of outlets including *New York* magazine, *Essence* magazine, Fashionista.com, TheSartorialist.com, and the *New York Times*. Recently, she cofounded the made-in-

Ghana outerwear line Exit 14. She is currently at work on a new novel. Learn more at nanabrewhammond.com.

GLENDALIZ CAMACHO is a 2013 Pushcart Prize nominee and 2015 Write a House finalist. She has been an Artist in Residence at Jentel, Caldera, Kimmel Harding Nelson, Hedgebrook, Lower Manhattan Cultural Council, Lanesboro Arts, the Anderson Center, and Kerouac House. An alum of the Voices of Our Nations Arts Foundation (VONA) 2010 and 2013 Fiction Workshops and the 2016 Tin House Summer Workshop, her work appears in *The Female Complaint: Tales of Unruly Women* (Shade Mountain Press), *All about Skin: Short Fiction by Women of Color* (University of Wisconsin Press), the *Brooklyn Rail*, the *Butter*, and *Kweli Journal*, among others.

ALEXANDER CHEE is the author of the novels *Edinburgh* and *The Queen of the Night* and the essay collection *How to Write an Autobiographical Novel*, coming from Houghton Mifflin Harcourt in 2018. He is a contributing editor at the *New Republic* and an editor at large at *VQR*. His essays and stories have appeared in the *New York Times Book Review*, *T Magazine*, *Tin House*, *Slate*, *Guernica*, and *Out*, among others. He is the winner of a 2003 Whiting Award, a 2004 NEA Fellowship in prose, and a 2010 MCCA Fellowship, and of residency fellowships from the MacDowell Colony, the VCCA, Civitella Ranieri, and Amtrak. He is an associate professor of English and creative writing at Dartmouth College.

MITCHELL S. JACKSON's debut novel *The Residue Years* won the Ernest J. Gaines Award for Literary Excellence and was a finalist for the Center for Fiction's Flaherty-Dunnan First Novel Prize, the PEN/Hemingway Award for Debut Fiction, and the Hurston/Wright Legacy Award. Jackson is the winner of a Whiting Award in fiction. His writing has appeared in the *New York Times Book Review*, *Salon*, and *Tin House*, as well as in the bestselling essay anthology *The Fire This Time: A New Generation Speaks About Race* (edited by Jesmyn Ward). His new book *Survival Math: Notes on an All-American Family* will be published by Scribner in 2019.

YIYUN LI's most recent book is *Dear Friend, From My Life I Write to You in Your Life*. Her debut collection, *A Thousand Years of Good Prayers*, won the Frank O'Connor International Short Story Award, the PEN/Hemingway Award for Debut Fiction, the Guardian First Book Award, and the California Book Award for first fiction. Her novel *The Vagrants* won the gold-medal California Book Award for fiction, and was shortlisted for the Dublin IMPAC Award. *Gold Boy, Emerald Girl*, her second collection, was a finalist for the Story Prize and shortlisted for the Frank O'Connor International Short Story Award. *Kinder than Solitude*, her latest novel, was published to critical acclaim.

ALLISON MILLS is a Cree and settler writer, archivist, and librarian with a thing about ghosts. She was featured in *Apex Magazine*'s Indigenous American fantasists special issue, and her critical work has appeared in the *Looking Glass* and

Archivaria, where it won the 2016 Dodds Prize. She currently lives and works on unceded Musqueam, Tsleil-Waututh, and Squamish land in Vancouver, British Columbia.

COURTTIA NEWLAND's first novel, *The Scholar*, was published in 1997. Further critically acclaimed work includes *Society Within* (1999), *Snakeskin* (2002), *The Dying Wish* (2006), *Music for the Off-Key* (2006), and *A Book of Blues* (2011). He is coeditor of *IC3: The Penguin Book of New Black Writing in Britain* (2000) and coedited with Monique Roffey the collection *Tell Tales 4: The Global Village* (2009). Courttia's short stories have been featured in many anthologies. His career has encompassed both screen- and playwriting; plays include *B Is for Black* and an adaptation of Euripides's *Women of Troy*. His novel *The Gospel According to Cane* was published by Akashic Books (US) and Telegram (UK) in February 2013. A collection of speculative fiction, *Cosmogramma*, will be published in 2019.

DENNIS NORRIS II is a 2017 MacDowell Colony Fellow, a 2016 Tin House Scholar, and a 2015 Kimbilio Fiction Fellow. They are the author of *AWST Collection—Dennis Norris II*, published by AWST Press, and other writing appears in *Apogee Journal* and *SmokeLong Quarterly*. Their story "Where Every Boy Is Known and Loved" was recently named a finalist for the 2018 *Best Small Fictions Anthology*, forthcoming from Braddock Avenue Books, and they currently serve as fiction editor at *Apogee Journal*, assistant fiction editor at *The Rumpus*, and cohost of the popular podcast *Food 4*

Thot. You can find more information at their website, www
.dennisnorrisii.com.

JASON REYNOLDS is crazy. About stories. He is a *New York Times* bestselling author, a National Book Award Finalist, a Kirkus Prize winner, a two-time Walter Dean Myers Award winner, an NAACP Image Award winner and honoree, a Newbery Honoree, and the recipient of multiple Coretta Scott King honors. His debut novel, *When I Was the Greatest*, was followed by *Boy in the Black Suit* and *All American Boys* (co-written with Brendan Kiely), and then *As Brave as You*, *Miles Morales*, *Long Way Down*, *For Every One*, and the Track series. You can find his ramblings at www.jasonwritesbooks.com.

NELLY ROSARIO was born in the Dominican Republic and raised in Brooklyn, New York. She received a BA in engineering from MIT and an MFA in fiction writing from Columbia University. She was named a "Writer on the Verge" by the *Village Voice Literary Supplement* in 2001. Her first novel, *Song of the Water Saints*, won the 2002 PEN Open Book Award.

HASANTHIKA SIRISENA is the winner of the University of Massachusetts Press's Juniper Prize for Fiction. Her debut collection, *The Other One*, was released in 2016.

BRANDON TAYLOR is the associate editor of Electric Literature's *Recommended Reading* and a staff writer at Literary Hub. His writing has received fellowships from Lambda Literary, Kimbilio Fiction, and the Tin House Summer Workshop. His stories and essays have appeared in or are forthcoming from Literary Hub, Catapult, *Gulf Coast*, *Little Fiction*, Amazon's *Day One*, *Out* online, *Necessary Fiction*, *Joyland*, and elsewhere. He currently lives in Iowa City, where he is a student at the Iowa Writers' Workshop in fiction.

PERMISSIONS